'Exquisite description of life's surprises as we wrestle with familial love and loss.'

STEVEN E. SANDERSON, SCHOLAR AND NOVELIST,
EPITAPH FOR SORROWS.

'*Family Impromptu* illuminates the quirky combinations of connection and rebellion that make up all families—beyond the binaries of happiness and unhappiness.'

LAURIE L. PATTON, PROFESSOR, POET, AND PRESIDENT OF MIDDLEBURRY COLLEGE

Family Impromptu: Collected Stories

Published by The Conrad Press in the United Kingdom 2022

Tel: +44(0)1227 472 874
www.theconradpress.com
info@theconradpress.com

ISBN 978-1-914913-23-5

Copyright © Rosemary M. Magee, 2022

The moral right of Rosemary M. Magee to be identified as author of this work has been asserted in accordance with the Copyright, Designs and Patents Act 1988.

All rights reserved.

All of the characters and circumstances in these collected stories are entirely fictitious.

These stories are works of fiction. Names, characters, and events are products of the author's imagination. Any resemblance to actual persons, living or dead, or actual events is purely coincidental.

Typesetting and Cover Design by: Charlotte Mouncey, www.bookstyle.co.uk
The Conrad Press logo was designed by Maria Priestley.

Printed and bound in Great Britain by Clays Ltd, Elcograf S.p.A.

Publications acknowledgements
'Arthur, My Cousin,' *Eclipse*; 'Double Helix,' *Atlanta Magazine*; finalist for story contest, *Fiction Magazine*; 'Extinction,' *Iron Horse Literary Review*; 'Fantasy Impromptu,' *Euphony*; 'Free Radicals,' *The Distillery*; 'Making Out,' *Fine Print*; prize winner, Authors in the Park Contest; 'Quantum Entanglement,' *EDGE*; Pushcart nominee; 'Spectacular Lies,' *Porcupine Literary Arts Magazine*; 'Suchness,' *Ellery Queen Mystery Magazine*.

FAMILY IMPROMPTU:

COLLECTED STORIES

Rosemary M. Magee

Dedicated to Ron Grapevine, dearest husband,
whose good cheer and constancy embrace me, always.

Contents

Double helix	7
Arthur, my cousin, who died last summer in Texas	18
Deep freeze	37
Extinction	54
Contamination	76
Fantasy impromptu	93
Spontaneous recovery	107
Making out	121
Free swim	133
Plan B+	150
Quantum entanglement	169
Earth Day	185
Spectacular lies	194
The family plan	214
Free radicals	236
Suchness	253
Summer solstice	266
Acknowledgements	271

'I do think that families are the most beautiful things in all the world.'

Louise May Alcott, *Little Women*

'All our roots go deep down, even if they're tangled.'

Naomi Shihab Nye, *Habibi*

Double helix

I know a woman who is in love with my husband. I'm jealous of her. I'm jealous of her because she feels this way about him. He seems oblivious to her intentions and emotions, or at least that's the way he acts around me. I want him to want her the way that she wants him. I know this is not the way it's meant to be. I know I'm supposed to resent their attentions to one another. But I like contemplating her feelings for him. It helps me recollect the pre-conditions of love.

The two of them are working on a research project together, so sometimes she comes over to our house in the evenings. We are just finishing dinner. The children have gone outside to play. I invite her to sit down at the kitchen table. She asks about my work. I have colourful finger paint smeared across my clothing from the rowdy classroom of preschoolers that I oversee three days a week. We have nothing in common – except my husband. She is a quiet and reserved scientist who wears black skirts. I am talkative and emotional. My husband is a subdued, pensive man. That is why it makes sense for them to be in love. They can spill their secrets to one another in sweet hidden spurts. I offer her coffee.

'No, but I would like herbal tea if you have it.'
'How 'bout some Constant Comment?'
'No thanks, that has caffeine in it.'

She cannot afford to have caffeine at night. It would keep her awake – thinking about my husband. The next morning, she would be bleary-eyed and irritable. In addition to this research project, she has a full-time government job that requires travel and frequent presentations. She must look refreshed each day.

'Well, what about some ice water?' I feel foolish that I didn't know that Constant Comment is not an herbal tea.

'That would be fine.' She smiles graciously. She wants to make a positive impression on me. It would not be good for any of us if she sensed I discovered what I already know. My husband becomes absorbed in clearing the table. He starts to wash the dishes absent-mindedly. She observes him with clear appreciation for a man who washes the dishes without being asked.

'Jamie, watch out!' my husband yells through the open window at our oldest son. 'Watch out when you ride into the street!' He worries that the children will get run over even though we don't have much traffic in our neighborhood.

'They are fine, Jim. Don't hover,' I caution. He shrugs off my words. His sandy-gray hair falls over his troubled eyes. Whenever I point out the relative safety of the boys, he likes to remind me that they can't always count on that security in life. They have to be prepared for other eventualities.

The woman who loves my husband scrutinizes these domestic activities with great concentration. She is quite pretty in a natural kind of way. She does not wear eye makeup, but I see evidence of some light blush on her cheeks and a trace of blotted lipstick. Her name is Eloise, which is not a name I cared for until I met her. It reminded me of my grandmother's best friend 'El,' who always picks her teeth at the dinner table while talking loudly. But now the name of Eloise sounds lyrical, lovely, and medieval to me. I use it often when I speak to her.

'Eloise, have you traveled any more lately?'

'Just to San Francisco and back last week.' She makes it seem so routine. I picture her on the airplane peering out the window as she looks forward to the next evening when she'll return to our home.

She doesn't ever utter my name. She never says, 'Yes, *Lucy*.' It's as if she can't consent to mention my name because that will make my presence more real, my feelings of greater consequence. She does not understand that I have splendid fantasies of her love for my husband.

'I'll finish up the dishes, Jim,' I offer. They need to get some work done on their project in order to make a presentation at the next scientific meeting in the early fall. That is the stated reason for her presence in our home.

All the males in my life have names that start with a 'J' – Jim, Jamie, and Jakie, our youngest. I wanted a girl so I could have named her Jenny, but we will not have any more children. I imagine Eloise pregnant with my husband's child. She would look very trim in a maternity business suit. I wonder at what point she would have to give up traveling because of her condition.

'Thanks, dear.' Jim kisses me in front of Eloise every chance he gets. 'Thanks for dinner.' He rubs my hip, letting his insistent thumb slip inside the waistband of my jeans.

I can hear Eloise shift behind us with a sigh. She wants my life. I want to give it to her. Not because I do not like it. Not because I want another life, but because it would offer her so much satisfaction. It's a good life – more than one person at a time can fully enjoy, more than enough for me.

They leave to go work in my husband's study, the door

halfway open. After I finish putting away the dishes, I sit in the family room and read *The New Yorker*. I dream of a bohemian nightlife in the big city. Every now and then I grasp the words of their serious discussion. They are stationed in front of the computer in a room otherwise darkened by the descending dusk of summertime. The bits and bytes shine all around them. They are caught in a secluded, intimate glow. I like the way my husband's voice sounds – a gentle monotone that could be invoking words of love. Instead, he compares tiny, twisted ribbons of DNA. Together, my husband and Eloise expect to discover a critical key to the mysteries of life, their combined contribution to the Human Genome Project.

My boys come inside from their haphazard games in the driveway. Even though they just had dinner an hour ago, they are hungry.

'How 'bout some ice cream?' I offer.

'Chocolate,' proclaims Jamie. 'Thrawberry,' counters Jakie. His *ss* get lost in a thicket of other combined consonants. 'Vanilla,' I hear from the study. Jim appears at the doorway and leans against the frame wearing cut-offs and a torn T-shirt. I admire the way his shorts hang low on his hips, as if they can barely manage to stay on him.

'Vanilla *and* thrawberry *and* chocolate for me,' wanting it all, I add to the ice cream chorus. I hear Eloise in the background laughing familiarly. She has learned our evening ritual. Jim joins the boys in the kitchen, and they invade the freezer.

'We all thream for i-thream,' they sing together.

I can discern Eloise's diminutive body now embraced by Jim's chair in front of the computer. She enters information quickly, as if there is no time in life for an ice cream break. She evidently believes he will love her back if she conducts this study for him. It seems she likes sitting in his chair because she rubs her shiny hair against it, hoping to leave dark strands with her scent, which she intends for him to savor long after she departs.

'No thrawberry!' I hear a wail from the kitchen.

Now I remember that we ate it all last night, that Jim and I finished it off after the boys had gone to bed. We sat at the kitchen table with the thrawberry carton in front of us. No bowls, only one large spoon – and we fed strawberry ice cream to one another as if it was the feathery pink-and-white cake at our wedding reception some ten years ago. We ate it so quickly that it gave me a jagged ice cream headache that vanished before we went to bed. So after my shower, we made love like ravenous honeymooners. I impersonated the wild, concealed emotions of Eloise – to myself. Who, besides my husband, knows his private fantasies? But I visualized her imagining what it feels like to be me, sleeping with him each night, his lust swaddling me.

'Yes, but we do have some marshmallows,' Jamie tries to console Jakie, interrupting my reverie. He wants to shut him up. He doesn't approve of his younger brother's frequent tears. The tactic works.

'Yummellows,' Jakie replies, immediately cheerful. Jakie will eat anything with marshmallows on top, even broccoli. Jim, ever the researcher, has examined their sugar content and is not pleased with this strategy, but we all use it anyway. I even keep marshmallows in the van so that we can make it to school and back without a temper tantrum erupting.

'What kind of ice cream would you like, Eloise?' She never

has any with us, but it would be rude not to offer even though she does not seem to eat much at all. She must hope that my husband finds secret pleasure in the linear shape of her body, as opposed to my solid, rounded geometries. She has not carried his children and breastfed them and eaten countless marshmallows on long car trips just because they were there.

'None for me tonight.' She leaves open the possibility that some other night she will partake.

Jim brings me ice cream after he scoops out some for the boys. Their spoons clang against the glass bowls and the Formica tabletop in the other room. He leans over the couch, his breath a fierce mixture of fire and ice as he nuzzles my neck, then bites the ridge of my ear. This gives me a throng of goosebumps; I shiver and shake inside. He takes his own bowl into the study and stands next to Eloise while she conscientiously enters data. He eats his dessert in big clattery slurps, and I know what she wants. She wants him to do to her what he has just done to me. And I want him to do the same thing. I want to see what it looks like – to experience furtive love and clandestine possessiveness.

It is time for the boys to take a bath. They struggle to divert me from this task by posing philosophical questions.

'Do flies have mommies?' This one from Jamie, a promising scientist like his father. The fly nervously skips around the light fixture overhead.

'Of course they do. Every living thing has a mommy.'

'Where is its mommy?'

'Someplace else,' I suggest tentatively. Jamie looks unconvinced. A fuller explanation becomes obligatory. 'At their home in Texas, I guess.' This state is far enough away to explain her prolonged absence.

'What about grass?'

'Grass?'

'Yep, grass. Does it have a mommy?'

'Well, not exactly.'

'Grass is living, isn't it?' His logical voice aims to argue with me. 'It grows, and we have to cut it.' He adds evidence to support his hypothesis while I collect his bowl and rinse it in the sink.

Jakie listens with suspicion as he picks up little bitty marshmallows and stuffs them into his cheeks. Soon his head is round like a cantaloupe.

'Careful, Jakie, or you'll choke.' He tries to smile at me, but little white puffs protrude from his pursed lips. He jams them back in with sweaty knuckles. Jim did not bother to wash the boys' hands before they ate, so now they are grimy from outdoor dirt and sticky with muddy ice cream. The fragrance of syrupy sweat in their yellow hair permeates the kitchen.

'To the bath, to the bathtub!' I chant with maternal authority. Jakie follows Jamie as he slips off his seat and escapes into their father's study. Jim is sitting in the faded wing chair monitoring Eloise's progress. The boys pound their grubby fists on his bare knees. His ice cream bowl clatters to the floor. Eloise does not look up. She cannot bear to see my husband wrestle with these two chubby hooligans who struggle relentlessly for control of our household and of our lives.

My husband tucks a wriggling body under each arm and transports them to the bathroom. I follow without question and turn on the water. Jakie is starting to wail once more, but his mouth is still full of marshmallows, so the sounds are muffled. The two boys, quickly naked, somehow land in the tub, and my husband disappears again without a word. I toss in plastic boats and action figures. I know I cannot leave the side of the bathtub, not even for a second. I have read too many stories of drownings when parents turned their backs to answer the phone. I will not have my life destroyed in that way.

I shut off the gushing water and listen attentively for sounds down the hall. I don't want to miss a moment of Eloise's private time with Jim either. Bad things might happen if I am not there to see them unfold. I study the streaks of dirt and ice cream dissolving into the bathtub water and turning it cloudy gray.

Jakie stands up and holds his arms out to me.

'Watch out!' screams Jamie, 'He's pee-peeing.' A pure golden thread of urine streams out of the tub onto the bathroom floor. I snatch Jakie up and try to place him in front of the toilet as I lift the lid and seat. It is too late. We are both standing in a brackish puddle. Jakie's predictable cries erupt as disintegrating marshmallows drip from his mouth into the toilet. I am wet all over, and the finger paint streaks are now transformed into a monstrous blob. I dip a squirming Jakie back into the tub.

'Ewww, get him out of here!' Jamie, nearly seven, has turned into quite the fastidious fellow. He does not approve of bodily fluids. I extract Jakie and wrap him snugly in a towel and bump straight into Jim's T-shirt.

'I'll take him, Lucy.'

Jakie holds on to my neck, but Jim tickles him under the towel, and they squeal down the hall towards the room that the brothers share so that Jim can use the spare bedroom for his research project.

I sit down on the toilet, forgetting that I had lifted the lid and seat for Jakie, and I almost fall into it. Jamie leans out of the tub and grabs my arms as the water drains from the tub. He wants to save me. Regaining my balance, I yank his towel off the rack and drape it around his shoulders. I steer him out of the bathroom. He scrupulously avoids stepping into the yellowish puddle that his younger brother created.

Jamie races down the hallway, pursued in flight by his sodden terrycloth cape, and I press my sore back against the wall. I am wet all over. I will need to clean myself up before I can lie down with the boys and read them a story. We are making our way through *Charlotte's Web* together, and I'm eager to finish it soon; I've forgotten what happens to Wilbur.

I hear the boys roughhousing with their father down at one end of the hall. At the other end, I detect a hesitant shadow.

Eloise stands in the doorway and examines me with scholarly curiosity.

'Are you okay?' she inquires.

She is accustomed to the pandemonium of our household, but tonight it must sound unusually uproarious – especially compared to the order and sobriety of science.

'Yes. Of course,' I respond with resolve, 'Jim is getting the boys into their pyjamas.' She looks confused by his abandonment of their joint project.

'He'll be finished soon,' I endeavour to reassure her. Somehow I have ended up with a towel in my hand, and I scrub my face with its musty dampness then drop it on the floor to absorb the wet trail of little boys.

'It must be difficult.' She is attempting to be sympathetic. But I sense her pity, her awareness that I look the way I look and she looks the way she looks. And her budding awareness that she is in love with my husband.

'Pretty much,' I agree without any energy.

'Jim talks about the three of you all of the time.'

I know what she knows. That he is trying to convince himself that he loves us as much as she loves him. But I will not play this game with them. I've seen the look she gives him. I am bewitched by the feelings it must awaken in him.

'Well, I've got to be going, anyway. Tomorrow I have an early meeting.' Her life has a predictable schedule with important deadlines.

'Eloise, let me see you to the door.' Just then I hear Jakie's shriek and Jamie's disgusted complaints. It sounds like they are jumping on the beds, but then there is a howl followed by a big bang.

'No, I'll let myself out. Tell Jim I said goodnight.'

Eloise turns and departs with a box of data tucked under her arm. Sometimes she works on this project on her own. I am pulled away from her to the boys' room by sudden silence.

Jim, now also saturated with sweat and leftover bathwater, is balanced on one bed with a sniffling Jakie whirled into his chest like a sad papoose. Jamie, on the other bed, has crammed his whole body, including his towhead, under the covers. I am relieved to see that there is no blood or major visible damage. I sit next to Jim on the bed, our thighs rubbing together with abrupt, lively friction. Jakie rests his head on my shoulder while Jim clutches his agitated body.

There is a solid second of stillness punctuated by the gasps of our merged, tired breathing.

I know this woman is in love with my husband. I want him to be able to love her in return, to disentangle himself from the strands of the chaotic life we have created. I want him to experience passionate desires instead of the weak exhaustion that binds us together. Jamie casts away the covers and stretches his leg across the empty space from his bed. He rests his big toe on his father's knee. Jim caresses and lifts the heel of this shy foot as he bows down his head to kiss it. Because of the intervening lump of Jakie's body, Jim cannot reach Jamie. He kisses the air.

I long to wrap my arms around these two freshly bathed boys to release my husband so that he can follow Eloise, the woman who is in love with him, into the separate night. I'm jealous of what they could have together.

Arthur, my cousin,
who died last summer in Texas

My cousin Arthur was executed in Texas by lethal injection for murdering a schoolteacher in front of her class during Social Studies. The schoolteacher was his wife. The governor of Texas saw fit to make these little girls orphans, not that their father would've done them much good in prison. Arthur was not even from Texas. He followed his wife Leslie from Georgia to Dallas after she left him. We were all surprised he had a gun, much less that he knew how to shoot it. Back when he was a boy, he had preferred reading history to going hunting.

'You girls go out and get some fresh air,' I call out from the kitchen into the den. There's no reply. Those two would rather mope around inside on a sunny afternoon with their noses stuck in a book than do anything else. It makes me wonder what I'm up against in life now that I've adopted my cousin's two children. I go back to browning the chicken breasts, and I hear them turn on the TV.

The oblong pieces of chicken take on a slick golden colour, and I drown them in the grey cream of mushroom soup. I pour pellets of rice into an iron pot of boiling water and watch steam gather as I put on the lid. The two girls stay mesmerized in front of the local news.

'Change the channel,' I call out. 'That's only violence and rubbish.' They switch the channel to the middle of an *I Love Lucy* rerun. Every now and then a choked giggle will emerge from one of the girls, which gives me hope. I start to work on the salad with fresh tomatoes from the backyard.

Arthur shot his wife Leslie while the schoolchildren in her classroom hid beneath their desks like they were expecting a nuclear attack. He thought abandonment was a worse crime than murder, or so he said to the newspaper reporters during the trial even though everyone was supposed to be under a gag order. I guess he was remembering the way his pa left his ma, my aunt, when Arthur was just a little fellow. And so he set out to fix things right for his own kids. While he was being executed, his two little girls watched *Gilligan's Island* in a hotel room with me.

I coat the tomatoes with oil and vinegar dressing and sit down at the kitchen table with my glass of sweet iced tea to take a break. I've already raised three kids here in the heat of South Georgia, which is where everyone in my family started out. My husband died of cancer a few years back. My retirement plan had been to travel and read trashy novels. But instead, I'm raising two more kids who are as skinny as refugees. Their hair is dark like their mother's, but their eyes are the colour of weak green tea like Arthur's. No matter how much I feed them, they never get any meat on their bones. The girls seem frail enough to break in two like the twigs in my yard, brittle from the drought.

That's the story of my life since I went to visit their grandma, Aunt Maude to me, out in Texas, who was minding the kids for Arthur and Leslie and who then took it upon herself to have a stroke. She attracted bad luck, my aunt did. Maybe her husband had known that years ago and left while he could, before his luck turned from bad to worse. Anyway, one thing led to another, and now I have a twelve-year-old and a fourteen-year-old on my hands.

The people in our town act afraid of two children whose mother was murdered by their father who was then executed. All of the sudden everyone remembers odd things that Arthur did as a child before he grew up and went to college just over the border in Tallahassee. In our town, he is a stain that can't be rubbed out.

I set the table for four places. Another strange thing about these children is that they never argue with me. With my kids, I prayed they would learn to hold their tongues. But these two are as quiet as baby field mice. They've turned off the TV and put their noses in some old books.

Then there's this other hitch. After my husband died, I got friendly with Edith down the street. To tell the truth, it was while he was dying that we'd go out at dinner for a change of scenery when my children would come to stay with their father. Edith and I would go see movies too. One night I started to cry in the car, and she held me in her arms and kissed me like a shy teenager. It was the first time I'd been kissed since Phillip took ill. I couldn't help myself from kissing back. When I came in the house, Phillip, who was in his final wakeful time, stared at me.

'You look pretty tonight,' he whispered. I pulled my fingers through my hair, still long but streaked with grey.

Later I sat on his bedside and held his hand, which was surprisingly hard and bony, unlike the rest of his body sagging in soft folds. We'd disconnected the various wires and fluids a few days before. They were only making him more miserable. The home nurse didn't ask any questions.

Phillip fell asleep with a deep snore that I hadn't heard in months. It used to keep me awake at night, but now it sounded like a lost lullaby. I took off my clothes and lay down next to him. He snored again deeply, a sleepy bear hibernating in the dead of winter. I looked at my own plump self, which I had not examined in a while. This fifty-six-year-old body of mine was not fully used for all of its intended purposes. I rubbed my cheek with the memory of Edith's touch. In the middle of the night, Phillip stopped snoring. I squeezed his hand and kissed him hard, like Edith had done to me. I wanted to share it with him. His tongue was still soft and warm, but there was no breath.

We lay in bed like that until morning when I called my son Phillip Jr who lives the next street over. My two daughters stay up in Atlanta and only come by on occasional weekends. I barely had time to get dressed before Phillip Jr arrived and kneeled at his father's bedside and sobbed. They had been mad at each other before Phillip took ill, and then they forgot what made them so mad. Phillip Jr started coming over every night after work. He sat and read to his father from the *National Geographic* as if someday they might go on a foreign expedition that would take them away from this sweltering place.

Now, the chicken is cooked, but the girls still haven't budged from the couch. I'm keeping watch on our street for the familiar green car. I guess you could say that Edith and I are having an affair, but nobody in town takes much notice when two women start keeping company. And we're in a fix. We've got these young girls with us on the edge of puberty, and Edith and I like to sleep in the same bed, a new one that I bought after Phillip died. My heart beats rapidly when I think of Edith. The girls are such heartbroken creatures that we don't know if they can even recognize love in their midst.

'Granny, can we have some pickles?' That's the twelve-year-old. They call me Granny even though their real Granny died, and I'm just a second cousin once removed or something.

'Of course, Belle. You can have whatever you want around here.' She comes into the kitchen and opens the refrigerator door. The pickles are on the side, but she keeps swinging the door back and forth.

'Close the door, Belle. You'll let all the cold out.' She shuts it immediately, forgetting about the pickles.

'Oh here. I'll get them.' I retrieve the pickle jar. She sits down next to her sister in the den. When I bring two fat green plugs over to them with some napkins, they each grab a pickle and start sucking as loud as they can. I'm just glad to hear some sound come out of them.

'Edith will be home soon, and then we'll have dinner.' They don't respond. Finally, I sense Edith coming in through the kitchen door. She and I go immediately into the bedroom to kiss with the door closed behind us. She smells like fresh produce. She manages the Piggly Wiggly in town and serves on the county commission. Edith is a mover and shaker, someone who knows how to get things done in life. Look what's she's done for me. She's never been married or had children – says she was just waiting for love to come her way, and here it came down the street. At dinner, Edith holds onto my knee under the table. It feels good to have something in my life good enough to hide.

We are going away together for the weekend, and Phillip Jr is going to take care of the girls. Edith gave him a gift certificate to the Piggly Wiggly. His wife June just loves a bargain. Phillip Jr said he'd take the girls bowling, and I said, 'Good luck, Mister.'

Phillip Jr recalls when he was a boy and his father got him on a league, and they bowled together. That was the last fun time he remembers with his father before the *National Geographic*. His own boys are too young to go bowling. Edith and I are planning to check in at a hotel, watch TV in bed, and hit the outlet stores. We'll buy the girls some new things. Maybe that will help them get friends at school.

Edith and I are packing our bags. It's nice to have a girlfriend instead of a husband. Neither one of us gives a hoot about negligees. We like big T-shirts and baggy slacks with elastic waistbands.

Bea comes in, sits on the bed, and watches me pack. 'How long y'all gonna be gone?' This is a long sentence for her.

'Not too long.' She peers hopelessly out the window. 'Just the weekend.'

She picks at a loose thread on the quilted bedspread. 'Can't me and Belle come?'

'Belle and I.' Even though my own grammar isn't so great, I can't resist the urge to correct hers. I wonder where Arthur and Leslie came up with these names, Annabelle and Beatrice, like they should be in the movies.

'Yeah. Us. We'd be real quiet.' There's a little whine in her voice.

'No, Phillip is counting on you girls to help out with his boys. It's all pre-arranged.'

'Oh,' she responds meekly then shuffles out of the bedroom. I try to make up my mind between the blue sweatshirt and my old green one. Edith pokes her head in the door with a dishtowel on her arm.

'Take 'em both. There's room.'

'Who? The girls?'

'No, not them. Both sweatshirts. There's room in the suitcase.'

'Oh.'

Edith withdraws to the kitchen. Bea's sad eyes made me start thinking about Arthur. How all the boys had been so mean to him just because he was younger, read books, and walked swishy like a girl.

When I go out to the den to look for my walking shoes, Belle and Bea are snuggled under a blanket together still watching TV. 'Don't y'all have any homework?' They like to watch *The Simpsons*.

'No, ma'am.' They respond in unison, and I just let them alone. They're not hurting anyone anyway. They'll have plenty to distract them over at Phillip's with those three wild boys. My own grandchildren live just a block away, and I hardly see them because of Bea and Belle preoccupying me. The 'BBs' is what Edith calls them like they were shot into our midst and we're still trying to estimate the damage.

Edith and I take off in her Pontiac Bonneville. It has a big trunk that will be put to good use if we strike some hot bargains.

'You think Phillip Jr will take good care of those girls?' I ask Edith as we drive out of town.

'They don't need much attention,' she reminds me. 'Just give 'em a book, some dill pickles, and turn on *The Simpsons*.'

Edith puts her pudgy, firm hand in the seat between us, and I place mine on top of hers. Women have this nice way of being together that seems natural. And everybody says that it's natural the other way. Things, of course, were always natural between me and Phillip. I never thought I would need anybody but him. We pledged our hearts and bodies eternally when we were only seventeen. I didn't figure on him dying before we got old. And I didn't figure on me taking up with the lady down the street. Sometimes I wonder if I'm happier now with Edith than I was before with Phillip. But happiness is too hard to measure because it sloshes around inside of you.

The afternoon is darkening into evening as we drive. Neon signs fly by us in a rainbow blur. Edith drives fast like a man. I'm ready to get to our hotel and watch cable TV and not have to worry about the girls. Sometimes I think they speak a special language that only the two of them can understand. Edith pulls off the highway and into the parking lot. We're staying at the Holiday Inn Express. They give a free breakfast buffet with muffins and fruit. She lets me register at the front desk. Nobody notices two middle-aged women staying together.

When we get to the hotel room, I head straight for the phone, which I didn't plan on doing, and call Phillip Jr's number. One of his boys answers the phone.

'Is Bea there?' I ask.

'I don't think so,' this little boy voice replies.

'This is Grandma. Let me talk to your mother.'

He puts the phone down. 'Mama!' he calls for her as he runs down the hallway. There is the loud clanging of pots and pans.

Edith brings in our suitcase. Lifting it to the bed, she opens it. A bottle of merlot wine from the Piggly Wiggly lies on top of our sweatshirts.

No one comes to answer the phone. I try calling out loudly. 'June! The phone. Come get the phone.' Edith and I don't have those fancy smartphones yet.

There is no response. The boys must be sitting down to eat. Edith watches me as I call out again, 'Hello. Hello there, somebody. Anybody.'

She digs in her purse for a corkscrew. I watch her take two plastic cups from the bathroom. She unwraps the paper from around them, expertly opens the bottle of wine, pours me a glass of deep purple liquid, and kisses the top of my head.

I continue to listen to dinner noises from my son's house; no one answers the phone. Eventually I hang up and take a big gulp of the merlot. It stings my throat like I've been crying. Edith is flipping through the channels. She stops momentarily on *The Simpsons*.

'I need to go back and check on those girls,' I state over the laugh track.

Edith doesn't utter a word. I try my home phone number, but no one answers.

'I just can't stand the thought of them being abandoned once more.' I drink the rest of the Merlot in my cup.

'Shirley, hon, you haven't abandoned them. We're just taking a weekend getaway. We'll bring them back some gifts.' She pours more wine.

'I keep thinking of Arthur before he was executed. I told him I'd take care of his girls.' This time I take smaller sips.

'You have been taking care of them.' Her cup of wine is still full.

'He said to protect them, and how do I know they're protected?'

'Well, he didn't seem to be too worried about their protection when he went around shooting up their mother.'

'Yeah, did you ever hear of anything so crazy?'

'I've never heard anything as crazy as your whole darn family. I always thought you were nice folks. Anyway, I love you, and that's all that counts.' She takes a sip and then another, swishing the wine around like mouthwash. Her lips are starting to turn purple. I pick up the phone again.

She pats the bed. 'Come here and let's watch TV before we go out to eat.' When I sit down next to her, she kisses me on the lips. Edith is always so warm, it makes me sleepy to be next to her, like she is a hot water bottle when you've got the chills.

After a little nap, we go to eat at Denny's then walk down the street to the outlet shops. They have everything from Ann Taylor with those short straight skirts for young professional women to a gigantic discount bookstore and also The Gap. That's where we find some T-shirts and jeans for the girls, which is all they seem to want – no dresses or anything fancy. They don't want to call attention to themselves.

It's nice wandering through the store with Edith. Women know how to shop together. Men just look for the one thing they have in mind then call a halt to it. Women know how to let things unfold, staying open to whatever surprise bargains might come their way. Standing at the counter in front of the cash register gives me a sense of accomplishment, even if it rings up more than I had figured in my head.

I'm happy to be with Edith until we return to the hotel room, and my stomach gets all knotted up. Here we've come all this way to get away from everybody else, but I can't get them out of my mind. I try the numbers back at home. There are still no answers. Edith flips through the channels in a hurry, just like Phillip used to do before he got sick. The flashing light from the screen is getting on my nerves.

'Stop,' I call out.

'Stop what?' she replies. She has also been rubbing the back of my neck where it is all tight and tense, which she does in time to the channel changing. I'm twitching all over.

'Stop fooling with the TV.' She quits the neck rubbing but continues with the remote control.

'I'm just trying to find something with both adventure and romance. Don't you want that?'

I'm silent. I know she wants to make me happy. I feel small next to her. Finally, I manage to say. 'It's just those girls, those darn kids.'

'What about them?'

'I keep thinking about Arthur.'

'Arthur?'

'Yeah, their dad.'

'Well, he's dead. What's there to think about?'

'About when he was a boy.'

'What'd he do?'

'It's not so much about what he did but what was done to him.'

She turns off the TV. The room is dark. We are lying on the bed facing each other. Her hand is on my hip. I want to smother myself in her large, soft breasts. I take off my glasses and rub my eyes.

Edith is not a person for much discussion. Like Phillip, she's more into doing things rather than thinking about them. Now she whispers, 'Tell me.'

I close my eyes and tune out everything else in life. 'The boys, my brothers and other cousins and even Phillip, they never did like Arthur. He got good grades and kept reading history all the time. He had toy soldiers, and sometimes he'd want to play battle games with the other boys. But they didn't want to play with all that strategy. Every so often I'd go out in the woods with him. He'd act out these exciting stories about the Civil War, and he didn't make me the nurse. I could be a soldier too.' I pause. 'We always got along real well.'

Edith takes both of my hands, clasping them between hers, then places them on her large chest. I can feel her heart beating with a solid assurance.

'Well, that explains the girls. Why you took them in.'

'They're like Arthur, always reading and thinking. You never much knew what was going on in his head, except for the stories. His mother was so proud of his big words. She didn't mind that he didn't like football or fishing.'

'Hmmm...' Her breathing had grown even deeper. I keep talking.

'They were close, Arthur and his mother. Sometimes I'd sit with them in the kitchen while she cooked, and he'd tell us stories about lost battles. Only when his father came for a visit, he made Arthur go outside and told him not to be a sissy.'

'Was he mean? The father.' Her voice had gotten deeper too.

'Oh, no more mean than the boys.' I stop to pull my thoughts together. 'One day, they followed Arthur out into the woods. I was hiding behind a big oak tree. They made a big circle around him and started calling him bad names. He was about ten or eleven years old. All the boys yelled things at Arthur. They made him take off his pants. And when he did, he just stood there in his shirt, jacket, and underwear. But they made him take those off too. Then they just laughed at him. Laughed and pointed. I couldn't bear to look. I didn't know what they were laughing at. After a while they grabbed a stick, and each one hit his bare behind with it. They didn't hit it too hard, and Arthur didn't cry. They ran off and left him alone.'

'Was that it? Anything else happen?'

'Not much. Arthur put back on his pants and lay down in a pile of leaves.'

'What'd you do?'

'Nothing. I didn't let him know that I'd seen everything. I was too ashamed.'

'Ashamed for him?'

I thought for a few seconds before answering, 'Ashamed of myself that I didn't do a thing. Didn't lift one little finger. The next day I went out to the woods with Phillip and let him kiss me all over.'

'Phillip had been one of those boys?'

'Yep, Phillip and my brothers. I didn't say a word to them then and never later.' I pause for a minute. 'It's a good thing Phillip died before Arthur acted up in Texas. He never would've let me go out there, and the girls would be orphans who knows where.' I collect my thoughts. 'So I think about the girls and how I never did help their daddy who was my cousin and my best friend. And now he's dead, and they remind me of him. I think about them being over at Phillip Jr's house with those three wild boys.'

'Those boys aren't big enough to hurt a flea.'

'But they don't have to be. They just have to scare you. Like Arthur was scared.'

Edith didn't say anything.

'I need to…'

'What's that?' Her voice is sharper now, as if she'd just been awakened from a nap. She holds on tighter to my hands.

'I need to go get those girls from Phillip Jr's house.' I push out of the bed and start to pack my clothes in the suitcase.

'They can get by one night without you, hon. Besides, I want you to stay here with me.' She sounds lonely.

Here's the way it's been my whole life: when I need to do one thing in particular, someone else is pulling at me in the other direction. I wish I could pray about it, but I've given up praying ever since Phillip and Arthur died.

'I've got to go. I'm just worried about the girls, and I'm worried about Phillip Jr too. He misses his father, even though he's still mad at him.'

'Why's he so mad anyway?'

'Don't really know. Phillip could be real rough with that boy like he never was to our girls. And now I don't want Phillip Jr to take that meanness out on anyone else. Maybe I'll tell all of them about watching Arthur that day.' I add in a quieter voice, 'And maybe I'll tell them about you and me.'

'About me? What's that got to do with anything?' She looks worried. 'What if the city council hears?'

'If people can't accept two people loving each other then they don't have any right to call themselves upright citizens. That's the way I look at it.'

'Don't you count on it,' she cautions. 'Besides, Shirley, I just want us to stay here.' Edith reaches out her hand to hold on to me. I never thought that she could act so scared or that I could be so certain. In my marriage, I had always put Phillip's desires ahead of everything else. But the girls had ended up with me, and as near as I could tell, they were here to stay.

'I need to see Bea and Belle.' I pull away. 'Then there will be a time for us.'

Edith eventually joins me in the packing process. She picks up hotel containers of shampoo, conditioner, and lotion, storing them next to an unopened bottle of merlot. I won't let her take the towel. It just isn't right. Somewhere you have to draw the line in life. We head off in the car. It's starting to rain lightly, which is good because we need it in South Georgia. I'm driving now. She sits back with her eyes closed and listens to sad country music. We hum along. Now that we are on the road, everything is comfortable again.

I don't know exactly what to say to those girls. But I want to tell them that I didn't help their daddy when he needed me way back when, and that the only way I can help him is by taking care of them. He did what he did because he missed them so much that it made him want to kill. What's done is done. None of us need to be punished anymore.

Edith opens the car door as I pull into our driveway. The house is alive with lights. We see people moving about in the yard in the rain. Smoke from cigarettes hangs over them in damp clouds. There is no sign of Phillip Jr's car, but he lives close enough to walk.

Inside the house, the TV and stereo are blaring with more noise and commotion than there has been in years. Where have all these kids come from? Edith is right behind me. She doesn't stop like I do to take it all in. She goes about checking each bedroom. Immediately youngsters of all shapes and sizes follow her out. She tells them to sit in the living room. I follow her into the kitchen where our two girls are sitting on the counter in skimpy halter tops like they own the place, each holding a beer. Two boys step away from them and look out the window over the sink into the wet night. The rain starts to come down harder.

'Where's Phillip Jr?' I ask. They shrug their shoulders in unison.

'Have you seen him tonight?' No response.

Edith marches back out to the living room. She soon has kids standing in line at the phone and calling their parents. They slump pathetically in their oversized jeans and T-shirts. The girls in the kitchen look unperturbed.

'I need to know where Phillip Jr is.'

Belle and Bea look at each other until Belle speaks up, 'He came by here with his kids. They were going out to eat and to the movies. When we said we'd rather stay here and watch TV, he said he'd come back by to check on us later. That's the last we saw of him.'

What happened to the bowling plan? It's 10:30pm, too late for him to be out with the boys. I break into the line for the telephone to call his house. June answers the phone in an exhausted voice.

'Phil just dropped us off. I've gotta get these boys in bed. They're cranky as all get-out. He's on his way to check on the girls.'

I put down the phone as rain-brightened headlights come up the driveway. I head out there to interrogate Phillip Jr, but it's one of the mothers.

'What are you doing allowing my boys to hang out with these escaped convicts?' Before I can respond, she grabs two bodies and stuffs them in the car. The boys hide their heads like they'd been arrested in front of TV cameras. Other cars start to show up. I see Phillip Jr, a lost, lonely figure, walking up the street. He's not in too big of a hurry. In the night, he doesn't look much older than these kids.

'What are you doing here?' he calls out.

'Just had a funny feeling that something wasn't right.'

He surveys our surroundings. His hair is plastered on his forehead from the rain.

'You always were pretty good with those funny feelings.'

'What are these two girls doing home alone anyway?'

'Doesn't look like they are short on company. Might do them some good.'

'Weren't you in charge of them?' I accuse. This conversation takes me back to Phillip Jr's high school days. Back then his daddy would beat him if he sassed or misbehaved. When he cried, his daddy would laugh in just the way he laughed at Arthur. All of this was piling up inside of me.

At least Phillip Jr isn't mean, as near as I can tell. He doesn't beat his boys. He just lets things happen to him rather than taking control. And right now, somebody needs to be in control of this situation, but neither of us seems up to it. We stand together outside getting wetter before wandering indoors where more lights are coming on. The air conditioning makes us both shiver. Edith has Bea and Belle picking up the mess. She's giving a good talking to whomever takes notice. 'What do y'all think you're up to scaring me and Shirley so much?' One of them starts to sniffle.

Finally, after all the other kids clear out, Edith places the two girls at the dining room table. All five of us sit down together like it's Thanksgiving dinner.

'We got something to tell you,' she says.

'Edith,' I whisper, though all can hear. 'I don't think this is the right time.'

'It was your idea, and the more I've thought about it, the more I like it. Everybody's been walking around here like they've got something to hide. And the minute we're out the door, these two come alive. We didn't even think they ever talked to any kids. Then there's Phillip over there who never says a thing since his daddy died. He just acts like everything is fine. Well, it's not fine. Except for one thing – and that's me and you. Yep, they might as well hear it because they already know it anyway.'

The girls look at their fingers as if checking for hangnails. They have this irritating habit of concentrating so hard on one task that you'd think they would just die of boredom. Phillip sits back in his chair with his eyes closed. 'Oh lordy,' he mutters, 'Now what?'

This is an open invitation to Edith. 'Well, here's what.' She takes a deep breath. 'Your mother and me. Well, we're what you call – we're in love. We love each other so much it's hard to be apart. That's what.'

Bea and Belle look at each other and start to giggle. I stare at them. I don't believe I've ever heard them laugh except at the TV. It makes me feel good inside. Even Phillip Jr watches them in wonder. He looks so silly with all that pitiful damp hair that I begin to chuckle. And then Edith, and the next thing you know Phillip Jr starts that full hoarse laugh of his that I haven't heard in forever. We sit at the dining room table laughing till we cry at something we don't even know what.

Ever since the girls threw that party, the phone has been ringing off the hook. I keep remembering those early days of worrying about them. Now I've got something new to worry about: keeping them away from boys. Edith has taken to holding my hand, no matter where we are, even in the Piggly Wiggly. We don't see much of June and the boys. They act leery of what Edith and I have together. Phillip Jr mostly keeps to himself. I think he's still missing his dad. There's no one to be mad at any longer. Every now and then, he'll come on over to our place to sit and talk with the girls while his boys run around like wild bandits in the front yard. I heard him once say to Bea and Belle that he knows what it's like to lose your daddy before you were really ready for it. And I think about everything that's happened in my life – about my cousin Arthur who died last summer in Texas and all he's done for me.

Deep freeze

The Monday she brought home her dead dog from the veterinarian was the day Ginger vowed she'd never smoke another cigarette. Life was too short to clog up her lungs with impure air. But that night Ginger could not sleep. A heavy darkness enveloped her. She couldn't accept the fact that Toby, who used to fidget in chase dreams next to her, who for years had greeted her with reckless frenzy each evening, was now dead – transformed into a cold, hard, inert lump in her freezer.

Smoking was the only activity that could alleviate this sadness. Ginger craved the wisps of smoke that formed soft, scented circles around her head. Earlier in the day, she'd taken all of the cigarettes out to the garage and hidden them on the shelf above the freezer. Now she pulled herself out of bed and wandered out into the garage, dressed only in a torn T-shirt and long socks. The cartons were stashed behind cans of dog food. Grabbing a pack from the box, she leaned against her car and examined the upright freezer.

At odd moments earlier in the day, Ginger had opened the thick freezer door to gaze at the brown-paper wrapped parcel. Again, near midnight, she tugged on the door. Cold air seized her lungs. She reached down to touch the wrapping. The frigid mass did not respond. Ginger shut the door quickly, pushing against it and shivering as she unwrapped the pack of cigarettes. She put one, unlit, in her mouth. She had thrown all of her matches down the disposal earlier in the day. She inhaled, not finding any relief.

Ginger placed the pack of cigarettes above the freezer and returned to the kitchen. She kept the unlit one dangling in her mouth. Putting Toby to sleep had been too hard, harder than splitting up with Jon last year. She'd never been in therapy, not even when going through the divorce. But here she sat at the kitchen counter in the middle of the night, browsing online sites. She wanted to find a stranger who would let her talk about Toby – about the way he looked at her with hopeful surprise even as his short breaths diminished into nothingness. She entered phone numbers but was too embarrassed to leave her name on some unknown therapist's voicemail.

The vet had been kind to her. He'd asked her if he should dispose of the body or if she wanted to do so herself. She'd astonished herself by saying that she would take care of it; his assistant had expertly wrapped the body in brown paper, placing Toby's velvety, warm remains first inside a dry-cleaning bag. He carried the package out to the backseat of her car and instructed her to keep it in a cool place until she could get him buried. That afternoon Ginger had cleaned out the bottom shelf of her garage upright freezer and placed Toby, still limp, carefully inside of it. Now his body had turned hard and heavy. Toby, all his life a short-legged runt, had grown bulky in the aftermath of his death.

Ginger abandoned the laptop on the counter and dragged herself into the den. On her cool leather sofa, she shook under Toby's comforter until she dropped into a fitful sleep, the unlit cigarette clutched in her hand. She woke up once with the dream of Toby's warm wet nose pushing against her chest.

When she arrived at work the next day, Ginger announced to Kathi the receptionist that she'd quit smoking.

'What possessed you to do *that* all of a sudden?' The two of them regularly smoked together in the covered garden outside the suite, despite signs declaring it to be a smoke-free area.

'Toby.'

'Toby?' she inquired. The office was starting to fill up with morning activity.

'Yes' Ginger twisted a strand of her dark hair tightly around the little finger of her left hand. 'My dog.'

Kathi showed no signs of comprehending. 'You weren't here yesterday,' she remarked as she turned to greet others as they arrived.

All of the computer programmers, except for Ginger, were men. She and Kathi liked to assess their personalities and physiques over lunch behind the building. While the men ran laps or shot baskets in gym shorts, the two women smoked and gossiped.

Just then the phone rang, and Kathi quickly grabbed the receiver. Ginger drifted into her own office. She closed the door behind her, turned on her computer, sat down, stared out the window, and longed for a cigarette. She usually left her office door wide open so that she could hear passing conversations in the hallway. The low buzz of business discussions helped her concentrate. Today she needed quiet.

Ginger had stuffed the cigarette from the night before in her pants pocket. She took it out, rolling it around the desk to straighten the wrinkles. The tobacco was starting to spill out of the dingy white casing, its pungent scent covered her fingers. The rich bronze colour reminded her of Toby when he was just a puppy from the pound. Jon had brought him home to her one summer day early on in their marriage, just after he had graduated from seminary.

Her office door opened suddenly; Kathi stuck in her head. 'We're having a going-away party for Martin in a little bit. His wife sent in some of her yummy spice cake.' She paused as if expecting some response. 'It will be in the conference room.' Kathi looked hard into Ginger's face. The disintegrating cigarette was in plain view on the desk.

'Hey, come on,' she added. 'Let's step outside and have a smoke before it gets too hot today.'

'No. I quit.' Ginger stared gloomily at the bright computer screen. 'Remember?' Noting the hoarseness in her voice, she picked up the cigarette and twisted the ends. 'Thanks anyway.' The filter dropped to the desk and then rolled on to the floor. Ginger squished it with the heel of her shoe.

'Such fast change can be upsetting. Usually there's a reason.' Kathi tended to pose questions without really asking them. Ginger had fallen for this tactic before. That's how she'd ended up telling Kathi about Jon and also about Rick, who was now her boyfriend, and the divorce. She regretted divulging so much. It is best to maintain one's privacy, especially at work.

Ginger picked up and contemplated the cigarette, which resembled a tattered joint. She sniffed it and inserted the limp stem in her mouth, clenching her teeth around it. 'I think I can handle this,' she stated.

'Fine. I'm sure you can. I'll see you at the party.' Kathi jerked the door closed.

Ginger rested her head on her desk. Tiny pinpoints of grief stabbed her stomach. She hadn't eaten anything but bananas and Pepperidge Farm cookies the day before, and today she'd skipped breakfast. But she had no intention of going to the farewell party, despite the promise of spice cake. She didn't want to explain anything or have to accept forced looks of sympathy – which was really pity for someone who mourned a scraggly dog like Toby.

When she arrived home from work that day, Ginger was immediately confronted by the electric humming sounds of the freezer. Its white metal exterior exuded frosty sweat. Peering inside, Ginger examined all the contents. The upper shelves were stuffed with lopsided cartons of snow peas, corn niblets, and broccoli spears. On the middle shelf, she had stockpiled chicken breasts and frozen meals. Her eyes came to rest on the bulky beige package secured with a taut string on the bottom shelf. She half expected it to twitch in a bad dog dream. A bright appliance light flickered in the back of the freezer like a beacon to explorers with teams of huskies on the South Pole. She quickly shut the freezer door.

Ginger reached for the opened package of cigarettes on the upper shelf as she made her way into the kitchen. Shiny hardwood floors greeted her; the housecleaners had come that day. Apparently, they'd retrieved from under a pile of old newspapers the note that Rick had written to her last weekend, and they'd left it in plain view. She picked up the notebook paper with scribbled lines to reread his words:

Q: Why don't southern ladies like group sex?
A: Too many thank you notes

This was Rick's idea of a love letter. Usually, she liked his sense of humour. He had signed his full name with a flourish, as if she would not otherwise know who had written it. He left the note for her to see early Monday morning before he'd taken off to Nashville, before she'd taken Toby to the vet – back when life still felt abundant.

Ginger changed into her exercise clothes although she had no intention of going to work out. The spandex shorts made it easier for her to breathe. She missed Toby's ever-watchful presence at her ankles.

'Scoot,' she whispered as she wandered through the empty house, 'I don't have time for you right now.' It was nice to pretend that her life was too full for Toby.

'Hey Gin.'

She liked the sound of Rick's voice on the phone. That was how she first fell for him, when he used to call to consult her at work on computer issues. Jon had never liked to talk on the phone much.

'Hey, yourself.' She lay across the bed and closed her eyes. He'd called her Gin from the beginning, as if she were an intoxicating, clear liquid.

'Hope you haven't changed the sheets on the bed yet.' He liked to picture her sleeping on the spots where they had made love.

Ginger did not answer his question. She pulled the edge of the bed comforter over her legs. 'What have you been up to?'

'Well, I went to a country music concert. Very noisy, lots of smoke and cowboys. Don't tell the folks at NPR that I liked it.' His job was to install computer systems at public radio stations.

She didn't respond.

'I'll be back soon. It doesn't look like they have any serious problems here. What have you been up to?'

'Um, not much.' The past couple of days formed a chaotic jumble in her head.

Rick parodied a love song from the concert and promised to send her an email in the morning. After they hung up, she lay motionless, wanting him to return from his trip, dig a hole, and place Toby's body in the grave. The parched Georgia red clay was too hard from the recent drought for her to attempt it alone. She hadn't told Rick about Toby, nor had she mentioned that she had quit smoking. Not a smoker, he wouldn't fully appreciate the discipline required, and for him, Toby was just an addendum to their relationship. She tucked the pack of cigarettes under her pillow. She also retrieved one of Toby's stuffed toys, a tattered rabbit, and buried it under the comforter.

Ginger called into work sick on Wednesday. It had finally started to rain. She remained in bed with one hand under the pillow and slept until noon. Even eating seemed like too much of an effort; she got up briefly for a cup of herbal tea and a few cookies. Thursday, despite continued thunderstorms, she forced herself out of bed and eventually made it to work. Kathi only nodded to her when she walked into the office. All of a sudden, it seemed they didn't have very much in common. Ginger kept her office door closed. Her pockets were stuffed with frayed cigarettes. She rubbed the loose tobacco between her fingertips and sniffed their bitterness throughout the day.

On the way home that afternoon, Ginger observed scattered twosomes of people walking their eager dogs in the remaining drizzle. She felt ashamed of Toby's frozen, immobile condition. She needed to take action and dig a hole near the overgrown garden by the fence, one of Toby's favourite outdoor spots for sniffing. When Jon moved into a condominium, he had left all the outdoor equipment in the utility closet in the backyard.

That's what she would do: bury Toby before Rick got back. Then they could get on with their lives without Toby in the middle of things.

She left the car in the driveway. As she entered the garage, the buzzing, vibrating freezer imposed itself in her path. When she opened the door, her eyes started to water immediately, and her nose began to drip. She reached for an old dog blanket on a nearby shelf and laid it over the bundle that contained Toby. She would wait until the weekend to bury him.

Ginger checked her emails. There was the promised one from Rick. He liked to quote erotic poetry to her, this time from Petronius – a poem that started out, 'Good God, what a night that was' and ended with 'If I could only die that way, I'd say goodbye to the business of living.' He concluded his message by saying he'd be back Friday evening. Maybe they could go on a picnic on Saturday. Ginger looked out the window. The rain was over.

She thought about Jon. They used to run into each other at the park near the church where he worked, but she'd stopped walking there with Toby in the fall. He'd given the puppy to her almost exactly twelve years ago. She named him after *Toby Tyler* her favourite movie as a child, where the boy runs away to join the circus. This puppy never ran away, however. He slept between them. Before they made love, Jon pushed the dog outside – but afterwards Ginger retrieved Toby, wiped his muddy feet, and brought him back into bed. They had talked about having children, but somehow had never gotten around to it. Jon was busy with the youth groups at his church, and there were too many other urgent distractions.

It took Ginger several tries to compose a message to Jon with the right tone and information. Finally, she went with the direct approach:

Jon, I wanted to let you know about Toby. I had to put him to sleep. He was so crippled from various lumps and hip dysplasia that he could no longer walk. The vet said there was nothing else to be done. Toby seemed depressed. The tips of his ears were turning white. Maybe I should've told you before I did it. I hope things are going okay with you. I had a promotion at work, but it just means that I'm busier than ever. I even have my own office instead of just a cubicle.

She didn't know how to close the note. 'Love, Ginger'? 'Sincerely'? She decided to leave it blank. He would know who had written it. After clicking the send button, she felt better. Jon deserved to know about Toby.

The next morning before breakfast Ginger checked her email messages. Jon had always been very prompt, but there was nothing from him. Maybe he was out of town. In the summers he frequently went to Camp Victory with the church youth group. She wrote Rick a note that the rain had stopped and a picnic would be nice that weekend. She did not mention Toby.

She checked once more before leaving the house. When there was still nothing from Jon, she felt a coldness accumulating in her chest. She craved a cigarette. Just then she heard a ping, and a short message from Jon appeared on the screen.

'I will come by your place tonight.' That was all he said. No closing words except for his trademark signature. His messages ended with the letters *WWJD*. Just seeing those letters again made Ginger's chin quiver. He had numerous T-shirts with the insignia inscribed on the front and the back. Either coming or going, Jon was always asking the world the same question: *What Would Jesus Do?* He even wore the T-shirts to bed. She thought that it was very unlikely that Jesus would wear a T-shirt that asked, 'What Would Jesus Do?' any place at all, much less in bed. But it was useless to pursue this line of thinking with Jon. He had majored in philosophy first before he studied theology and had plenty of answers.

When Ginger returned home from work that day, she felt suddenly energized. Soon Jon would be there to help her with Toby. Damp patches of perspiration from the brutal June humidity had accumulated under her arms. A shower would feel good. On her bed, she placed her old peasant top and faded jeans, the ones she used to wear on the church campouts with Jon. Straightening up the bedroom a little, she hid the book on sensual massage that Rick had given her for her birthday; she also tucked his aftershave and deodorant behind the towels in the linen closet.

Ginger was washing her hair in the shower when she heard familiar sounds. She poked her head, full of suds, out the shower door. She could make out Jon's lanky presence in the bedroom. He tossed a small, black, rectangular object on the bed.

'I came in when no one answered. I knew you were home because your car was in the garage.' He stared at her then looked away. 'You know, you shouldn't leave the house wide open, especially now that...' His voice trailed off as they both conjured up Toby on one of his ferocious barking sprees.

'Oh.' She rubbed her eyes with her wet hand so as to see

him better. 'I'll be out in a bit. Help yourself to something… to drink…in the kitchen.'

He stood motionless for a moment. The steaming shower water sprayed out of the stall onto the tile floor. He took a step in her direction. She watched him kick off his shoes, unbuckle his jeans, and let them fall to his feet. He kept his underwear and shirt on. It seemed like the most natural thing in the world for him to do. They had often showered in this very place together. When he entered the tile stall, she turned toward him. The soap was running down her face. He scrubbed her back with his callused palms and rinsed her hair. She couldn't tell if it was tears, shampoo, or hot water that made her eyes burn. She rested her head against his shoulder and tasted the wet, salty fabric of his T-shirt, right above the *WWJD* emblem. It was the first time her insides had felt warm all week. Neither one of them spoke, but large unintelligible sounds erupted from her throat.

When the water turned lukewarm, then cold, Jon twisted off the faucet as he reached outside the door to grab a large towel. He pulled her from the shower and wrapped it around her two times, leading her without a word to the bed where her clothes had been laid out. He was still dripping wet in his shirt and underwear. Jon tugged on the towel, and she turned in an uncertain circle. He vigorously rubbed first her hair with it and then his own before letting the waterlogged towel fall to the floor. Picking up the peasant blouse, Jon guided it over her head and tied the drawstring. He took hold of her jeans and navigated them over her still-damp legs. They were loose on her. She hadn't eaten much of anything all week. He handed her the hairbrush from the dresser while he yanked off his soaked T-shirt, stepped out of his underwear, and threw the drenched clothing in a pile with the towel. Jon pulled on his own jeans. He picked up the book, a familiar tattered New Testament, from the bed and stuffed it in his back pocket. Puddles of water had gathered around his feet.

Ginger observed Jon's actions with awed recognition. His strawberry blonde hair was long, curling up on the ends in wet ringlets. Even after the shower, he smelled just like the musty pine trees following a rainstorm at Camp Victory. She'd loved it there – until she didn't anymore. His focus on philosophy and theology had been fine with her, but the constant expectations the youth ministry placed on him were just too much. For her.

Her eyes itched, and she knew they were swollen and red. Her straight, black hair had tangles that she could not get through with the brush.

'Tell me about Toby.' Jon was staring at the torn ears of the stuffed rabbit peeking out from the covers on the bed.

'I can't explain,' she responded after a moment's hesitation. 'I'll have to show you.'

Ginger grabbed his hand and pulled him through the house. Their moist bare feet made sucking noises on the wood floors. As they passed through the kitchen, Ginger was embarrassed that she had left the note from Rick on the counter next to her teacup. The white paper glowed against the butcher block countertop. She guided Jon down the hall towards the garage. They stepped onto the concrete floor. The freezer compressor was pumping out acrid air.

'In there,' she pointed at its massive door.

Jon's face turned sombre. Ginger worried all of the sudden that he might pray as he tended to do when people were upset. She squeezed her eyes shut.

'Would you like a cigarette?' Jon asked in a low voice.

'I've quit.' She breathed in relief and opened her eyes. They still stung.

'Is that so? Since when?'

'Since Monday – when Toby died.'

'Hmm.' He rubbed his chin where his beard used to be. He'd shaved it off after the divorce. His neck looked white, bare, and bony without it. The rest of his face and shoulders were sunburned.

'Well, I don't smoke very much anymore either. I don't want the kids at church to see me.' He paused and swallowed hard. 'And it's dishonest to do things behind their backs.' He glanced away from her then let his eyes rest on the sleeve of her peasant blouse. 'Anyway, they can smell it on you.'

Ginger pulled the drawstring of the blouse tighter. Her eyes watched the tip of Jon's nose that wiggled when he spoke. The reddish hairs on his chest, still damp, now were highlighted with touches of silver.

'But,' he continued, 'I sure could use a cigarette right now.' He turned towards her, away from the freezer. Ginger reached up to the shelf where she'd sequestered the cartons. Several packs fell to the floor.

'I don't have any matches,' she confessed.

'Oh, I have a lighter in my pocket,' he offered. She realized that he had some new, fine wrinkles around his hazel eyes. She wished she could rub them away and that they could start all over, back to the time when Toby was a puppy and things were simpler between them.

As she picked up one of the packs, he fished the lighter from his pocket. Moving together in a dance that was choreographed from their past, he leaned against her car, their hips nearly touching. He lit the cigarette, took a long, grateful puff, and handed it to her.

'So, tell me about your promotion.'

'I skipped work two days this week.' She inhaled slowly then returned the cigarette to him.

'Were you sick?' He flicked ashes onto the floor as he released smoke from his lungs. He knew she never missed work.

'No, just couldn't get up in the morning. It wasn't like I had to feed Toby or anything.'

Her fingers brushed his thumb as he gave her back the cigarette. She grew conscious of the fact that neither of them wore any underwear. The smoke made her dizzy.

'Your parents doing okay?' He'd always gotten on well with her mother and father.

She took one final puff. The familiar tobacco fragrance was calming her down. 'Yeah, just fine. I haven't told them about Toby yet. You know, they didn't really like him.' She paused. 'They thought we spoiled him.'

Jon did not reply. He squatted down and snuffed out the cigarette butt on the concrete floor. She studied the crown of his head; his hair was drying full and fluffy on top. It was thicker than hers.

'How about your work at the church?'

He stood up straight and concentrated on the freezer as its humming came to an abrupt stop. 'The kids are great. But I'm no good at the politics.' He spoke in a muted voice now. 'There's always some controversy – plus, I don't make very much money.'

Ginger breathed deeply, surprised he mentioned this. She had always made more money than he did. He'd claimed that money wasn't important to him, that he had a calling.

He leaned towards her. 'What do you think we should do with Toby?' His long arms hung at his side, as if ready for some action. She desperately wanted another cigarette. She couldn't allow this pure, close moment to vanish.

'Umm, I was getting kind of used to having him in here. I have a hard time imagining him anyplace else right now.'

'I can see that.' He rubbed his naked chin again as if searching for the missing beard. 'But you know, Ginger, you can't leave him in your freezer.'

She looked at him with scepticism. 'It's just that he seems bigger now.' The warmth of the cigarette was fading, replaced by an icy chill in her gut.

'Like everything,' Jon said in a serious voice, 'Like time.'

'What's that?' He tended to speak in confusing ways.

'Oh, that's just what Sartre said – you know, "Time is too large."' His thoughts always came as a complete surprise to her. She could never think of an intelligent reply. He added, '"It refuses to let itself be filled up."'

'Well, I don't know about that,' she finally countered. 'My time at work does.'

Jon was now appraising the freezer.

'But you could be right. That's what happened to Toby. He's gotten bigger. Plus, I feel something cold and hard in my chest all of the time.' She placed her hand on her blouse.

Jon turned his attention back to her as she kneaded the soft tissue above her heart. He'd always been one to study other people. She recalled how special it made her feel when he observed her, like she was pretty and important.

'Can I see?'

'What? See what?' Her hand fluttered on her chest.

'Toby.'

'Oh. Of course.'

When he pulled the freezer door open, the wrapped package no longer seemed so large to her. It nested at the bottom there – innocent and impassive. Jon ran his right hand slowly over the wrapping as if giving it a blessing. He placed his strong arms under the weight and lifted as he stood, turning towards her. The package exuded a coolness that filled the space between them. With a soft sigh, the freezer door closed.

'How 'bout if I take care of him for you?'

She hesitated before she responded, 'What are you going to do?'

'Oh, I don't know. I'll think of something.' His hands clutched together reverently under the frozen bundle. 'I'm the one that found Toby at the pound. Maybe tomorrow I'll bury him in the woods near Camp Victory. You know, where we used to go for walks on Saturday mornings.'

'Could I come with you?' She knew she sounded like a child pleading for an undeserved favour. She refused to let herself think about Rick, who by then would be coming back from his trip, his very existence a nervous intruder in her thoughts.

Jon stared at her then looked away. She combed through her hair with her fingers. She needed to look more composed, more in control.

'I don't know about that.'

'Why not?' Her fingers were stuck in a tangle. She tugged hard on it. Her scalp tingled.

He hugged the bulky parcel against his chest. 'Let's just say it's about me. And Toby.' His voice faltered then found its depth.

'I found myself missing Toby when I moved to the condo.' He added in a whisper, 'It seemed easier than missing you.'

Ginger wished she had not left the note from Rick out on the counter. She knew there was no way she could take it back, any of it. She furiously scratched her tender scalp.

'I think it would be best for everyone if you just let me take care of Toby,' he stated. He was accustomed to taking care of difficulties for others.

Jon spun away from her in his bare feet. He cradled the package in his arms like a newborn. The black book bulged in the back of his jeans. Ginger pictured his prized T-shirt, along with shoes and underwear, in a dazzling damp heap in her bathroom. She reached for the cigarette pack from the top of the freezer as she retrieved Jon's lighter from her pocket, hurriedly lighting another cigarette while he placed Toby's body in the back of his pickup truck. He climbed inside the cab, his hair lifted by the hot summer breeze. She leaned inside the window, handing him the lit cigarette as he started up the engine.

Jon's chest hairs shimmered in the rays of the evaporating sun. She yearned to nuzzle her face against their warmth. It was comforting to know that Toby's frozen body was also swathed in the late afternoon sunlight. The truck backed away from her down the driveway. Ginger grabbed another cigarette and flicked the lighter with her thumb. The flame, erupting in her hand, vanished into the tip of the cigarette. She watched Jon's regular rhythms of putting his truck into gear and moving forward as smoke filled her lungs and circled her head. When her shoulders shook, she knew that they had unearthed a cold, deep place in each of them – the one that never changes, that never stops hurting or pretending. She smoked in time with him.

Extinction

The air conditioning clicked on overhead. Gusts of recirculated air twisted around Ben's head before landing on the tight spot at the base of his neck. He swallowed an exhausted yawn, refocusing his attention on the woman seated across from him. His eyes concentrated on her tiny movements.

Donna pondered her short dull fingernails before she spoke again. 'I like the ones in the Hawaiian print swim trucks,' she confided with solemn conviction, 'Even if they are a little baggy.' She put her thumb in her mouth and nibbled on the cuticle. 'Those are the men that I like.' She indicated her satisfaction with this conclusion by nodding decisively. She inspected her thumb in the draft of cool air. The tip was bloody red.

Surely, Ben ruminated as he scrawled quick notes, this will all lead somewhere new. They hadn't talked about the swimming pool before although he knew she went there with her children. He glanced at the clock on the wall then checked his watch, his gesture to indicate that their time was up, then shifted in his seat.

'Yes,' Donna sustained her thought processes. 'I like to watch the men dive off the boards – as if they were teenagers. Some, you know, are still graceful. Even if they are bald and round. I don't like the ones who wear those skimpy Speedo swimsuits, especially old men. That seems vulgar to me.' She was now rubbing the bleeding thumb into the fabric on the couch. Ben sat forward and put down his notepad. He started to search for a handkerchief in his pocket but stopped himself, reaching instead for the Kleenex on the corner of his desk. He handed her a soft beige tissue. She wrapped it around her thumb, then took it off to blow her nose. She deposited the tissue, now turning damp pink, on the couch cushion next to her.

'Donna, our time is up for today. Maybe we could start here next week.' She looked up at him with alarm. He relaxed the tone of his voice. 'Do you want to come again – say, Monday morning at this same time?'

Her hand floated reflexively to her mouth, the thumb finding its resting place on the end of her tongue. An unpredictable world waited out there, and they both knew that she had used this time to discuss men's swimsuits. Donna jerked her head up and down while she collected her belongings and rushed out the door as if she had done something wrong. She left behind the soggy wad of stained tissue on the couch.

Ben's sore shoulders sank into the rough upholstery of his chair. It would be nice to take a nap on the couch. He stretched out his arms then refolded them to scribble the date on his notes. He picked up the telephone receiver as he scanned the entries on his calendar. The rest of his day looked jumbled up.

There was a rapid tapping noise, and he glanced up to see a spirited shape in a floral dress appear in the doorway. He dropped the receiver in its cradle. The new receptionist stuck her head into his office. Kate, Katie, Kathy…Katrina? He couldn't remember her name. She had fuzzy, rust-coloured hair that always looked as if she had forgotten to fix it, yet he'd seen her brush it at her desk with brisk strokes in the mornings. Long hairs clung to her desk and file folders. She was shedding. Sometimes a tangle of wavy crimson threads stuck to his trousers. They disturbed him. What he really wished to do was to take some of those lost hairs and paste them to his bald spot that was starting to expand into a shiny blotch in the midst of his dusty blonde hair. Frequently during the day, he stroked the smooth skin with his fingertips, hoping to inspire the roots to sprout new growth. He wore a baseball cap after work and on weekends.

'Your next appointment is here, Dr Ben. Should I send him back?' He sat up straighter in his chair. This new receptionist annoyed him by appearing in his doorway and referring to him that way. This Dr Ben stuff sounded juvenile and at the same time too friendly. He wondered if she did that to everyone else in the suite. He hadn't been paying much attention to what was going on around him lately.

'Yes. Fine.' Usually, he walked into the lobby to meet the people waiting to see him, but not today. He selected a file folder from the loose stack on his desk. 'Thanks,' he added as she withdrew from his view.

Ben had wanted to call home to see if he had any messages, but there was no time now. His wife had not called him for three weeks except to leave cryptic communiqués on their voicemail when she knew he wouldn't be home. She and Noah had gone to visit her family in Birmingham at the end of the school year, after she had handed in her grades. Ben had talked to his son a few times. They discussed baseball scores. Ben missed Noah's sulky presence in the shadows of the house. Cindy's messages concerned paying the bills and checking on the pets. When he called back, she always whispered as if to suggest they had something to hide. He couldn't think of anything to tell her, so they compared notes on the weather.

He felt certain she'd be back soon, before the planning period at the start of the new school year. Plus, Noah was to begin marching band practice in a few weeks. But thus far, Cindy had been noncommittal. Birmingham was a hot and dull place to be in July, or at least that's way it seemed to him. What could be so entertaining to her?

Jeremy Spalding strode into the office. Ben stood up abruptly, stuck out a welcoming arm, then yanked it back. He usually didn't shake hands with people who came for therapy. His wrist collided with Jeremy's elbow as he grabbed the discarded tissue from the couch and tossed it into the trash. His timing was off today, but Jeremy didn't seem to notice. He wore a new pin-striped business suit and carried a small electronic gadget as if it were a trophy. At least he would not try to extend his appointment. Jeremy was to be the CEO of a new company, yet he'd been experiencing overwhelming physical sensations: rapid heartbeat, sweaty palms, disorienting headache. At first, he thought it was a heart problem, but everything seemed fine when he had it checked out. The cardiologist suggested panic attacks and referred Jeremy to Ben for therapy.

'So, how did your week go?'

'Good! I convinced the bank to increase the loan. I hired a business manager. We're going to rent some space. Lots of interest in the software system. It's gonna be fantastic. Want to invest?' Ben couldn't tell if Jeremy was serious or not, so he decided to ignore the question. They'd been discussing anxiety disorders.

'How about the panic attacks? That's what I mean. Did you have any of those this week?'

Jeremy placed the PalmPilot on the carpet next to his shiny black shoes. He coughed as he sat back up. 'Last Thursday when I was driving a potential investor around in the car…' His voice dissolved. He cleared his throat then began again.

'You see, when I got to the highway, I had to pull over to the side of the road. I thought I was going to get sick right then and there.' Jeremy paused and closed his eyes for moment. 'I don't think I can face him again. I had a hard time driving after that. My clothes were soaked through with sweat. I needed to go home to change.' He brushed his hand over his forehead and ploughed the thickness of his straight brown hair. His eyes blinked rapidly, flashing worry signals despite the ever-present smile. 'Do you know what you were talking about when this occurred?'

'I can't remember a thing.'

'Hmm. Was anyone else there?'

'Just Julie, my assistant, in the backseat.'

'Could you ask her?'

'No. Absolutely not. This is embarrassing enough already.' Jeremy crossed his legs and then uncrossed them. He put his hands on his knees as if to hold them still.

Ben proceeded from a different angle. 'What time of day was it?'

'Afternoon. Right after lunch, I think.'

'Do you remember what you had for lunch?'

'Um, can't quite recall. Probably a burger. I don't know.'

'Caffeine?'

Jeremy shrugged his shoulders. His long fingers tapped on his pants leg. They seemed to be searching for something to do.

'Alcohol? Did you have a beer or glass of wine?' Ben persisted.

Jeremy looked uncertain. 'Probably not.'

'Well, you know, you have to pay attention to these things. You could even keep a record, a journal.' Ben's tone grew insistent, 'Maybe you could use that – for notes to yourself.' He pointed to the small rectangular object at Jeremy's feet.

Both of them stared at the PalmPilot. Its silver casing, nestled against the nubby blue carpet, beamed a shiny significance throughout the room. Jeremy rubbed his hands on his knees.

'Remember?' Ben inquired with forced patience. 'We discussed all of this before. It will help us if we can figure out what's triggering these episodes.'

'Maybe I just need some medication. Something to calm down my nerves.'

'Yeah, maybe. We discussed possible side effects. Besides, the medication mutes all of your reactions. Which is fine, if that's what you want. I can refer you to someone else, or we can try to figure this out.'

Jeremy looked at him with scepticism. He crossed his arms over his chest.

Ben had no desire to talk him into anything. Maybe a referral wasn't such a bad idea. Who cared if emotions were muted? He looked at his watch. Only seventeen minutes had passed. Jeremy sat across from him expressionless; his face looked vacant without a smile. Ben rubbed his bald spot, which felt tender. The second hand on the clock struggled forward.

'I once had a panic attack,' Ben stated quietly. Jeremy uncrossed his arms and studied Ben. He squinted his eyes. This was their third session. They really hadn't found a rhythm or rapport yet.

'Just once?' Jeremy queried.

'No, actually a series of things happened.' His stiff fingers combed the residue of hair on his scalp. It was okay to say this. Yes, fine because Jeremy wouldn't know how unusual this admission was. 'It just lasted a short time but affected everything I did.' He slowly collected molecules of air into his lungs and pushed them out again.

'Is that so? What sorts of things?'

Jeremy was a natural at this, Ben realized with surprised envy. Clearly, he was the kind of person who inspired trust in fellow travellers. They'd reveal their secret lives to him – even on short airplane rides.

'Oh, just about everything, lots of stuff at work and at home,' Ben responded vaguely, inhaling again. 'I can't really say.' His thoughts turned inside out. Things like having the energy to play catch with Noah. Or wanting to make love with Cindy. He recalled what it felt like to have her sleeping beside him but never touching. Surely it was better to have panic attacks in a car with a business associate than at night in bed with your wife.

Jeremy looked even more at ease now. He shook loose his long thin legs, taking care to avoid kicking the electronic device on the floor. 'Well, you need to remember these things, Doc, if you want to do anything about them.' He smiled at his own cleverness. 'Would you like to borrow my PalmPilot?'

Ben had difficulty taking his next breath. His heart and lungs took over his body. This was getting harder and harder for him. On his own travels, he'd started telling strangers that he was an economist. They sought financial advice, and he told them things he didn't even realize he knew. Before, when he had admitted to being a psychologist, people had automatically covered their mouths – as if to capture wayward Freudian slips before they erupted.

He swallowed hard, contracted his internal organs, then

contrived to steer the session back on course. They discussed Jeremy's various anxiety incidents. There was no predictable routine. He had panic attacks in the car, at the movies, with clients, with his girlfriend at the lake, on Saturdays as well as Thursdays. Finally, when Ben checked the clock on the wall again, his shoulders relaxed. Their time was almost up.

'Okay. Next week we're going to start the process of helping you manage your anxiety. The first step is for you to remember everything that happens when you panic. What triggers it, what you feel like as it's happening, what you do afterwards. I need for you to write everything down.' He forced himself to sound convincing.

Jeremy stood up in front of Ben and towered over him. His suit was not even wrinkled. Ben had smeared ink on his own tie; the waistband of his pants sliced into his middle. Jeremy's full head of hair made him seem even taller than he was. He dropped the PalmPilot into his pocket and turned away. Here was a man with a mission. Ben admired his sense of direction in life. He probably had sex with his girlfriend several times a week, but they had not discussed these matters. Ben didn't like to talk with other men about sex, even in therapy sessions. It was easier with women. They talked about sex as if it were a mystery, one that might never be solved but still worthy of intense investigation.

Ben glanced at his watch. Noontime. He had over two hours before his next session. There was time to carry out his plan.

Closing his empty briefcase, Ben buzzed the receptionist. 'I'm going out for lunch then to a meeting. I'll be back by two o'clock. Please take messages if I get any calls.'

'Sure, Dr Ben. Have a good lunch.'

He wondered why he felt obliged to tell her where he was going and what was on his mind when he couldn't even remember her name. One of the problems with his line of work was that other people always assumed you cared what they were thinking and feeling. He grabbed the scuffed briefcase, locked his office door, and headed towards the elevator. That's the way it had been with Cindy when they were first married. Everything was on the table all of the time. Recently, he'd discovered that it was better not to talk about feelings. Cindy had stopped telling him things as well. He'd begun to savour the silence between them. Even Noah, who used to be such a chatterbox, had grown into a taciturn teenager. Their lives were much calmer and quieter nowadays.

The elevator was filled with couples who stood close together. He rarely had lunch plans. He'd learned to accept that it was not easy for therapists to form friendships, even with one another. The lunchtime crowd opened up to make room for him. He clutched the hard briefcase tightly against his chest. This was a perfectly respectable thing to do – to go home for lunch. He would check the mail and feed the pets.

Ben dropped the briefcase just inside his front door. The contrast of the cold, bright air with the penetrating, humid heat outside sent chills across the tightness in his neck. He immediately headed for the kitchen. In Cindy and Noah's absence, he had let the newspapers and mail stack up on the counter. At first, he had kept nice, neat piles and even paid the bills immediately upon receipt. Lately, he had not bothered to open the envelopes. Today, he tossed the most recent bills on the top of the heap. They slid off sideways to the floor.

The house was beginning to have the lonely, desperate appearance of the day after Christmas. Most of the newspapers were turning yellow, still encased in plastic bags. There was no worthwhile news anyway, just sordid reports of corruption, terrorists, and homicidal maniacs. The sink was clear, however. He had managed to keep his dishes washed. He only had cereal and juice for breakfast and usually bought fast food for lunch and dinner. In the evenings he drank beer and watched baseball on television, carrying on strategy debates with Noah, who wasn't even there.

Now that he was home, he didn't know what to do with himself. He had not stopped for lunch, so he searched through the refrigerator and pantry. The cheese was mouldy; the luncheon meat looked suspicious; the bread stale. Eventually his hand landed on a can of Campbell's chicken noodle soup, Noah's favourite. They liked to slurp it together on nights when Cindy had PTA meetings. Ben poured the contents of the can into a bowl and stuck it in the microwave. The idea of the soup seemed nourishing but better for winter than for summer.

This was not turning out to be a good summer for him. Others in the office had taken vacations, and some of his therapy clients had made exciting plans. Ben dreaded hearing about their cruises. Jeremy was going to the French Riviera soon, and he made sly references to nude beaches when describing his itinerary. Ben's stomach ached just thinking about it. His wife and son had been away almost a month. It seemed easier to go into the office each day rather than come up with something else to do in life. He sampled the undiluted soup as he observed hyperactive birds in the trees in the backyard. The broth scorched his tongue, so he set aside the soup bowl to cool. Without Noah around it tasted too salty, almost bitter.

Ben decided to wash some clothes. After they first left, he had done several loads of laundry. Pairs of Noah's socks and Cindy's underwear got all tangled up with his T-shirts. He re-washed them each time he started another load of light clothes. He liked rolling up the long white athletic socks together. He fingered the toes. He smelled their freshness, seeking the pure aroma of Noah when he first got up in the morning. He hid some of Cindy's lingerie under her pillow in the bed. At night when he watched CNN, before he fell asleep, he rubbed the lace. In the morning he stuffed a pair of her satin bikinis in his pants pocket instead of a handkerchief. This slippery sensation made her seem more present to him. His body throbbed when he thought of her, even though they had not had sex for weeks before she left. He didn't think it much mattered to her, but he wasn't sure.

The sound of the phone startled him. Ben let it ring three times before he responded. He walked around the house with the receiver clasped tightly to his ear. He stopped at the bedroom door.

'Hello.'

'Oh. Hi. What are you doing there?' Cindy seemed less surprised than he'd expected.

'I forgot...I forgot something, so I decided to come home at lunchtime.' He moved to the pantry.

'Well, I was just checking in – planning to leave a message, you know.'

'How's the weather?' he questioned immediately.

'Sticky. How about there?'

'Looks like there's gonna be a storm this afternoon.'

'Yeah, we had one earlier, so it must be moving in your direction.'

'Is Noah nearby?' Ben's voice turned high and hopeful, as he now hovered over the television in the family room.

'No, he went to the store with my mother. They're going to pick up some fried chicken.'

'Oh, I see.' He paused, fiddling with the buttons on the VCR. 'Well, I just made some chicken noodle soup, and I thought of him.'

'Isn't it kind of hot for soup?'

'Yeah, I suppose.' His voice trailed off. He couldn't remember what he had needed to say to her. He wandered back into the kitchen.

'Well, I've gotta be going. I don't want to run up my parents' phone bill. Don't forget to feed the fish and turtle.'

'Of course not.' He hadn't checked on the fish in days. 'Umm…I guess I'll talk to you soon. Tell Noah…tell Noah…'

'Yeah, bye.'

The distant calmness in her voice terrified him. Those heart palpitations, the ones Jeremy had been describing, seized Ben now. He gasped for air. He felt dizzy. Here was the thing about life. There was no way you could count on anything; nothing was reliable. You never knew what to expect. All of these people came to see him in therapy because they couldn't deal with what life threw at them. What he really needed to tell them was the truth – you can't figure it out, so don't even try. People panicked because their lives were unpredictable and scary. 'Accept it!' he wanted to scream at them, 'Just accept it. That will solve your panic attacks.'

Ben leaned against the kitchen counter where he'd been folding laundry. He was overcome by the quiet emptiness that surrounded him. He looked around the room, and his eyes landed on the translucent barrel of Noah's paintball gun leaning in the corner. He could count on Noah. He knew the boy would come back for this prized possession. He'd begged his mother to let him take it to Birmingham, but she'd said absolutely not. The nearby canister of paintballs was nearly full.

Ben took off his jacket. He draped it on the back of the kitchen chair. He loosened his tie. He put on Noah's Atlanta Braves baseball cap that was perched on the stair post. The scent of his son's cast-off perspiration coated his head. He picked up the paintball gun. It was still shiny. Noah had just managed to save up his money at the end of the school year. The gun had hardly been used before his mother whisked him away to Alabama despite his protests. It had the serious look of a real gun. Ben had always hated guns. He objected to Noah buying this toy. He had refused to touch it when his son was at home; now he looked down the empty barrel and nervously pulled the trigger. There was a pleasant popping noise. He tried it again. He liked the way the paintball gun felt cool and calm in his hand when he had expected it to be hot and explosive.

Ben stopped when his watch read 1:42. He had to hurry to get back to the office, but he felt satisfied. He had hit his target in the backyard nearly fifty percent of the time. He kept track with a line of pebbles on the deck. Aiming at the big oak tree, any strike on any part of the tree counted in his favour, and so he added a pebble to his pile. The birds scattered to new treetops in neighbouring yards. He was pretty good at this.

He'd decided he could use thirty paintballs, and Noah would never know the difference. The ones in this container were all hot pink. He admired the psychedelic colour smashed against the canvas of green leaves giving the tree the festive appearance of being tie-dyed. He enjoyed the way his fingers felt after he had pulled the trigger. His shoulders no longer ached. Each hit made him eager to try again. He was exuberant, now fully awake.

There was no time to change his shirt and put on fresh deodorant. He didn't wash his lunch dishes either. He'd only eaten half of the bowl of soup, so he grabbed a bag of potato chips to snack on in the car. He kicked aside the weightless briefcase on his way out the door. It was not a good idea to be late for therapy sessions. People thought you didn't take them seriously, and the whole point was to let them know that you were considering their lives with the utmost seriousness. He crushed the baseball cap against his scalp. His own acrid adult sweat mingled with Noah's fresh adolescence. Leaving the paintball gun behind was hard; just touching it had made him feel closer to Noah. For the first time all summer, Ben was looking forward to returning home after work.

The rest of the week Ben spent his lunch break at home. When the phone rang, he did not pick it up to answer. Later he checked messages and listened to Cindy's flat Alabama drawl that deepened with each phone call. He did not attempt to return her calls at night anymore. He let the laundry accumulate in shapeless piles. He had other things on his mind. The best time to shoot paintballs was in the middle of the day. The sun was bright, the neighbours were at work. He'd had to cancel a few lunchtime appointments in order to maintain this schedule. His aim was getting better and better.

On Saturday and Sunday, Ben kept to this regimen. He only allowed himself to shoot paintballs at noon. In the afternoon he ran out to the sports store to pick up some more ammunition, white and blue paintballs this time. Despite threatening storm clouds, there had not been rain all week, so the oak tree was splattered with paisley ink blots. They looked lovely and revealing to him. He started searching for new targets. At the store he discovered additional fittings and elaborate equipment for the gun.

The following Monday after breakfast, he grabbed Noah's hat, then placed the gun on the passenger side of the front seat. He planned to use his lunchtime to find some new attachments. Ben had been looking forward to this expedition all weekend. Noah would be impressed when he returned. Ben could hardly wait to see the look on his face.

That morning, the weekly session with Donna made him feel like he was caught in a slow-motion video. She'd had a manicure since the last visit, but her fuchsia fingernail polish was already chipped. She gnawed on it during their session. Something seemed to be extremely upsetting to her, but Ben couldn't determine exactly what it was. They focused their discussion on her six-year-old son Christopher. This child kept the whole family up at night with his erratic wanderings. Donna worried that he might fall down the stairs or venture outside in the middle of the night. There were purple circles under her eyes. The nail polish further disintegrated as she chewed on her fingers, leaving dark specks on her teeth. She confessed in a sad voice that she had contemplated locking Christopher in his room.

'I want you to start keeping track of the times of these wanderings,' Ben instructed, 'You and your husband should take turns on this, so at least one of you gets a good night's sleep. Okay?' She nodded as if in a trance.

'I need to know how often they occur and at what intervals. Also, when you put him back in bed, don't argue or cajole.' He watched Donna's creased face as she grabbed a tissue from his desk and rubbed her bloodshot eyes with it. Black mascara smeared across her cheek.

He wanted to reassure her. 'You know Donna, Christopher will learn to stay in bed. And even sleep soundly through the night. We just have to help him along.'

Ben's thoughts turned to Noah who had been afraid of closed doors when he was little. Nowadays he kept his bedroom door tightly shut at all times. Ben remembered with a sinking feeling the abandoned goldfish on Noah's cluttered dresser.

Donna said nothing. She stuffed the dingy tissue in her purse.

'Are you all right?' he asked gently.

'Do you think it's anything I said or did that is making him act this way, Dr Hodges?' she whispered.

She had the look of the guilty. Ben had observed that babies these days arrived fresh from the birth canal with the posture and demeanour of prosecuting attorneys. By the time they reached kindergarten, they knew how to keep their parents on the witness stand.

'Well, we talked about all this earlier. Can you think of anything that might have scared him at night?' She shook her head sorrowfully. 'Then let's not worry about that right now. We'll just concentrate on his behaviour.' Her face struggled to manufacture a weak smile, which he returned with further encouragement. 'Donna, you know, I'm certain we will figure this out.'

It pleased Ben that he was able to give her some comfort, some hope. Donna collected all of her things, and he escorted her into the lobby. He was feeling better these days, more in control of things. The nice part about his profession was that sometimes you could actually help people deal with the challenging things in life.

As Donna left, Jeremy arrived, filling the reception area with exuberance. He seemed to suck up all the unstable air around him. He carried a smooth leather briefcase. Together they moved towards Ben's office.

Jeremy paused in the doorway.

'Nice hat, Doc.'

The Atlanta Braves cap rested upon his desk. It had smudges of colourful paintball droppings on the brim. Ben smiled proudly. It was one of the few personal items in his office. The other, a picture of him with Cindy and Noah on the bookcase, was at least four years old. The photograph had faded, but all three of them looked energetic, as if they were waiting for life to unfold. Otherwise, the office was full of manuals and files. Anyone could have conducted any kind of business in it.

The two men sat down opposite one another. Ben picked up the hat and brushed its brim. Dense body odours escaped into the air.

'This belongs to my son. But he's letting me borrow it.'

'Must be a good kid.'

'Yeah, he's great.' Ben wondered how much Noah had grown

over the summer. The boy had been nearly Cindy's height when they'd left. He gazed at the hat as he set it down on his desk. Maybe he'd drive over to Birmingham soon to see them for a surprise visit.

'How has your week been?'

'Excellent. No anxiety attacks.'

'None?'

'Absolutely none.'

'Well, that's good. I suppose.' He hesitated. 'And did you have a normal week otherwise?'

'Yeah, pretty normal, I guess. Work and golf – that kind of thing. Jessica and I are getting our vacation planned. Next Friday and I'm out of here.'

Ben's stomach felt queasy. It was getting close to noon. Time for lunch and for his paintball errand.

'Did you write down all of the anxiety-causing events that you could think of?'

Jeremy rested his briefcase on his thighs and opened the lid, unveiling its hidden contents. The PalmPilot sat securely on a stack of papers. He picked it up and in a surprisingly reckless move pitched it to Ben. It glided through the air, a determined missile, landing on top of the notepad in his lap.

'Nice catch, Doc. Everything is right in there.'

Ben stuck his pen in his shirt pocket. He opened the top of the PalmPilot.

'How do you work it?'

'Like this, Doc. Here's what you do.' Jeremy set down the briefcase and leaned towards Ben with a sharp stylus in his right hand. As he pushed buttons, the device emitted beeps. Ben watched in fascination. He reached for the baseball cap and placed it securely on his head. It released the essence of wild sweet onions into the air.

They both stared at the words that emerged: a list of six situations that had previously set off anxiety symptoms. Ben struggled to process them.

'Isn't this great, Doc? Don't you just love it?' With the stroke of a button, the anxiety symptoms vanished from view and Jeremy's crowded appointment calendar appeared in its place. Jeremy kept pushing other buttons, and new screens with notes and phone numbers materialized.

Ben had to admit that the digital display was impressive. But he was starting to feel anxious himself. The session was slipping by him. He had an important errand to run. This man seemed more interested in demonstrating the latest technology than solving his problems. The two of them kept getting diverted.

He slumped in the chair still clutching the device. He pulled off the hat and tossed it on his desk.

'Jeremy.' Ben rubbed the tight bare skin on the top of his head.

'Yes?' Jeremy smiled at him.

'Let's try to make some progress here.'

Jeremy snatched the PalmPilot from Ben then sat back and crossed his legs. He appeared to be waiting for something important to happen.

'In our first session I told you about the process of desensitization.' As he reiterated the main points, Ben sat up straighter and straighter. 'Gradually, over time, if we go through these steps your anxiety symptoms will diminish – through the discipline of learning to relax and also focusing on your feelings and behaviour.' He spoke with deliberation, his head nodding vigorously. 'Then careful, planned exposure will lead to extinction of the anxiety.' Ben enunciated each word. 'That's what the strategy is. Surely you remember?'

'Exposure,' Jeremy repeated slowly. 'Extinction,' he added with pleasure, licking his lips and lifting his feathery eyebrows. The sound of these powerful words seemed to renew his optimism.

'I'll tell you what, Doc. How 'bout we see how this vacation goes and worry about anxiety when I get back. Maybe it's just up and cured itself, gone and got extinct while I've been doing other things.' He lifted his hand and waved the PalmPilot triumphantly in the space between them.

Ben turned his chair towards the paperwork on his desk and away from Jeremy. He couldn't believe that a person would pay good money to come to see him and then take that attitude. Jeremy must be hiding something behind his cheerfulness. He'd seen this kind of pretence before. But it was impossible to make people do what they didn't want to do in life. He'd learned that a long time ago from his wife and son.

'Fine, Jeremy.' He deposited his notes for the session in a file folder. 'If by chance you have a panic attack while you're gone, it would be a good idea if you'd write the circumstances down. Are you bringing that with you?' They both stared at the PalmPilot, now poised on Jeremy's leg.

'No siree. Jessica wouldn't stand for it. She's jealous enough as it is. I'd be checking my emails day and night. Plus, I won't have a place to keep it. No briefcase – not even pockets in the Riviera.' Jeremy seemed to enjoy to teasing Ben. No doubt about it, his life was tantalizing.

'Well, a piece of scrap paper and pencil will do just fine. Okay?'

'Yep. I'll call for an appointment when I get back – if I need one.'

Ben let Jeremy find his own way to the reception area. This man was grating on his nerves. He preferred openly miserable people like Donna, people who could take advantage of what he had to offer. Jeremy's perfectly pressed suit and Italian leather briefcase and electronic devices and sexy girlfriend were all so excessive. Besides, he thought he could fix his own problems. Right. More power to him.

Ben waited until he was certain that Jeremy had left the office suite, then he grabbed his keys. He pressed the musty baseball cap back on his head. He no longer needed to tell the receptionist where he was going. She had learned his lunchtime routine. He remembered that her name was Kitty, which made him want to stroke her outrageous hair to see if she would purr. Instead of the elevator, he'd taken to using the building stairway. It was only three flights, but he was beginning to lose the weight he'd gained. Mostly he just had a milkshake for lunch and soup for dinner.

He located his dusty silver Volvo in the parking lot. The black leather interior was so hot that Ben let the car idle with the windows down and air conditioning turned on full blast. The sports store was only a few miles down the interstate. He had plenty of time to get there. The paintball gun waited expectantly for him on the passenger seat. It shimmered in the blazing sunlight. Ben ran his fingers along the eye set. Its curves were sleek and smooth. The plexiglass barrel was full of a random assortment of paintballs, all the colours he'd acquired in the past week. His car was starting to exhale the accumulated heat, and the interior temperature grew milder. As he let himself relax for a few minutes, he picked up the gun. The paintballs looked like spheres of juicy chewing gum stuffed in the drugstore machine. He was tempted to taste them to see if they had distinct flavours. Ben tenderly stroked the barrel. He rested its hot metal tip on his lips.

Just at that moment a forest green Jaguar crept into his line of vision. The vehicle inched along the parking lot in his direction. A familiar head turned his way. Ben saw Jeremy's eyes peer out with wonder from underneath the shock of brown hair. They locked with his own, startling him as he massaged the gun's trigger. His index finger twitched, then vibrated. The gun, with its own intentionality, now turned direction and pointed outward from the window of Ben's car. A rapid sound, like that of fretful popcorn, erupted in his ears. Pink and blue and white spots appeared in a pattern of crazy magic against the approaching green shape. The polished car stopped with a lurch. Ben could detect the drenching shine of perspiration on the upper lip of the driver, above the smile that had turned to a grimace. Ben could predict the vapours of sweat and vomit that were to come. Finally, something he did had caught Jeremy up short.

Ben backed his car out of the parking space, immediately finding the exit that led to the highway. He planned to stop at the sports store, then proceed to McDonalds for a chocolate milkshake. From there he figured he had two hours. That's how long he calculated it would take him to get to Birmingham.

Contamination

She showed up in my office shortly after being evicted from her boyfriend's loft apartment.

'Hal says I can't stay there anymore.' Holly's lovely face looked so pinched with worry that I couldn't bring myself to ask questions. My advisee had many wonderful qualities, like beauty and brains, but not good judgment – at least in men, it seemed. I looked up from the grind of grading papers.

'It was his place, after all,' Holly explained with an exaggerated shrug. 'I was the interloper.' Usually so self-contained and statuesque, Holly looked ragged with her clothes wrinkled and her blonde bangs covering her eyes. She parked her hiking backpack, a computer case, and a crate in the corner and asked if she could sleep on the office couch over the weekend.

True enough, I was going out of town for a few days; there was no real inconvenience to me. She had earlier served as my teaching assistant, so I knew her to be highly organized and conscientious. When I stopped by the following Monday afternoon to pick up some files, her computer had established itself on an upside-down crate with toiletries nearby in a bucket and a few blouses hooked on the back of the door.

'A room is available in the grad student co-op, but I've got to wait until the beginning of the month,' she clarified. 'Just a little while.'

It was actually almost two weeks until the first of October, but I was on sabbatical that semester, traveling a lot for a book tour and trying to finish up research on rites of passage for girls in American life. In between trips, I was working at home. Holly was just a graduate student trying to finish her dissertation, after all, with limited resources. The bathroom was right next door and the departmental lounge with a microwave across the hall. Holly could water my withering African violets.

On Thursday when I went by to check my mail before heading out of town, the door to the office was cracked open. Quiet voices crept into the hallway. I knocked before poking my head in. The faint smell of incense tickled the inside of my nose.

'Excuse me,' I interrupted. 'Just wanted to pick up some of my files.'

Another young woman lounged on the couch facing Holly, who sat at my desk. A new pillow, throw blanket, and footstool had been added to the décor, along with a flourishing spider plant and some herbs on the windowsill to keep the African violet company.

'Oh, hi.' Holly looked up from a paper that she was reading. 'This is Kim, she's in the class I'm TA-ing this semester. We're just going over her paper.' She sat back in the chair. 'It's quite good,' Holly added, with an air of authority.

'No need to stop,' I countered. 'I just came by to pick up some files.' My gaze landed on a set of folders, formerly dishevelled, now stacked on the coffee table with a teapot resting on the top of the pile. There was steam rising from the spout.

The papers on my desk had also been rearranged into neat piles, and the blinds pulled up higher; the sun washed through the window with a clean brightness. Holly's boyfriend had no reason to complain about her housekeeping abilities.

'I'm so grateful for the use of your office that I took the

liberty of straightening it up a bit,' Holly explained. I noticed Kim, a petite person with straight, dark hair, staring at me. When I reached out to retrieve the files, she steadied the teapot.

'It's from Korea,' Kim volunteered with a midwestern accent. 'Celerian. I gave it to Holly. But it's really for the office. Would you like some ginger tea?' When I did not reply, she added, 'It's good for the digestion. Or so my grandmother says.'

'Oh…No. I mean no thanks,' I mumbled, retreating to the doorway. 'Everything looks so…um…nice in here.'

'Some of your advisees stopped by,' Holly informed me. 'I initialled their drop/add sheets. I wanted to save you the trouble of having to come in. It's the least I could do.'

'And my mail?' I inquired, trying to sound casual.

'It's in the wooden tray on the bookshelf, which I've labelled "inbox." Nothing important. Just a few departmental fliers. I'll keep you posted if anything official-looking shows up.' Everything seemed so exquisitely well-ordered that I couldn't find words to object to these changes. Only when I left my office did I notice above my nameplate on the door a bumper sticker proclaiming, 'Imperialism is not the Answer.'

My latest book was a huge success, at least in the popular press – although barely noticed in academic circles. That was good enough for me. I had tenure and an endowed professorship at Western. The news media had picked up some selections concerning the relationship between girls and nature. My research study showed positive correlation between the amount of time girls spent in unstructured natural surroundings and their success in science. The message was distilled into a sound bite by CNN – send your daughters into the woods or to the beach for the summer and quit worrying about music lessons, volunteer work, SAT preps, and reading lists. I had even been invited to talk shows, which impressed my grown daughters, although none of us had ever spent much time in an unstructured natural environment unless that concept included the neighbourhood swim club or a condo at the beach. My study at home was a natural enough habitat for me – a back porch converted into a sunroom. In addition to a large old-fashioned desk with my computer and shelves of books, there was a comfortable easy chair, which was perfect for reading and napping. But the chair was always so covered with books and files that I never got around to sitting in it.

All the same, I had everything that I needed at home. The college and my office were becoming increasingly irrelevant. Holly was certainly capable of looking after things for me, at least for a short time. Otherwise, my daughters were both elsewhere working on their MBAs. Their father, my ex-husband, stopped by regularly for a glass of wine. Once or twice a week, Nathan spent the night. Sex with him was as good as ever. And there was no one else to worry about, except the middle-aged Irish setter Terry. Neither Nathan nor I mentioned to the girls that we saw one another occasionally. We'd split up shortly after they left for college for reasons that no longer seemed important, especially when we slept together.

The cell phone in my purse was ringing. I rummaged through the cluttered contents to rescue it. 'Um, hello.'

'Dr Bennett?' The voice was vaguely familiar.

'Yes?'

'Campus security wants to speak with you.'

'Excuse me?' Loudspeakers in the airport droned out excruciating details of flight delays.

'Campus security. They're trying to locate you.' It was Sam, the temporary receptionist for the sociology department.

'Me? About what?' I hadn't been going to campus, much less parking my car illegally. I'd been issued a warning the previous semester that the next time I parked in the service driveway my car would be towed.

'I think it's important,' Sam insisted.

'Well, I'm on my way out of town. Give me their number.'

I wrote down the number on a scrap of paper and stuffed it in my pocket. I would call back once I checked in during the long wait required for security. Apparently, there was a high alert due to some bombings that had occurred in Canada in a train station. It was getting harder and harder to go anywhere these days.

My neighbour's son, who took me to the airport, had agreed to walk the dog and water my lawn. Jamie was a nice kid. I paid him $50 per week, even when I was in town, just to ensure his availability. I also told him that he could watch old DVDs from Nathan's collection on my big screen TV, if he liked. Every now and then, I saw evidence that he'd watched James Bond or some other indecipherable adventure movie with lots of guns and shooting.

As I boarded the airplane, I realized that I'd forgotten to call campus security. There was no hurry. What could be such an emergency? I had other pressing matters on my mind. Holly, Jamie, and Nathan were perfectly capable of handling whatever came up. Besides, I was on my way to New York for an important interview and to meet up with my sister; we'd planned to see a few plays and go to museums. On the plane, I browsed through the current *New Yorker*. When I landed, I saw several more missed calls listed on my cell phone, including some from my ex-husband. I felt pestered.

'Moira, some people are trying to track you down.' Nathan's voice implored when I called him back.

'What kind of people?'

'The security office at Western. They called me. I guess you still have me listed as your emergency contact.'

'Of course I do, who else?'

Nathan didn't respond. We'd each had a short list of barely significant others in our lives since the divorce but nothing substantial. He remained the beneficiary on my life insurance policy. He was a financial analyst, so I could count on him to take better care of the girls than they could care for themselves.

'By the way,' I added, 'Could you go by and check on Terry? Since I've been traveling so much his appetite is off. Might need to see the vet. Jamie has been looking after him.'

We both knew that I could've taken Terry to the vet myself in between trips. I avoided doctors, dentists, and veterinarians like the plague. Nathan had been in charge of all medical affairs when we were married. I still called him to pick up my prescription when I had a migraine.

'Yeah, sure. This call has something to do with your office.'

'Oh, they're probably wanting to use it for the new visiting professor. I'm avoiding everyone in the department.'

'Moira, I think there's something else.' Nathan was a worrier at heart. And he had a big heart with lots of worries stacked up in it. 'After all,' he continued, 'it's the security office, not the department, and they wanted to know your travel plans.'

'Well, I hope you didn't tell them anything.'

'That would be hard since I have no idea what they are. Where are you anyway?' When I didn't answer, he continued, 'You'd better call because you don't want them contacting the girls.' Nathan and I had a longstanding policy about not troubling our daughters with superfluous information about our lives.

He gave me the number, which I'd already received several times from the department secretary in the long listing of missed calls. I noticed that I also had two from Jamie, the dog-walker. I knew Nathan would be in touch with him, so there was no need to respond.

After collecting my luggage, I decided to use the time in the taxi, which was zipping toward Manhattan, to return the call to campus security. I simply had to say, 'This is Professor Moira Bennett.' They immediately put me through to the sergeant.

'Dr Bennett, were you aware that someone is using in your office?'

'Certainly. The department often allows visitors or graduate students to use offices when faculty are on sabbatical.'

'We mean sleeping in it. Staying there.'

I didn't reply.

'Do you know someone by the name of Holly Nix?'

'Yes, she's a graduate student in my department. Surely you know that already.'

'We need to speak to you as soon as possible. When will you be back home?'

'Not until next week.'

There was static on the phone. I opened the window of the

taxi. We were going through a tunnel. 'You're speaking to me now,' I talked into the air, not knowing if he could hear me.

'It might be a good idea to come back before then.' The wind was hot for late September.

Given that they were in the midst of an investigation, apparently he couldn't give me much more information. My sister already had tickets for us that evening to a new play on Broadway. I wanted nothing to do with Holly, security, or the sociology department for that matter. I was entitled to my sabbatical. Besides I had a major TV interview set up, bringing much-needed credit to the school. There was no reason that they should be making things difficult for me.

'I'm sorry. I have vital business to attend to here in New York. I can't come home any earlier.' What were they going to do – arrest me?

'We actually are working closely with the city police. They have a search warrant for your office.'

'A search warrant? That's absurd. An infringement of my rights. Preposterous!' The whole matter had turned into an intrusion that needed to go away.

The sergeant was quiet for a few seconds, but I could hear voices and electronic beeps in the background.

'We don't have a duty to inform you. I'm just doing so as a professional courtesy.'

Actually, beyond the principle, the idea of a search warrant didn't bother me much. There was nothing I had in the office to hide – no pornography, no confidential memos, no lurid love letters, certainly no deep dark secrets or illegal substances. Of course, there was Holly. Who knew what she was up to? But it had nothing whatsoever to do with me.

'I'm sorry,' I responded. 'I can't be there. I'm imploring you to stay out my office.' With that, I switched off my cell phone.

While talking to Lindsay over dinner, I suppressed the impulse to check messages on my cell. If the girls needed anything, their father was easily accessible. Once I turned on the phone, people would expect me to do something. Lindsay and I made a point of not talking about anything important on our annual fall trips. Family gossip, however, was okay. Our first cousin was marrying our second cousin on the other side, and we spent some time analysing mating habits and customs. Lindsay was an anthropologist who worked for the Smithsonian where she was supposed to be a curator for Native American art, but she spent most of her life answering emails and preparing budgets, which appealed to her desire for order in life. When we were children, she'd constantly tried to correct my carelessness.

We'd just seen the Jeff Wall exhibition at MoMA, and his large-scale backlit photographs, especially the one of the dishevelled woman's room, among his earliest, captured her attention. The next day we were planning to go to a matinee and an evening Broadway performance, but we didn't have tickets yet. Our plan was to check out the half-price ticket booth to see what was available. Not having a plan was our idea of a vacation.

I slept well in New York. The bustle of the city was like white noise for me. The thought of spending time in the wilderness, as recommended for adolescent girls by the research in my book, was not the least bit appealing. I was willing to study it but not to live it, which made me part of a fine scientific tradition. My doctor, the one that I avoided, was at least forty pounds overweight. I, on the other hand, managed to stay thin with a diet fuelled by Lean Cuisine while at home and too-expensive restaurants with small servings while traveling.

My sister Lindsay had younger children and a temperamental husband, George. She felt more obligated than I did to stay in touch with her family. On the third night we were there, she handed the phone over to me. George's voice was insistent, 'Moira, Nathan is trying to reach you. Give him a call. Or at least answer the phone, for God's sake. He asked me for the phone number to the hotel also.'

Although he was a worrier, Nathan was not the kind of person to try to track me down, even when we were married. We just didn't have that kind of relationship, which had been fine. But now that he was trying to find me, this behaviour felt oddly reassuring, like something we should've been doing all along – keeping track of one another rather than wandering around on our own – although I couldn't stand it when anyone asked me questions about my whereabouts, especially Nathan. Still, he had many endearing qualities, including keeping up things in the house, which was starting to fall apart in his absence. When he spent the night, he often replaced burnt-out light bulbs and watered the plants before he departed, always leaving a change of clothes behind. At one point, before the divorce, we had talked about additional renovations following the transformation of the sunroom, but the house was old; taking the trouble to abate lead paint or asbestos, better left undisturbed, had gotten in my way.

If Nathan found my increasing messiness unnerving, he was willing to overlook it for the nights we spent together. He was a much more attentive lover than any of the others I'd sampled in the past few years, especially the academics who would just as soon talk about their libido as do anything about it. Nathan had focus.

'I stopped by to check on Terry last night,' Nathan said immediately after I reached him.

Now I was worried. Maybe there was something wrong with the dog.

'Yes?' I questioned, impatient as always with his roundabout manner.

'There were some people at the house.'

'What do you mean "some people"?'

'Well, they were watching movies with Jamie.'

'I told Jamie he was allowed to use the TV. I guess he had his friends over. To be fair to him, I never said he couldn't do so.'

'Well, they seemed a bit older. They were all kind of out of it when I got there.'

I didn't say anything.

'This girl and her boyfriend were sleeping on the couch. Holly, she said her name was. They had some boxes and stuff in the sun porch. Jamie seemed kind of out of it too.' He paused. 'But the other really weird thing was…'

'What about Terry?' I interrupted him.

'Well, it seems he got into some brownies that were left on the cocktail table.'

'Brownies? Dogs can't eat chocolate.'

'And not just any kind of brownies.'

'Oh God!'

I wished I had never turned the phone on. I was scheduled to be on *Good Morning America* the next day. There was a 4am wake-up call. That one interview justified the trip to New York as a research expense. But Terry was a big a price to pay.

'How's he doing?'

'Marginal but the vet says he'll live.'

We both paused, breathing in relief. Terry was the dog we rescued after the girls went to boarding school, then to college. He was supposed to save our marriage. Nathan would take care of him.

'What was the other really weird thing you mentioned?' I whispered, afraid to hear the answer.

Nathan talked so slowly that I had a tendency to rush on to the next thing before he finished what he was saying.

'The house. That was the funny thing.'

'Funny?' I asked. 'In what way. Is it still standing?'

'Oh, yes. Definitely.'

'Then what…?'

'It's absolutely spotless. Spic and span. And new plants throughout. You'll love the way it looks.'

'You may think I'm a somewhat irresponsible person,' I told the lawyer recommended to me by my sister's husband George. I called him after the television broadcast, which lasted for a total of 4.5 minutes, my time cut short by the nationwide high security alert due to the Canadian train bombings and the news surrounding it. 'But I've actually spent my life being responsible. All I asked for was one simple thing in life. An uninterrupted sabbatical.'

'Well, unfortunately, you've gotten yourself mixed up with some creepy people,' he replied, 'They suspect the graduate student of peddling marijuana and possibly other substances to undergraduates. Your office has become quite the hangout.'

'Well, that's really too bad. But I'm not mixed up with her. I just tried to help when she was in a fix. Surely, she's in jail by now.'

'Actually, she's out on bond.'

Nathan picked me up from the airport in my car; it seemed very natural for us to be together during a crisis. I was continuing to get a steady stream of calls on my cell phone, which I mostly didn't answer. As we were heading towards the house, a new number popped up.

'Dr Bennett?' The voice sounded small and quiet. 'This is Holly.'

I did not respond.

'Dr Bennett, are you still there?'

'Holly, I'm sorry but I don't really want to talk with you. Have your lawyer get in touch with my lawyer.'

'I just wanted to let you know that there's been a terrible mistake. Hal, that's my boyfriend, brought me over to your house to drop off your office key, and we started talking to that kid who was watering your lawn. You know, um, Jamie.'

'Yes, I know Jamie.'

'That's all that happened. It was all very innocent.'

'Great. Tell that to the judge.'

'Well, anyway, some of my stuff is still at your house. And I'd like to come by and pick it up.'

'Not on your life.'

'Well, you see, there's my computer with a draft of my dissertation, plus a check from my parents stuck in one of my books. I kind of need it. You know, to move into the co-op.'

I glanced at Nathan. He stared straight ahead. I pictured Holly homeless, on the streets, her dissertation never completed, still stored in the computer in my possession.

'We'll be home in fifteen minutes. Be there. You can collect your things. Then as far as I'm concerned, this whole big mess is out of my hands.'

Holly and her boyfriend pulled up in an ancient diesel Mercedes-Benz as we turned into the driveway. They had bags and boxes stuffed in the backseat. He zoomed off in fog of exhaust after she got out.

'Where's he going? And I thought you had broken up with him.'

'Yeah, well, I guess you could say that we're still together, just not living together. He'll be back.'

'Holly, it's none of my business, but you've made it my business. This is not a good situation to be in.'

Her blue eyes filled up with tears, which she brushed away with the back of her hand. I resisted the impulse to pull her long dark hair out of her face.

Nathan was getting my suitcase. He did not even acknowledge Holly as she and I walked into the house together. He was fixated on speaking to Jamie's parents when they got home from work. Terry sprawled listlessly on the rug in the foyer, his favourite spot. I bent down to pet his limp ears. His eyes were gloomy, reminding me of all that had transpired. My hand started to twitch. Standing up, I regained my momentum.

'Get your things,' I ordered Holly, as if she were a child. She scuttled away.

As I wandered through the house, I realized that Nathan

was right, it looked magnificent. Much better than when the monthly cleaning group swept through it. Holly's stuff was arranged in a neat pile in my study. Other than that, my books and papers had been completely reorganized. The drapes in the family room were pulled open; the dining room table shiny and sleek; the kitchen floor brilliant with a new sheen.

'How did you get in here to begin with?' I asked when I sensed Holly's presence behind me in the kitchen.

'Well, the key was on the ring with your office door. I didn't think you'd mind if I stayed here a few days while you were out of town after they hassled me in the department. I told the neighbour boy, you know, Jamie, that it was fine, that you'd given me the key.'

'Hmmm.' I now remembered he'd tried to call me a few times.

I began to imagine how my office in the department must look: a place where order had been restored after almost thirty years of accumulated of piles and files. I kept picturing that pretty cerulean teapot with steam coming out of it.

Holly was collecting her things in the sunroom. When I joined her, she reached out her hand to touch my arm.

'I only wanted to make things better for you,' she said with an air of hopeful resignation, 'To show my gratitude.' She was a little older than my daughters and much more interested than they were in my state of mind – or the condition of my house or office.

'Holly, this is a big mess that you've created. I really don't want anything to do with it. I'm your academic advisor, nothing else. This relationship is not supposed to be contaminated by other issues.' My therapist had explained this concept of contamination to me when I invited her to a fundraiser that I was co-hosting for a camp for homeless children. 'It is important to observe the various roles that we have in life,' she had admonished. 'And not to mix them up.' At the time, she had seemed unnecessarily inflexible when such a good cause was at stake.

'I really needed a place to stay for a couple of more days.' Holly looked as lost and vulnerable as Terry had when we had first discovered him at the pound.

'What about your boyfriend?'

'Well, he has a new roommate. The kind that pays half of the rent.' Behind her, the spotlessness of the house sparkled.

'I didn't get to the upstairs,' she apologized.

I pictured my daughters' rooms, still filled with assorted notebooks, abandoned school projects, stuffed animals, and out-grown clothes. I'd been meaning to pressure them to go through their stuff but with no luck. I couldn't bear to tackle it on my own.

Nathan was rustling through the kitchen. 'What about the dog?' I asked, 'Do you expect me to overlook the fact that you poisoned my dog?'

Holly stared down at her feet in worn out flip-flops. Her toenails were painted bright pink. Terry appeared at Holly's feet as if to offer forgiveness. He licked her hand.

'Not to mention implicating the neighbour's kid in all of this. He's going to be in big trouble too,' I added with vengeance. 'And what about the police charges?'

'That was all a big misunderstanding.'

'I'll say,' I glared at her. I heard Nathan open then close the refrigerator in the kitchen.

'Dr Bennett,' she spoke quietly. 'I know how to cook.' While I took a deep breath, she added, 'My parents owned a series of B&Bs. It's a family business. We all had to work in it. I was the youngest of five.' She peered at me, her eyes now dancing. 'The first to go to graduate school.'

Part of my emerging research was on the positive effect of chores on girls' future success. My own daughters had been rather coddled in that and in almost every regard. Neither Nathan nor I enforced rules very well.

'Want some lunch, Moira?' I heard Nathan call out. 'There's a refrigerator full of food. And a beautiful bowl of fruit.' He paused, opening and closing the door to the laundry room. 'Gosh, and the shirts that I left here last week are all ironed.'

Holly smiled sweetly, 'I'm also pretty good at grocery shopping and laundry.' She disappeared into the kitchen to help Nathan while I slipped into the comfort of the easy chair in my study – to contemplate its newly established order.

Fantasy impromptu

Our father quit his job as a traveling electronics salesman in order to sell discount shoes at the local strip mall. We needed him to be closer to home. My brother's abduction had changed our lives. One afternoon, an unknown somebody stopped at our side yard and yanked Reynolds into a strange car. Or so we later put it together. After a long and dreadful two days and two nights, Ren showed up at the big Safeway store the next town over, and from all appearances none the worse for wear except for chocolate stains on his T-shirt. Reynolds, who'd just turned four, was too young to explain what happened.

I was the one who found him in the Safeway when Mama sent me to search up and down its aisles for the granola that she said would sustain us in this time of trial. There he was, perched on the bottom shelf with an empty bag of Doritos, his lips and tiny fingertips turning orange.

'Hey, Ren,' I called out quietly to him.

'Sadie,' was all he said with that sad crooked grin of his. He came running to me and latched onto my hand so hard that it ached. Later on, I was declared his saviour, and we smothered Reynolds in our everlasting love. Papa never travelled out of the state of South Carolina for business after that. Mama, too, changed her course in life. She quit her job as a hostess at the Piccadilly and worked as a seamstress at home. Despite Angie's and my protests, she also decided to home-school the three of us, which only made us hope to get kidnapped, especially if it meant we got our pictures in the paper again.

The next year when she turned a teenager, however, Angie was shipped off by my parents to the strict Christian boarding school down in Georgia on scholarship. She'd gotten so she wouldn't do any of the schoolwork or housework assigned by Mama, and she looked at herself a lot in the mirror while she sang. She kept trying to hitchhike into town to go to the county junior high. Angie had dreams of becoming a singing majorette. Throughout all this, Reynolds and I continued to be local celebrities. We'd both been featured on TV and in the newspaper. Angie had no similar claim to fame, except towering behind us in photographs with one elegant hand planted on each of our heads as if she were in charge of keeping us from growing up.

In the late summer when Papa drove off in the Impala with Angie and her footlocker, she insisted on sitting by herself with her stuffed animals in the backseat. Mama swept off the front porch. Reynolds and I ran after the car as far as we could go before we fell hard into the grass. I scraped dirt from under my fingernails, my bare legs shivering even though it was a hot August day.

When you are famous enough to show up on the 6pm news, it is hard for real life to regain such early promise. My brother Reynolds and I had achieved fame before we even knew it was owed to us. The police never found the kidnappers, and Reynolds confounded all of our attempts to drag the story out of him. Small for five years old, he wasn't much of a talker to start with. After the kidnapping, he had this strange way of gazing up at the sky when we asked him questions as if he'd been abducted by aliens or angels. The police and my parents weren't above bribing him with candy.

'Was it a green car, Reynolds?' He'd suck on the green lollipop they offered and smile sweetly. A lady police officer showed him pictures of men and women in storybooks. 'Did they look like this?'

Reynolds nodded yes to all questions. Back when the kidnapping happened, Angie and I had been shocked that anyone would choose Reynolds, who still wet his pants and smelled sour most days. We considered ourselves much better prospects. We could've helped the kidnappers rob banks or abduct other young children as we were used to being brave and sneaky. When I found Reynolds at Safeway, the true miracle was that he had on dry underwear, and he never ever wet his pants again.

Being left at home with Reynolds, especially with Angie off in boarding school on a music scholarship, was more wounding than I could bear. The excitement of Reynolds' celebrity status, and my role in finding him, was starting to lose its dazzle. We did receive a $100 gift certificate at the Safeway, which Mama quickly took possession of. Sometimes I'd get Reynolds to play cops and robbers with me to see if he might re-enact his disappearance. Mostly, he just did what I told him to do, and there was not much thrill in that.

Angie wrote that she was studying Chopin and Mozart at boarding school. She'd always been something of a musical child prodigy, stating her goal to be a gospel singer when she first started Sunday School. All of the other girls piously proclaimed their hopes to become nurses or missionaries. From boarding school, she wrote that her music teacher had been classically trained at the world-famous Juilliard School before she met the Lord. She believed young minds disciplined enough for music would carry on the Lord's work wherever they went. Angie seemed to like this idea and shifted her tastes quickly to classical music, sending us audio tapes practicing the piano. We listened to them at night after dinner, proud and envious that someone from our family could be so accomplished in a faraway place.

Even though she had just arrived, Angie was to be featured in the annual school piano recital in November, the weekend right after Halloween. In a postcard, she wrote 'Hey Sadie and Ren, Come see me, and I'll show you around.' Despite her welcoming words, she sounded homesick to me when we talked on the phone, her voice very quiet. As much as we despised Angie when she tried to boss us around, Reynolds and I missed our trio; we still weren't allowed to go to school in town, although the kidnappers had snatched Reynolds right out of our side yard.

'It's unfair of Mama and Papa to torture us this way,' I moaned to Reynolds. He stuck out his lower lip, which was the closest he ever got to being mad. He was excited, however, about going to visit Angie. He carried a picture of her around in his pocket along with other treasures. For the recital, we planned to wear our Halloween costumes that Mama had sewn. Mine was a police officer's uniform and his was a pirate's outfit, complete with eye patch. We wore them for three days straight before Halloween, even to the bank and to Safeway and to the farmer's market. There were some advantages of not going to public school. My best friend Julia who was a sixth grader, a year ahead of me, said that they didn't let you wear costumes to school anymore because of Satan. Halloween was about worshipping the Devil, which Mama apparently had not heard about. She let us go trick-or-treating before it got dark, Papa following closely behind.

Before she married Papa, Mama had gone to the community college and had learned how to be a library assistant. Books were her sincere passion in life. She made us read storybooks every night before we went to sleep. Reynolds did not like to read out loud, so I did his part with lots of expression. Even Mama would laugh at my big fancy words and foreign accents – and also at the stories I made up afterwards.

On the Halloween outing, wearing our costumes, no one took us for the famous kidnapping case. And so it became our plan to return to celebrity status and to reverse our fortunes. Later on, much later, after all that was to happen came undone, with my brother as sick as death with bronchitis, Mama threatened to send me off to boarding school with Angie. I would have none of that.

'The two of you just can't be trusted together,' as if I'd had something to do with Ren's original kidnapping. On that fateful day, Mama had been at work, and I'd been watching TV in the basement while Reynolds played outside with his salamanders. Afterwards I told Mama that I was reading a book at the time, as we weren't allowed to watch TV during the day. Maybe if the TV had been off, I could've heard all that transpired. In addition to finding him after his ordeal, I was the one who discovered he was lost to begin with, the salamanders deserted in their shoe box filled along with sand, grass, and a teacup with pond water. Angie had been playing the piano, although rock music instead of the hymns she was supposed to practice for Sunday mornings.

Our family did not go to church, but on Sundays we did sing 'Praise God from Whom All Blessings Flow,' and my father read from the Bible. My mother told stories about the old days when settlers came to South Carolina and made do with only what God provided in a new land – no Dr. Pepper or mascara from Wal-Mart. At the end, Angie would sing 'God Bless America.' The rest of us knew the words, but her voice was so beautiful that it seemed a sin to sing along. Reynolds brought all of his little creatures with him to our Sunday gathering – the salamanders, worms, a vicious-looking beetle, and his sparkly quartz rocks. Mama approved because they were part of God's great creation. When I found Reynolds at the Safeway after the kidnapping, tiny quartz rocks were still tucked in the pockets of his shorts, and it soothed me to know that they'd been there during his mysterious rapture. Nobody, whatever else they might've done, could steal his precious treasures.

Reynolds talked more to me than anyone else. But he worshipped Angie. I was just someone he would play make-believe with. We planned to rescue Angie from boarding school. I knew how to drive from riding the tractor with Papa on the weekends. I was good at things like that – and I was tall for my age. In our costumes, no one would know who we were. We figured that Angie would want to complete her recital pieces since she had practiced so much and loved to perform and be the centre of attention. When her part was over, she wouldn't even care about listening to anyone else, and we'd find a way to get backstage. Reynolds had a sword for his pirate costume, and I had some pistol caps and handcuffs for my police outfit. We planned to put a blanket over Angie's head and drive off in the car. If we mentioned Nashville, she'd go with us in a flash, boarding school and the Juilliard music teacher left behind.

It would take a little while before our parents realized we'd gone missing. And so, for starters, we'd head directly to Wal-Mart for more supplies and to get lost among the other children wandering the aisles. Angie was mature and smart enough to look like she could be in charge. Reynolds and I had even managed to save nearly $22 from selling lemonade and old books on the corner by our house where Mama could watch us from the dining room window as she sewed curtains. Plus, we'd become experts at collecting loose change and stockpiling extra food. All our plans were coming together nicely.

It wasn't that hard getting the car keys from our mother, who did the driving on family outings. Papa liked to study maps. Reynolds and I sat very inconspicuously in the backseat; he played with his shiny quartz rocks, and I gazed out the window. We'd allowed Mama to wash our Halloween costumes in preparation for this day, stubbornly refusing to wear anything else. Worried about Reynolds because he had a cold, especially with the pirate shirt so thin, Mama threw his jacket in the backseat. But he wouldn't wear it because of ruining the pirate look. Every time he got sick, Mama became nervous that he might vanish again.

When we pulled into the parking lot, I helped my mother gather our stuff. Papa and Reynolds walked on ahead of us. As we got close to the auditorium, I stopped in my tracks.

'Mama, Reynolds left his jacket in the car.' She halted. Mama's hands were overflowing with packages for Angie, including her favourite lemon squares.

'Oh dear. Sarah Diane, can you go back and get it?' I nodded helpfully. I felt grown up when she called me by my full name.

In addition to obtaining the car keys from Mama, this ploy allowed me to retrieve the jacket, which was now intended to serve as the blindfold for Angie.

'Thanks, lovey. I have my hands full.'

She looked flustered, like all of a sudden rearing three children – one nearly kidnapped for good; home-schooling two of them; sending the talented, rebellious, and beautiful daughter off to boarding school; plus having a husband who sold discount shoes – was more in life than she had bargained for. We all did have nice shoes though, better than any of our friends. They were a source of pride to us, especially for Angie when she went to boarding school. She gave shoes to her classmates for birthday presents.

I opened the car door, checked under the front seat for the extra food, including Doritos for Reynolds, and grabbed his jacket. I then ran back to Mama with my most wholesome, trustworthy look. She smiled at me, 'Bless you, Sadie. You're quite a good rescuer.' I pulled the brim of my police hat over my eyes so that I'd look more official.

All of the boarding school girls were dressed in Sunday school clothes, and the boys who were visiting with their families sported clip-on bow ties. Reynolds stood up straight, proud to be a pirate, but I was starting to worry about the police outfit. I didn't want Angie to pretend she didn't know us like she used to do in town. She sat with her friends towards the front of the auditorium. When she saw us, she stood up, squealed, and pointed. I couldn't tell if she was excited or embarrassed. I figured she'd go early in the program because Angie was the kind of person who always volunteered to go first. Her whole name, Angela Maria Andrews, was printed in the program. I made a point of sitting on the aisle. Reynolds was tucked in between Mama and Papa. I still had hold of his jacket. His cue, after Angie played, was to say he needed to go to the bathroom. We were all still so relieved that he didn't wet his pants anymore that we let him go immediately whenever he needed to.

Angie played like a genius – two hard pieces by Chopin, one that sounded like soldiers marching and the other like a dream getting ready to come true, a fantasy. Beside her name the program stated 'Fantaisie-Impromptu.' The music teacher, sitting next to Angie and turning the pages, acted like Angie was her own special invention. Mama had hand sewn the recital dress, and it was prettier and fluffier than all the store-bought dresses put together. The matching pink ribbon in her hair made Angie look like an enchanted princess or an old-fashioned movie star. But underneath the classical music that she played so cleverly, we could all picture a country music star ready to burst out.

The applause for her was so loud that Reynolds had to repeat himself. 'I need to pee.'

Papa looked helpless. Mama was enthralled with Angie's performance, proving right the decision to send her away from our small town to a grander fate in life.

'I'll take him,' I volunteered. Ren was scooting out of the seats just as the next girl stepped forward.

'Wait for him. And don't come back in during the middle of a piece,' Mama instructed. She was big on manners. The next girl in the recital line-up was too plump for her short dress. I figured she'd play for a long time and that she had a big family who would applaud forever, even if they had never cared a thing about Beethoven's 'Moonlight Sonata' before. Then the music teacher would move quickly to another performer, and there would be no way for Reynolds and me to get back in place. The car keys jingled in my pocket. I'd noticed that after taking their turns, the girls did not return to seats in the auditorium but disappeared backstage in preparation for some big deal at the end.

Reynolds headed up the aisle for the bathroom, which he had already used once before the program started. When he went to the door, I called out, 'Hey, not now. We have to hurry.'

'But I have to go.'

'Well, make it snappy.' I was holding on to his jacket and staking out the hallway. Reynolds always took a long time in the bathroom, which none of the rest of us could figure out. Eventually he reappeared, just as I was starting to panic. Praise God from whom all blessings flow, I had not heard any clapping yet.

'This way,' I commanded. We reached the side stage door. Only four girls were in there so far watching the performances from a monitor. Angie sat in the middle of them like a goddess.

'Psst,' I hissed. She looked at us and rolled her eyes. I could tell she did not approve of the costumes.

'We need to talk to you.' I kneeled down next to Reynolds as if I were comforting him from some inconsolable loss, which I knew would pull on Angie's heartstrings. She walked impatiently over to us. We tugged her outside the door. Although I had grown nearly as tall as Angie, she had on the pink high heels that Papa sent to her. I wore black Reeboks to match the police pants. I had a time trying to blindfold her with Ren's jacket, and I knocked askew her pink hair ribbon. Reynolds finally moved into action by taking the handcuffs and yanking Angie's hands behind her back. He'd been practicing on me with the handcuffs a lot lately.

'You're going with us,' I informed Angie, who pushed into my stomach with her hard head. Reynolds and I shoved her out the backdoor. She seemed too surprised to put up much of a struggle. Plus, she didn't want to interrupt the recital taking place in the next room. She did sputter something under the jacket that sounded like major curse words I had not heard her use before.

'Hush up,' I commanded. She banged her head against mine.

Reynolds had one arm crooked in Angie's arm, and in the other he carried his sword. I kept my left arm interlocked with Angie's and my right hand on my holster. The large Impala was parked near the rear entrance to the auditorium. We stuffed Angie in the backseat, keeping the jacket on her head. We didn't want her to comment on any part of the getaway as she always saw a better way to do things. Reynolds, flushed with anticipation, sat in the front seat with me, the maps spread out on his legs. In the evenings, he liked to snuggle with Papa in the big chair and read maps. We'd already marked the way to Nashville.

I had no trouble getting the car started. What I hadn't figured on was so many vehicles packed all around us. Back at home with the tractor, we were the only ones in the field. I put the car in reverse and turned the steering wheel real sharp.

'Watch it!' Reynolds cried out. The side mirror scraped along the side of a minivan.

'It's hot under here,' Angie's insistent voice called, 'Let me out.'

We ignored her. I pulled forward and tried again. I was able to back it straight out, but I could not turn the car either way. Things were not going well. Angie was crying and swearing some more.

'I have to pee,' Reynolds announced. His nose was starting to run.

'You just went.'

'But I couldn't go then, Sadie. Now I really need to go.' This was a long, feverish speech for Reynolds.

Angie had managed to get her hands out of the plastic handcuffs and was pulling the jacket off her head. I could see in the mirror that her hair fell right back into place, though the ribbon had lost its bow. I was at a complete loss.

She blinked her eyes and assessed the situation.

'Here's what you do,' she said without hesitation, 'Leave the car like this. Toss the keys in the grass over there.' We followed her finger pointing to some picnic tables. 'We'll go back to the concert. You come sit with me, Sadie. And when it's all over, you can tell Mama that someone must've stolen the key when you weren't paying attention. That will explain the car looking like this.'

Reynolds and I did not have the wherewithal to compete with Angie's quick thinking. He was already headed back to the auditorium, knowing exactly the location of the restrooms. After tossing the key into the grass where I could find it again, I followed more slowly with Angie.

'Nice costume.' She rested her hand on my slumped shoulder.

I looked down at the police officer's badge. The shirt was all wrinkled. Even with the messed-up ribbon, Angie's hair still looked pretty, and her pink shoes had not even gotten any grass stains on them. Her dress seemed to float around her.

'I wanted to save you from all this.' I swept my arms around me, trying to encompass the grounds of the school. 'Plus, I thought we could make you famous.'

'It's not so bad here,' she said. 'Just after night-time prayers, that's when it gets lonely.' Angie and I had always shared a room. Sometimes, like when Reynolds was lost to us, we slept in the same bed with our arms wrapped around each other.

'Maybe you can come and spend the night soon,' she offered. I looked hopefully at her. 'But you'll have to wear a uniform.' She glanced over at me. 'I mean a school uniform.'

'What about Ren?'

'He's too little, besides it's a girls' school.'

I sighed, knowing I could not bear to go anywhere overnight without Reynolds. He'd escaped once before when I wasn't paying enough attention.

Entering the building, we waited for him to leave the restroom and get safely into the concert hall. I followed Angie to the side room where we could watch both the stage and the audience on the monitor. Reynolds slipped past my old seat, into the one between Mama and Papa. I thought I could hear him coughing hoarsely.

At the end of the program, all of the girls assembled back on stage. Together they sang 'This Land is Your Land' to wild applause. For the encore, Angie belted out a solo verse of 'God Bless America' as if she were at the Grand Ole Opry. In the side room, I stood at attention in my police uniform. Angie was where she belonged, where she could perform in front of an audience to her heart's content, where she could find her own special kind of glory. Reynolds looked small, sweet, and sickly in between our parents, his eye patch having slipped down around his neck. Even from a distance, I could tell that Mama was crying and that Papa was lost in thought, as if trying to find the right road back home. All alone, I felt brave and expectant – fully prepared to shower fame and fortune on my family, whatever it took.

Spontaneous recovery

My grandfather got up out of his wheelchair – the one he had been sitting in for three years – he stood up and pushed the chair out of the nursing home when the fire alarm went off. Subsequent versions of this event mentioned old ladies that he escorted through the doors, as if his skills as a Boy Scout had not diminished with time. Later, when I asked Grandfather about that day, he said, 'I smelled smoke. Where there's smoke, there's fire. When the alarm sounded, I knew I'd best get out of there.' He smiled coyly as he added, 'And help others.'

It was such a matter-of-fact statement that casual listeners would not realize that Grandfather required daily assistance just to move from the wheelchair to his bed at night, then back again in the morning. The grease fire that erupted in the kitchen had quickly been contained but only after the alarm sounded, thereby allowing Grandfather to perform his miraculous feat.

Grandfather's daily care had become more than my grandmother could handle. He had first been confined to the wheelchair with a home attendant and then, after his last stroke, dispatched to the nearby nursing home. I visited him frequently. My special assignment was to read to him from magazines and *The New York Times* due to his failing eyesight. Often, he nodded his head, as if he'd been sleeping, but then he'd clarify a point I'd just read about the Electoral College.

He'd made me take him to the polls to vote during the 2000 presidential election. I agreed to do so on the condition that he wouldn't vote for George W. Bush. He later claimed that he was the only person in his precinct, known for Republican retirees, who voted for Ralph Nader.

'Al Gore could've used your help, Grandfather, and then maybe we wouldn't have ended up at war, with members of my generation getting shipped off to Iraq.' I couldn't help rubbing it in that the state of Florida had not done its part for freedom and democracy.

'Every generation, Christopher, has its war,' he replied.

'Yeah, but at least you get to be a member of the Greatest Generation,' I countered. He beamed proudly, which only egged me on. 'I'm part of Generation X, or is it Generation Y? Or maybe Z by now. What kind of glory is there in that?'

'I just call 'em as I see 'em,' he responded as if life were a baseball game. This was his standard response if he couldn't think of something better to say.

Not a serious match for Grandfather, I surrendered quickly. What I really wanted was another fire to come along while I was there so that I could take my grandfather's picture with the new digital camera he'd given to me for graduation as he got up from his wheelchair and walked out of the nursing home. I'd print out multiple copies, one to mount in his room, another for Grandmother, and still another for submitting to a photography contest to make him famous. We needed to know, the world needed to know, that he still could do whatever was required to take care of himself – and save others along the way.

Grandfather's feistiness made him a favourite with the elderly ladies. Together, they figured out a way to listen to the music of Glenn Miller and dance in their wheelchairs. When Grandmother came to visit him, they'd all whisper about her. 'Such a pretty girl,' one of his neighbours commented loudly, as if Grandmother were a debutante. She had been a beauty in her youth and retained the stately magic of good-looking people along with an innate willingness to be treated as a celebrity. She and Grandfather, it seemed, were made for one another. The clippings that she kept in her scrapbook showed that Grandfather had been a football star in college and a handsome pilot during the war before he became an uncompromising newspaperman. I lived with my grandmother that summer when I had a job working construction nearby. She presided at bridge club and book club meetings, her life so full of activities that I'd wondered when she'd had time for Grandfather all of those preceding sixty years.

One of Grandfather's favourite topics of conversation had to do with the dog they'd inherited from their neighbours a few years back. Curtis, the black-haired mutt, had taken a liking to my grandparents – they saved dinner scraps for him. After meals, he'd regularly visited the back door, and eventually he started coming inside to watch TV. Most dogs under these conditions, especially who had been left outside all day, would quickly fall into slumber. But Grandfather claimed that Curtis only liked watching certain shows – and that was how the dog coped with his seemingly incurable case of insomnia.

'In fact,' Grandfather proclaimed, 'I've never seen Curtis sleep at all, except for occasional catnaps when he's sitting straight up. His head drifts off to the side, then all of the sudden he straightens it back up with a little yap. Strangest thing I've ever seen, a dog with insomnia. Can't sleep worth a darn.'

'Guess he's a watch dog,' I inserted, not pointing out that I'd observed Curtis taking a nap every so often while Grandfather snoozed.

He ignored me, not really open to a solution for the quandary. 'I could've used Curtis nearby when I still had kids at home and stayed up late worrying myself sick about them. But that's not my fate anymore.' He concluded with a sigh, '*Longtemps, je me suis couché de bonne heure.*'

'Huh?' I replied. Grandfather spoke French, as well as snatches of Italian and Portuguese.

'You know, son – from Proust, the opening of *Remembrance of Things Past*. Don't they teach anything in school these days?'

'Nothing much useful. What's it mean?'

'Quite literally "For a long time, I went to bed early." That is, since I've been in the nursing home. Just don't tell Curtis.'

After the neighbours moved and left their dog with my grandparents officially, Curtis maintained his normal routine. He was put outside in the morning to roam the neighbourhood, then brought in for dinner and evening TV. An article in *The New York Times* that I read to my grandfather reported on animal researchers who had discovered that some border collies with special training could understand dozens, maybe even hundreds, of words ranging from 'slippers' to 'water' to 'bone' to 'bed'. When there was an unknown object, these smart dogs could even figure out the unfamiliar name that applied to the new object. Curtis was part border collie and part something else that was indecipherable in his DNA. Grandfather claimed that Curtis's preferred programs on television weren't animal shows but the History Channel and *I Love Lucy* reruns. It was a further sign of the dog's intelligence that Curtis liked the same programs Grandfather did and that he wasn't partial to the cooking channel or talk shows that Grandmother preferred.

After Grandfather went to the nursing home, he developed a plan that involved Curtis. 'Christopher, you can sneak him in here one night. Put him in your duffle bag and bring him on in. Explain it to Curtis in advance, and he'll cooperate fully.' Grandfather's plan did not involve just a visit on the patio, which would have been too simple. He wanted Curtis in his room to watch TV with him at night. 'I'll let him stay in the bed with me, even if he can't sleep.'

Sometimes it seemed to me that Grandfather missed Curtis more than anything else. He had numerous pictures of the dog on the window ledge in his room, only one of Grandmother in her wedding dress on his bedside table, and none of me.

The following weekend I brought Curtis by during visiting hours. We met up on the patio, Grandfather steered there by an accommodating orderly. It was a lovely summer afternoon, one of those bright days when each of us can think of something special we had done at an earlier moment in our lives that we hope to do all over again. A few other elderly 'inmates,' as Grandfather called them, and their visitors talked nearby.

'Hey Curtis, old boy,' he said when we arrived, barely acknowledging my presence. Curtis's ears perked up in delight. Grandfather had me attach two leashes to his wheelchair – one on each side – and let Curtis pull him around. Curtis was strong and proud for his size. Grandfather called out 'gee' and 'haw' when he wanted the dog in this makeshift harness to turn. It did, indeed, seem that Curtis could understand exactly where he was supposed to go. They meandered along Grandfather's favourite paths towards the pond filled with koi. Grandfather tossed bits of bread, stored in his shirt pocket from lunch, into the water, and Curtis barked as the koi congregated.

If only Curtis could read the *NYT* to Grandfather, then I'd have been relieved of my duties – although I looked forward to reading news stories out loud. I was learning a lot about the world. Neither one of us could stand the sensationalism of television news, but we both loved the nuances beneath the clear black-and-white print of newspapers. Sometimes, just to test my grandfather, I'd rewrite the pieces as I was reading them, to make them more fantastic.

'Firefighter from 9/11 marries pregnant ninety-year-old wife of a survivor,' I read one day.

'Why on earth would anyone ninety years old want to get married?' Grandfather asked, chuckling.

The article had actually read 'nineteen years old,' but I thought my version was more newsworthy. I was starting to appreciate writers who embellished the truth to create a better story. I'd learned in college from my history major and English minor that the distinction between what really happened and what could have happened is minuscule. I'd also learned that the job market was every bit as soft as reported, despite the more prosperous version politicians running for re-election put forth. So, here I was, living with my grandmother, working part-time for a home remodelling company and reading to Grandfather almost every day. My parents said that the reading would account for my room and board. In addition, my grandparents separately slipped me bills of various amounts for 'mad money.' I saved up the secret funds rather than spending any on women or wine. My plan was to go to law school like both my mother and father, although I was starting to consider facts and details tedious. With Grandfather, I found the interpretation of events, of civilization, of intentions, and of deeds to be increasingly absorbing.

As a pastime, I decided to work on a story to submit to the local paper – a human interest piece that featured my grandfather and Curtis performing noble acts together. After the story was published, I imagined when the Fourth of July came along, Curtis and Grandfather could lead the parade in our small town. None of us in the family were particularly patriotic, but I envisioned a red bandana around both of their necks and an American flag attached to my grandfather's wheelchair. Curtis would confidently draw him along the parade path. My grandmother would cheer from the sidelines, and I'd take numerous pictures, one of which would surely win first prize in a contest. While remodelling kitchens, I embellished this idea. Staying with my grandparents that summer made me feel important, as if an essential responsibility to observe and report life's proceedings had been conferred on me.

The plan for Curtis to come stay with him was Grandfather's favourite fantasy; it began to take on large and independent momentum. Eventually, perhaps inevitably, Grandfather convinced me to give it serious consideration.

'Just one night, Christopher,' he pleaded with uncharacteristic humility. 'That's all I'm asking, just *one* night. Then I'll let it be.' I looked at him sceptically.

'Do *not* tell your Grandmother, not under any conditions,' he added. 'She's never been one to break the law or keep secrets. She'd have the FBI or CIA out here in no time flat.'

'Grandfather, this is hardly the CIA's jurisdiction – or the FBI's for that matter.'

'Don't you think for one minute that will stop your grandmother. The first time she turned me in was way back when we were dating and I tried to sneak in her window. I was banned from the dorm for an entire semester. Why, she tells on herself.' He shook his head in dismay. 'Confessed to the IRS once, and she wasn't even going to be audited. No use trusting someone like that with a secret.'

I tended to downplay these conspiratorial sessions, although it did seem to me that Curtis and Grandfather deserved one another. They both loved being the centre of attention, and because they were so much alike – with even the same wavy, wayward hair – they didn't find it necessary to compete.

Sundays, when the newspaper was the thickest, provided my longest session with Grandfather. After we completed reading the paper and working on the crossword puzzle, I'd drive back to the house to pick up Grandmother for Sunday dinner. She always brought one of Grandfather's choice dishes, like sweet potato soufflé, as if attending a potluck dinner. She never went anywhere empty-handed, even to the nursing home. They'd sit and talk at the end of a long table pretending no one else was around. Oftentimes while they ate, I'd go for a run in the woods nearby. When I got back I showered in Grandfather's room as they watched baseball. Grandmother loved baseball more than Grandfather did, although she got the teams confused. She enjoyed the quiet symmetry of the game. 'It reminds me of bridge,' she once told me, 'You know. All those diamonds and clubs. Plus strategy.'

After my shower that Sunday in late June when I collected Grandmother from the nursing home, I picked up my duffle bag with wet, sweaty clothes in it. Grandfather was eyeing the size of the bag. He winked at me and smiled. No wonder he'd been such a celebrated leader in sports, the military, and the news business; people instinctively wanted to be on his side. Only Grandmother could resist his charms.

After our visit to the nursing home, I took Grandmother home, then drove aimlessly around the countryside. My father and mother had constantly reinforced the concept that 'rules were rules' in quiet opposition to the influence Grandfather had over me. I was his only grandchild, and therefore, more extraordinary than anyone else on earth. I'd had a younger brother, but he'd died as an infant. I had no memory of him, but the watchfulness of my parents served as a constant reminder of Justin's brief life.

When I was seven, Grandfather decided I was a budding genius, and he let me drive his brand-new Cadillac while he sat in the passenger seat and calmly browsed through the Rand-McNally road atlas.

'We'll go on a trip together, Christopher, one of these days. Just you and me. We'll leave these other crybabies behind.' Grandfather looked down on people like my parents who were not adventurers. I kept focused on the small gravel path in front of me, not wanting to lose Grandfather's confidence. I could only reach the pedals by standing up with the driver's seat pushed way back. He'd let me practice steering before in his lap; now I had to put all the disparate pieces together. Driving in the hot sun gave me a headache, but I kept pressing forward. When we reached the road at the end of the driveway, Grandfather declared, 'Well, Christopher, you got us where we needed to go.' He hopped out to get the mail from the mailbox, then made me scoot over so he could drive back, whistling as he steered the car.

'The boy can drive like a pro,' he announced at dinner. I had hoped he'd keep this little episode quiet, but he was much too proud of me. My mother rolled her eyes.

'Can't you control him?' she later asked my father when she thought I was asleep. All three of us were staying in Father's old bedroom at the lake cabin.

'Never could and never will. The only one who can control him is Mother, and she picks her battles. What's the harm in a little driving practice?'

Unimpressed, my mother replied, 'Maybe at sixteen but hardly at six. I can't trust them together even for a few minutes.'

That night I got out of my bed and wandered through the cabin until I found Grandfather sleeping in front of the black-and-white TV showing old war movies. I climbed up with him, wanting him to know that we were a twosome, a gang of thieves, not managed by the cautious forces of civilization. Thus, fifteen years later, as I drove around the flat humid countryside dotted by lakes in central Florida after dropping Grandmother off, I decided that there was no reason for Curtis not to be fully initiated into our gang. He exhibited the appropriate mix of spontaneity and respect for secrets.

Grandmother kept her bridge club schedule on the refrigerator, which I checked that evening. The next day she'd be going up to Vera's house, just around the corner. She would not need me to drive. I'd merely have to track down Curtis, who would be roaming the neighbourhood, but even that shouldn't be too hard. Curtis loved to ride in cars.

I went to bed early that night so I could arrive at my job first thing in the morning, from which I'd get off by noon. Grandmother was certain to play bridge until at least 3pm. She wouldn't be expecting either me or Curtis to arrive until dinner time. Even later, Grandmother would not be too suspicious when Curtis didn't show up – we all suspected he had a love interest, the golden lab on the next block.

As anticipated, I had no trouble tracking down Curtis. He tended to loiter along the paths that neighbourhood kids had created. They often discarded wrappers and crumbs along their way. He was a playmate with the children, who made me promise to bring Curtis to their school for a visit in the fall. This dog made enchanted friends wherever he ventured in life.

Curtis was nosing around the azaleas near the bus stop when I spotted him. All I had to do was open the car door and whistle. He must've already heard the familiar sound of Grandfather's old Cadillac, because he ran directly through the open door and situated himself on the passenger seat as if preparing to navigate. I started thinking about the cross-country trip that Grandfather had once predicted we would take. We had never gotten around to it. Perhaps the perfect time would've been between high school and college, but by then Grandfather had suffered his first stroke.

While I had brought the duffle bag for Curtis with me, I realized that I didn't need to use it yet. I could bring Curtis to the patio as I had before, tie his leash to one of the lawn chairs, which were bolted down, then collect Grandfather somewhat earlier than usual. He'd call the shots from that point on, which would only make him more pleased with the situation.

Since we'd been through this part of the routine before, Curtis cheerfully complied. At the nursing home, I filled a discarded Styrofoam cup with water from the spigot for him. After finishing it off, he sat expectantly, knowing full well that he'd be seeing Grandfather soon. I tethered him to a post nearby.

Just as I entered the front door of the nursing home and signed in, a piercing siren invaded the air space around me. 'Fire drill,' the desk attendant said quickly to me. 'We must get all of the oldsters outside.' He added, as if to calm my nerves, 'Just a drill but we have to act as if it's real.' I could see Curtis shaking his head back and forth outside, but he did not seem to be overly disturbed by the screeching noise

Apparently, the facility had not satisfied the fire marshal's expectations the month before, so it all needed to be replayed. I nodded and went to find Grandfather, figuring I might pass him in his wheelchair along the way. If so, then he and I could take Curtis for a walk instead of waiting in the parking lot with everyone else. I did not find Grandfather in the front corridors where nurses and orderlies were swiftly pushing beds and wheelchairs through fire exits. Some of the elderly women were crying and laughing simultaneously, in the manner of teenage girls on amusement park rides. Almost no one spoke.

Grandfather was not in his room although his wheelchair was there. Pleased that I'd remembered to bring my digital camera, I took a picture of the vacated wheelchair. I pushed it aside and found my way to the nearest emergency exit. I walked around the perimeter, seeking my grandfather in the midst of the elderly and infirm. There were many grey-haired men, even more women, but no one who matched my grandfather's grandeur. As I approached the patio, I could see Curtis whining and pulling at his leash. He was looking away from me but seemed to sense my arrival. He sat down on his black tail, which normally flapped gleefully from side to side, and stared straight ahead.

On the other side of the patio doors was a figure dressed in khakis and a light blue buttoned-down Oxford shirt leaning into the sliding glass door, the figure's face distorted from being pressed into the glass door. Moving closer, I could make out Grandfather's sky-blue eyes under eyebrows that were fierce and funny at the same time. His whole body pushed hard against the sheet of glass. Several orderlies behind him were trying to coax him gently into an extra wheelchair. He was so rigid with determination that they could not easily bend his knees. I stood at an angle that would allow him to see both me and Curtis, my camera in my hands behind my back.

Eventually, the attendants were successful in forcing his body into a sitting position. I slid open the door and helped them bring the wheelchair outside to Curtis, who I let off the leash. Curtis crawled into Grandfather's lap. I took their picture. They both fell sound asleep, Grandfather never to wake up again.

One orderly told me that before lunch he had helped Grandfather dress into his best outfit that he normally saved for Grandmother's visits. 'We're not sure how he got to the door. Suddenly, there he was in the side hallway, whistling and lurching towards the patio. He never stopped – just kept moving towards that dog, ignoring the sliding glass doors between them.'

'How could this happen?' I asked incredulously. He shrugged his shoulders, as if I'd been accusing him of neglect, offering no explanation for how Grandfather got to that door, just as there was no accounting for most of his behaviour.

'These things just happen sometimes,' is what the distracted director of the nursing home told me later. 'They call it "spontaneous recovery," but it rarely lasts. Sometimes things get better, often worse.'

There was also no explanation for the fact that Curtis stopped roaming the neighbourhood afterwards and stayed home, close to Grandmother. In the fall I went off in Grandfather's old Cadillac to New York City in search of adventure and a newspaper job in lieu of law school. Curtis stayed behind. At night when Grandmother fell asleep in front of the television, he slept nearby

Making out

My mother is fading away. She is getting smaller and smaller and farther and farther away. She is the teeny tiny woman, but ours is not the teeny tiny house. It is quite large and old, and if she keeps up her disappearing act, she will be like a speck of ignored, ancient dust in it. As she gets smaller, I get larger until I can nearly contain the whole household in my tight fist. If I squeeze hard, shrill shrieks will emerge from my mother slipping through my fingers. So I must be careful. My father believes he can prevent her disappearance by looking away just as he did when I was a terrible toddler and threw myself into tantrums on the kitchen floor. It's my job to keep track of her now.

When I come home from school today, my mother has prepared a sandwich of bread and honey with a glass of chocolate milk. I am surprised and pleased that she is able to make an appearance for me. I smack the sandwich loudly in my mouth so that she will remember my special sounds. Usually I take care of myself after school. I break a handful of Oreos into a bowl and then cover them with milk. I spoon the soggy cookies into my mouth as I read the comics. Today over sweet sandwiches, my mother remembers to ask me about my homework in the manner of all dutiful parents.

'I have to memorize the state capitals,' I inform her, the honey spilling down my arms in golden rivers. She has poured it on thick, recalling the way I liked it when I was little – before she started to disappear.

'Bismarck,' she proclaims immediately, as if she were an explorer who had discovered new land.

'North Dakota,' I automatically reply, between sips of chocolate milk. The thickness of the honey coating my tongue has turned the cold milk bitter.

'Portland,' she announces.

'Oregon,' I answer with pleased certainty.

'No!' she reacts, 'It's Maine.' She adds a triumphant, 'Gotcha!'

She seems to think it an accomplishment to outsmart a nearly-thirteen-year-old. I am so pleased for her that I do not insolently insist 'Augusta,' which I just remembered to be the capital of Maine. Instead, I take the last bite of my sandwich. I even eat the crusts to make her happy. I decide to answer her next question wrong to further tether her to my world, to prove my need for her. But she has lost interest in the capitals and begins to pull crackly dead leaves off a poinsettia plant leftover from Christmas. Her fingers are nimble at this task, in just the way she used to braid my hair before my aunt took me to the salon to have it cut into a bob that would be easier to care for. I rub my head softly wishing for the braids again. She never touches me anymore.

I pick out my books for homework from my backpack, shoving aside the dishes on the table. I am bound and determined to learn all of the capitals before the end of the week. This assignment will be easier than the spelling bee, which I failed miserably at because my parents did not practice with me. After all, there are only fifty tried-and-true capitals to memorize instead of an infinity of words with crazy combinations of letters. My best subjects this year are geography and especially vocabulary where I am the class prodigy. My mother starts to clear my dirty dishes then stops as if she just remembered an important task she needs to finish. I hear her moving up the stairs with footsteps muffled by her peach satin bedroom slippers.

A little later, my father brings home some Kentucky Fried Chicken. He and I eat it straight from the box, the way we do every Tuesday night. It tastes better that way to us. We like the dark meat, so we gnaw on the drumsticks. My mother does not make a reappearance. She's found lots of hiding places in our house. My father, who has given up searching for her, prepares a plate of the chicken breasts and coleslaw. He carefully covers her supper with aluminium foil and places it in the refrigerator, which he calls an icebox just like his mother, my Grandma Libby, used to when she lived with us before she died. This is her house with its fragile, twisted, antique furniture that I must not scratch or break.

'Ask me the state capitals,' I urge him. He is reading the newspaper as he tears chicken off the bone in thin, slippery slivers. He does not acknowledge my request but turns the large pages with each bite. He has not bothered to change out of his work clothes. I worry that he will get grease on his shirt, and I'll need to wash it for him before the weekend. He only has three good shirts. The others are frayed at the collars. I bought him new ones for his birthday. My aunt, his twin sister, took me to the mall, and we picked them out from the sales rack, along with a striped tie that he wears when he has an important meeting. Two blue shirts and one white. My mother will not go shopping anymore. The mall is a police state. The guards collect credit card receipts so that they can keep track of our every move and purchase. They will use this information against us, to hunt us down and imprison and then torture us. I paid cash for my portion of the shirts with money I earned from babysitting for Jasper and his puppy down the street. The puppy is more trouble than Jasper, who is four and happy to sit still and watch colourful cartoons with me.

'The capitals,' I prod him as he turns another page.

'Excuse me?' he asks politely.

'The state capitals. I have to memorize them.'

'Oh, that's easy. How 'bout Montgomery?'

'Alabama.' That's where he was born.

'Baton Rouge.' He sits back in his chair.

'Louisiana.' That's where he went to college.

I've studied the Southern states first since they are close by and familiar to me.

'Chicago,' he asserts, as he begins to read the sports page. The kitchen table is littered with old bones and napkins sticky from the dribbled honey. His favourite baseball team is the Cubs, and they are getting ready for spring training. He inspects the injury list.

'Hey, wait a minute. Chicago? That's not a capital.'

'Sure it is.'

'Nope.' I rub my greasy hands with a dishtowel and retrieve the atlas from the floor beside my feet. 'See?' I poke my finger smack dab on top of Illinois in the middle of our sprawling country shaded nut brown and forest green on the map. He pushes his glasses up over the bony bump on his nose.

'Well, I'll be.' He seems genuinely surprised, not just teasing me. 'It used to be Chicago. Back when I was a kid.' He watches me with renewed interest as he squints at the map.

'So what is it now?'

'Springfield,' I inform him with authority. 'Besides, they don't just go around changing capitals.'

'Is that so?' He returns his gaze to the sports page, then looks up. 'Sure they do. The capital of Georgia used to be Milledgeville, and now it's Atlanta.' He's better at history than geography.

I slam shut the atlas. I don't want any more questions from him. I know all about Milledgeville. My neighbour Brady, who is two years older than me, tells me my mother will be going there soon if she doesn't straighten out. That's the place for loony tunes, he insists, and I think about the nonsensical cartoons that Jasper and I watch together. After he tells me this, I won't let Brady kiss me anymore. He doesn't really want to kiss me anyway. He's just practicing for Sylvia who lives on the other side of him. She is sixteen and drives her father's old red sports car. Brady figures that if he learns to kiss, he'll get to ride in that sports car. He's spied on Sylvia making out with other boys in it. From our nearby front porches, we observe tangled arms and legs in the dazzling moonlight. We keep track of her night activities like private investigators hired by her parents who have thrown up their hands because they don't know what else to do.

Even though I've made the resolution about kissing to protect my mother, I miss doing it. I miss the way that Brady smells — like wild onions on the other side of the road, and how his tongue rubs hard like gritty sandpaper against my lips, hunting for my mystery tongue, hidden safe behind the cage of my solid straight teeth. The dentist says they are so perfect I won't even need braces, which Sylvia used to wear before she turned sixteen. I move out on the back porch with my atlas. It has not kept up with the new countries in central Europe that we learned about in social studies, but it's just fine for stable state capitals. Brady is mowing his backyard, and he pretends not to notice me. He keeps looking dreamily in the direction of Sylvia's house, Sylvia with the long blonde hair. My hair is short and light brown, but my aunt tells me that I have very fine features like the Hughes side of the family, their side. From this, I take it that I am not to be beautiful like my mother and Sylvia, which is another reason to study the capitals, so I will be smart and travel to brand new places that are not filled with dreary, brittle antiques.

Because the lawn mower is noisily churning up the air, I can call out the capitals loudly to myself and nobody will hear if I make a mistake.

'Sacramento,' I scream.

'California,' I shout back, not at all intimidated by such an outlandish place.

'Florida,' I reverse the order to trip myself up.

'Tallahassee,' I recall after a second. That is where my aunt went to school, so I should know about it. Brady does not take notice of my accomplishments. The grass bits ejected by the lawn mower release the scent of juicy ripe watermelon, newly cut open.

The New England states are the hardest because there are too many of them, and they are so petite that the words don't even fit within them on the map. Plus, the names sound foreign or from the olden days – Montpelier, Concord, Providence. I like best the states that are tricky, like Illinois with its Springfield.

And then there's Pennsylvania. You just know the capital of Pennsylvania should be Philadelphia or even Pittsburgh, but surprise, surprise, it turns out to be Harrisburg of all places. What a joke Pennsylvania has played on the other states and schoolchildren all across our land.

My father comes outside to sit with me in the porch swing. He has changed into his white T-shirt and faded blue shorts. His stomach tumbles gently over the top of his waistband. He is still carrying the sports page in his hand. He studies the statistics each night, just like at work where he calculates mortgages for expectant young couples who want to buy a house and start a family.

'Will we go to Harrisburg someday, Daddy?' The swing moves swiftly backwards, propelled by his long, hairy legs.

'Harrisburg? Why on earth would anyone want to go there, honey? I don't even know where it is.' We rush forward then back again, stirring up the early spring air as we move through it.

'Sure you do. It's the capital of Pennsylvania.'

He frowns in a worried way. This clearly baffles him. Like me, he must've been thinking Philadelphia, the cradle of American democracy, city of brotherly love, home of the cracked freedom bell. He pulls off his glasses and stares into the dusty twilight.

'Your mother and I went up north to New England when we first got married.' I hold my breath to concentrate on his words.

'It was fall, and the trees were turning more colours than you can name on a Sunday. She collected leaves in a paper bag and later used them to make wreaths and decorate the house.' I breathe again. He pauses to squint his eyes, as if struggling to spot some minor, forgotten detail in a history book. He puts his glasses back on and adjusts them over his nose. 'She's always had a special touch for pretty things, you know – although your grandmother didn't fully appreciate her talents.' And he smiles sadly at me all the way through his glasses, from a dark place behind his tired charcoal eyes. I put my hand on his arm then remove it to hug the atlas as the swing slows down. He has forgotten to push again.

'Brady says she's going to Milledgeville if she doesn't watch out.' I can't help myself. I need to warn someone of this nearby threat. I add in a scary sounding whisper, 'To the loony bin.'

The lawnmower starts back up again. My father takes off his glasses and critically examines the skinny boy who is making plush diagonal lines in the grass next door. Brady, who has grown tall this year, now looks distant and tiny to me. The swing has come to a complete stop.

'How old is Brady, these days, Mary Elizabeth?' The evening air feels suddenly cold, and I start to tremble inside. My father only calls me by my full name when he is cross. He is not looking at me, and I can barely hear his disappointed voice over the uproar of the lawnmower. My teeth start to chatter.

'About fifteen, I guess.' I manage to say something, anything. I know Brady's exact age, even his birthday, which is coming up this month. I have dreamed about what he might like for a birthday present.

'And how old am I?'

I study my father's creased face. I remember that my mother is thirty-five because I saw it on a form that we had to fill out for medical insurance the last time she went to the hospital. I struggle to recall the candles on his birthday cake, but I can only picture four burning stems poked in thick chocolate icing, which must have been Jasper's cake.

'Thirty-six?' I question. Husbands are supposed to be older than their wives. I know that much about marriage. Just like Brady is older than me.

'No, ma'am. I've been around longer than that.' He seems pleased with himself.

'Forty?' I try again. He does not dye his hair, so there are lots of silver clusters sprouting out here and there. My aunt, his twin sister, has no grey hair at all, not one speck. She insists that is the difference between men and women, which is not the way Brady explained it to me last summer.

'You're getting hot.' He puts his glasses back on again.

'Forty-two,' I answer decisively, as if I just remembered a little-known fact.

'Forty-three,' he informs me. 'When I was growing up, my parents would never tell me their age.' He looks down at me through his bifocals.

'Back then it was considered disrespectful to ask.' I want to correct him because I hadn't asked. He was the one who asked me. Could that also be considered disrespectful?

'And who do you think knows more? Me or Brady?'

I consider Brady's curly black hair falling over his pale forehead. This question is harder to answer than it should be. I believe with all my heart that my father knows more than Brady, but he may not tell me everything he knows. And I also believe that Brady tells me things to get me to do what he wants me to do in the fort we have in the woods where he keeps his magazines. But I am certain of the answer my father is seeking.

'You, of course, Daddy.' I sit up straight and adjust my rumpled T-shirt. My aunt bought me a bra at the mall, and I can't get used to the funny tight pressure across my chest. When

I look down at the new bulges, I keep thinking that I'm wearing someone else's body that doesn't quite fit me. So I focus my eyes on Brady's yard work. My father is silent. I repeat myself to convince us both, 'You, Daddy, *you* know more.'

'That's my girl, M.B.' This is the name my father usually calls me by, short for Mary Beth and even shorter for Mary Elizabeth, named for my two grandmothers. When he says it with his soft Alabama accent, it sounds like 'mebbee,' the way he says 'maybe.'

He then adds heavy words like he is making a speech that he wants me to memorize forever, 'You let *me* worry about things around here, honey. About you, about us, about your mother. Not Brady. He doesn't know as much as he thinks he knows.' To erase all the unanswered questions, he rubs the back of my neck with a firmness in his fingers that makes me warm and sleepy like a baby. He goes back to studying the paper. His legs push the swing as far as it will go, then he lifts them up from the wooden floor and we fly forward again into a gust of pure air. When we glide backwards, I close my eyes and anticipate the next time that Brady will kiss me. I keep Tic-Tacs in my pocket so that I can pop one in my mouth when he gets near – just in case.

The lawnmower shuts off, and the silence is harsh and startling in the cool March nightfall. Up above my head I hear a window open, and a voice reaches out like a search light on the seashore at Jekyll Island where we used to go on vacations with my cousins before my grandmother died.

'Anchorage,' my mother has made her evening arrival. I cannot see her above us, so I picture her framed by the window, wearing a long, silky, lavender nightgown, her hair flowing around her shoulders, down to her waist, in loose honey-coloured waves, like angel pictures in my grandmother's old Bible.

'Alaska,' I send back upstairs the answer with utter, happy confidence that I can hold on to her tonight. For now, I ignore the cold truth of Juneau as I shiver with gigantic goosebumps and picture sugary white polar bears and chubby native families eating fish around a fire.

'Pierre,' she sings lovingly, and I imagine someone on the other side of the world observing us with curious interest from beneath a lopsided French beret.

'Montana,' I return to America and start heading west. My father pushes the swing again while under his breath he whispers, 'South Dakota.' I'm happy that he wants to join us on this journey.

'Columbus,' she calls out celestially.

'South Carolina,' I reply with earth-bound conviction about our next-door neighbour state.

'Ohio,' she instructs, softly satisfied that she is correcting me, giving me additional knowledge to face the world. I realize that she also likes the tricky places; two states have capitals that are almost the same, like twins.

The window drops back down again. My father smiles at me, and I know this has been a good day for us, one of our finest, one we'll want to remember in the days to come. I yawn mightily with my whole face, then remember to cover my mouth.

'Our family,' he coughs then starts again in a braver voice, 'We're doing just fine, aren't we M.B.?' He folds the tattered newspaper under his arm and leans back with a long growling sigh from within his stomach. He massages its rounded folds.

'No matter what Brady says, our family is making out okay.' He reaches behind me with his other arm and hugs my shoulders until they ache. I press the sharp binding of the atlas into tender new flesh over my heart. And I nod as I swallow to hide my inside smile at what he says.

Through sparkling clear teardrops, I notice Brady stealing a glimpse at our house, at the window upstairs where my beautiful mother must still be looking into the falling sky. Then he stares hard at me. But I push my head into the side of my father's immense chest, which smells of fresh lemony deodorant, and I deliberately turn away from Brady's probing, penetrating eyes. I slip a Tic-Tac under my tongue and swish its slick tartness behind, over, and around my perfect teeth.

I don't mind him practicing on me for Sylvia. I don't mind it one little bit. Just to prove this, I'll even meet him in the fort tomorrow after school with my atlas. I'll show him the special places. Because here's what I've figured out. Here's what he doesn't know about me – not yet anyway – I'm practicing too. I'm practicing for something bigger in life than Brady, something majestic, far far away in one of those surprising places, places like Harrisburg, Springfield, Columbus, Sacramento, even Pierre – one of those distant, clever, romantic state capitals.

Free swim

Mother was a minimalist. Our trips to the neighbourhood pool required only an old towel, swim goggles, and magazines. Sunscreen was sparingly applied before we left. Anything additional we'd have to carry ourselves *both ways,* which she emphasized with a frown strong enough to banish frivolous thoughts from our heads. Walking the three blocks instead of driving, we formed a self-conscious, petulant parade. Neighbours, dressed in designer swimwear, whizzed by in minivans hauling pool toys and large coolers. Over our swimsuits, we wore the raggedy T-shirts Father had cast away.

I learned about Minimalism in Art History 101 my freshman year of college. The spare beauty of the Conceptual works of that era looked strangely familiar to me, although I had not studied art before. My roommate Virginia helped me come to new understandings of life.

'I think of my mother when I see the work of Mary Cassatt,' Virginia mused as she flipped through the pages of my stiff new textbook. 'The women are so lovely and sensual.' She smiled. Lounging on her dorm bed, she focused on one painting in the book, her eyes obscured by straight hair as sleek as velvet.

'I saw this one at the Museum of Fine Arts in Boston.' She held up the book so I could view a round, dreamy woman bathing her equally round child.

'My mother had taken me there,' Virginia confided with a meaningful nod. 'I thought she might simply walk into the painting like, you know, Mary Poppins.' She sighed as if disappointed her mother had not vanished into art.

I flipped through the art history book searching for what I could offer as an appropriate response. When I found the chapter on Minimalism, my mother's life suddenly became clearer to me.

'Here's my mother,' I told Virginia as I pointed to the picture of a wall sculpture with simple repetitive cords extending with lanes from a wooden frame to the floor.

'Eva Hesse,' I proclaimed as I read the label. 'Of course,' I improvised, 'you know her work. *Addendum.*' She stared at the spot where my finger met the glossy page, then quickly turned away from the book. She didn't ask me much about my family after that.

Throughout my childhood, fifteen minutes of swimming each hour at the neighbourhood pool transformed Mother from a vigilant parent into someone who would stop at nothing before her time was up. She swam laps with such focus that even blatant misbehaviour on the poolside did not distract her. Once, when my little brother Chevy pushed me into the water after I'd stolen his Eskimo Pie, Mother navigated an effortless breaststroke around me and the disintegrating chocolate blob. The lifeguard blew her sharp, unforgiving whistle, and I paddled to the side where Chevy howled tragically. I was supposed to be looking after him.

Mother had made it to the Olympic swim trials before we were born. Efforts to relive her past glories as an athlete were futile once she had children, like treading water in the strong currents of Edisto Island where we went for a week each summer. Father, who loved the freedom of our vacation beach trips, never came to the neighbourhood pool – except to pick us up from swim lessons. He remained at home reading the paper, baking cookies, or mowing the lawn. Chevy started staying home with him once he was old enough to state his own opinions. I did not have that kind of willpower.

Mesmerized by mother's single-mindedness, I counted laps during those fifteen minutes; she easily outlasted the other moms who paused to chat. I half-listened to their stories of love, disappointment, and grocery sales – not willing to lose track of the laps. When I was younger, I would run up the sides and back in time to her swimming. After the whistle signalled free swim, I jumped into the water with a planned, chaotic splash. Mother would then play underwater tea party with me. Our puffy faces smiled over pretend teacups and scones – no conversation required. Effortlessly, she had returned to my childhood reality until the whistle once again announced adult swim again. Mother's pattern was to indulge in two of these protected pool episodes every summer afternoon, unless lightening threatened. Only acts of God could intervene.

Later when I was a teenager, after Father moved out of the house without explanation to Chevy and me, Mother got a year-round job at the library. Sunscreen was no longer required as she swam in the summer evening hours. I was a teenager then, mad at both my parents for their separation and also having created me – an imperfect being, someone who was messy and uncertain – and Chevy, who needed more attention than any of us seemed able to provide. They should've done a better job of making us in their image, spontaneous like Father or mysterious like Mother in her unfussiness.

The last summer before my parents split up, Father ran over my kitten Cleo. I'd left her in a liquor box in the driveway behind the car while I went off to my friend's house. Father didn't even realize what had happened as he drove off to his job as an English teacher at the community college. Mother had seen the events transpire from the kitchen window. All that remained of Cleo was a flattened coat, turned dark orange from the blood mixed with her summer-yellow fur. We watched Mother carefully place the crushed, limp kitten into one of Chevy's shoe boxes. Shocked by the sudden intrusiveness of death, Chevy whimpered while I covered Cleo with dandelions and grass clippings. When Mother called Father at work, he came home immediately, tore off his shirt, and dug a hole under the oak tree in the backyard.

Surrounding the shoebox in the newly created hole, we allowed Chevy to pray 'Now I lay me down to sleep,' which he had learned at our neighbour's house. The part about 'dying before I wake' made my throat ache, but I was determined not to cry in front of my whole family. Cleo had been wide awake and curious when I had last seen her.

'Let's sing some songs,' Mother suggested. Father, with his warm, deep baritone, started the melody of 'Where Have all the Flowers Gone?' He'd belonged to a folk group in college and knew songs for every occasion. The rest of us sang sadly off-key with broken voices. We all held hands in the late afternoon sun, the pain and guilt of losing Cleo transformed into the sweet sorrow of standing in a circle with my family and singing together. I didn't want the song to end, and so I kept it going round and round, long time passing with flowers, young girls, young boys, soldiers, then flowers again. Mother finally declared 'amen.' Father cancelled his classes and did not go back to work that day.

'Let's go get some flowers for Cleo,' he offered as I sat disconsolate on the lump of fresh earth. He ruffled my hair with his sweaty hand, the two of us culpable for the loss of Cleo. With Chevy left at home watching cartoons, Father took me to the nursery where we bought some marigolds. I picked them out, selecting yellow and rust shades that matched Cleo. Father also bought potting soil and a small trowel. That afternoon, I planted them one by one in a colourful cluster.

'Water them every day, Cissy.' Father often called me by the nickname Chevy given me in place of Cecelia. 'They'll need your constant care.' I sniffled in sullen response. I was determined to fulfil my duty.

Afterwards I went up to the pool with Mother. I begged Chevy to join me. Now that he'd gotten older, free swim had become more fun as he invented games for us to play while Mother watched from the side. He rebuffed me today though. Mother swam faster than usual during adult swim while I dangled my toes in the water. We skipped the tea party and interlocked our arms as we walked home, skirting the dark spot in the driveway where my kitten had earlier played. Cleo sacrificed her life for us, for my family, so that we could come together one more time. The thought of a kitten dying for us was even more profound than Jesus, whom we did not talk much about in our house. Cleo, by contrast, was a cuddly, playful creature we had all held and adored.

A few years later, college brought new kinds of knowledge to me – mostly about my body. Virginia walked around the dorm room without any clothes. I had never before seen an adult person completely naked except in the changing room at the pool in the quick transition between clothes and swimsuits. Early on I had learned how to change mine underneath the cover of father's vast T-shirts, a talent that came in handy in college. It was hard to concentrate on art history, psychology, or English with Virginia so nonchalantly naked around me. Her breasts were full of an independent life, her hips magical, alluring. She made me want to have sex with anyone who noticed me.

James became my steady boyfriend that first semester. He was smart, scrawny, and younger than me by almost a full year. He'd skipped a grade and was equally hungry with untested desire. We never did manage to take off all of our clothes for one another and walk around naked like Virginia. We did manage to have sex in darkened corners of the campus, a feat that made me proud of my body's secret courage. But I was also nervous as James and I clearly did not love one another – not even in the quiet way Mother and Father still must have loved one another, even after their separation.

I went home that Christmas determined to talk to Mother about love and sex. There were stories, facts and insights I needed to learn, the kind of thing that was a mother's obligation to teach her daughter. I was not prepared, however, for the fact that Chevy never left our house over Christmas vacation. He watched television, read, and played computer games. His skin had turned grey. He did not eat at the table with us.

'How's he doing in school?' I asked Mother while we were standing outside waiting for the mail one day, anticipating the latest issue of *National Geographic* while I awaited cryptic notes from James. There was still the darkened spot on the driveway that I believed to be the remains of Cleo's presence among us. Chevy was a junior in high school by then.

'Talk to your father when you see him, Cecelia.' She never called Chevy or me by our nicknames. 'School is his department.' She looked away, saying nothing more.

With Chevy around so much, there was no time or space for confiding in Mother, no possibility for untangling life's mysteries. Father joined us for Christmas dinner as he always did, even after the divorce. He insisted that Chevy sit at the table as well. He described final essays from his freshman writing course. 'The students love semi-colons these days; they're quite the rage,' he admonished, 'as if random punctuation marks could improve otherwise bad writing.' Mother passed the green beans cooked with bacon.

'Eat something, dear,' she coaxed Chevy.

'No thanks,' he responded and passed the dish on to me. Chevy had become a vegetarian and refused to eat anything that meal but Waldorf salad, cornbread, and the chocolate pecan pie that Father had baked. Mother asked me politely about my classes. I knew they would be pleased when they saw my grades, but I did not divulge anything. Being a student was as easy for me as breathing – and certainly simpler than living at home. Gazing out the dining room bay window to the backyard, I could still detect the remains of marigolds faithfully replanted each summer in memory of Cleo and the rare pure moment when my family formed any kind of circle.

Christmas did not seem like a holiday that year. Instead of presents in fancy wrapping paper, Chevy and I both received envelopes filled with cash. Mother and Father exchanged cards. When I headed back to college, I made up my mind to have sex with other people than James, who had begun to irk me with his innocence. Somewhere in life, there had to be true emotion that matched my idea of love. I longed for it to be released by touching. I tried dating some of Virginia's friends, yet always came back to James. His familiarity reassured me.

I managed to stay away from home until May, when my return became unavoidable. I needed to earn some money to help with my tuition. Trips to Europe to see great art, which was Virginia's plan, or an internship at a newspaper with no pay, which is what James set up, would not work for me. That summer, the library offered me a job entering information into a database. I could carpool with Mother. The forty-hour interval of work was painless compared to the gloomy time I spent in the house. Chevy still would not leave the house during the day. Increasingly he stayed locked in his room except for clandestine meetings with unidentified associates at midnight and beyond.

'Aren't there counsellors who help with this kind of thing?' I asked Mother one day as we were driving home. She told me he had not been attending his high school classes. 'You know, like at community mental health centres. They don't even charge you much.'

'Sometimes, Cecelia,' Mother replied, almost inaudibly, 'it's not easy to know the right thing to do.'

Chevy wrote me notes at night when I was asleep and left them on the kitchen counter. The notes consisted of lists, requiring me to bring home from the library entire sets of books by a single author. Over the summer these sets ranged from Ayn Rand to Henry David Thoreau to James Baldwin to Carson McCullers. When Father came over, he brought fresh-baked chocolate chip cookies, and they sat in Chevy's room talking for hours about literature. No one seemed to acknowledge there was anything odd about Chevy's behaviour. I had once been punished for skipping a single day in my senior year of high school. My friends and I had gone to Daytona Beach and returned home gloriously sunburned. I now looked at this pale, frail creature living in our house as if in a cave, and I worried about the Unabomber, whom I'd learned about in a sociology course. Was this how he, too, had gotten his start? Equally terrifying, his brother had turned him in to the authorities. I could never, ever do that to Chevy.

'He'll snap out of it,' Father responded to my worried inquiries. He added, 'We're just homeschooling for a while.' Mother raised her eyebrows, quietly extracted a beach towel from the dryer, slipped into her flip flops, and prepared to walk up to the pool.

'Would you like to join me?' She extended this invitation with a forced smile. I shook my head and watched her disappear down our subdivision road. Father drove off in his well-worn Jeep. Every item owned by any member of our family looked as if it had already served a useful life before being pressed into extended service. I, on the other hand, was drawn to new, shiny, extravagant possessions, so much so that I had a hard time saving my summer money for the following year of college. I collected shoes that I might need for a party, CDs of the latest indie music artists, makeup in preparation for a date with a man I had not yet met. Newness made me feel more optimistic.

I went into the kitchen and poured myself a beer, kept in the refrigerator for Father's regular visits. I also poured one for Chevy. Balancing the two beer mugs, I knocked on his door with my elbow.

'What do you want?' he snapped at me.

'I have something for you.'

'Nothing I need, I'm sure.'

'Well, you just never know.' I remembered that the old Chevy from childhood couldn't stand a mystery.

'Oh, forget it, come on in.'

'I can't, my hands are full.'

The door opened quickly, the smell of pungent incense enveloping me. Magazines, books, and papers were stacked all around Chevy's room. There was no place for me to sit. I'd only had brief glimpses of his room lately when he darted in and out on his way to the bathroom or kitchen. How could Father sit in here with him several times a week? It was a fire hazard. Chevy was too young to be so weird.

'Here,' I handed him the beer that I'd already taken a few sips from.

He put the glass on a wobbly pile of library books that threatened to spill over onto his bed.

'Mother's up at the pool.' I informed him.

'What's new about that?'

'You want to go and surprise her?'

Chevy took a sip of the beer, which I marked as a triumph for me. I was sure he also was remembering that disintegrating Eskimo pie.

'You know, we're old enough now.'

'To drink? Not me. Not you either, for that matter.'

'No,' I clarified, 'we're old enough for adult swim.' Something that resembled Chevy's sweet smile from years past struggled to emerge from his tired face.

'We could take some beer up there and see if she – or anyone else for that matter – would say anything to us.' He leaned forward thoughtfully. I could tell he was listening.

'Why?' He had been the King of Why as a little boy. Why do you get to go first, why does mother swim by herself, why did Father run over Cleo? He seemed to think I had the answers.

'Well, just because we can. And should.'

'No thanks, Cissy,' he replied politely. 'Not tonight. I have other plans.' Chevy now half-reclined on the bed, his feet falling to the floor, which left a spot for me to sit as together we finished our beers. I left to put on my swimsuit but ended up reading *Vogue* magazines in bed.

Chevy was not really a bad kid, I tried to convince myself. He just didn't have any get-up-and-go. Mother and Father had been too wrapped up in themselves in recent years to pay sustained attention to either one of us. I didn't head to the pool that night, or any other night for that matter. I'd given up keeping track of mother's laps. When school beckoned at the end of the summer, I found my way back to campus, glad to be on my own. Virginia and I were still roommates. Despite our differences, we suited one another. I developed a plan involving her and Chevy.

'I'd like my brother to come up and visit sometime this semester. He's a senior in high school, you know.'

'Hmmm. Where is he thinking of going to college?'

'Well, he's not sure yet. There are lots of choices for a smart kid like him. Maybe we could go out together. You know, me and James and you and Chevy.' I had not managed to find a new boyfriend yet.

Virginia shook her hair from her face, looking at me with sceptical interest.

'He's not much younger than James – and very mature.' I continued, 'You'd like him. A literary type.' Virginia was an English major. The more I talked about it, the better I felt about this idea. Virginia was manageable; she'd eventually surrender to my plan out of desire for adventure. The harder part would be getting Chevy to comply. Mother would be relieved to get him out the house; she'd agree to anything, even if he needed to borrow her car because his could not be trusted on the highway. He drove the old Impala our parents bought when he was little boy. He had insisted back then on being called Chevy instead of George, our father's and grandfather's name. For many months, he pretended that he was a car, pulling up to the kitchen table for refuelling and into the bathroom for an oil check. He zoomed all around the house. This was the phase before he thought he could fly like Peter Pan, leader of the lost boys.

'Chevy, have you ever smoked pot?' I called him at home while Mother was at work. Most of the time he didn't answer the phone, but I let it ring for so long that not even Chevy could ignore it. He did not have or want a cell phone.

'Why do you ask?'

'Just curious.'

'Maybe,' he murmured. I waited. 'Maybe once. Or twice. Why?'

'That's the great part about college. You can smoke at night or in the mornings or in between classes. It even makes calculus interesting – and art history fabulous.'

'That's nice.'

'I have some now, you know, really good stuff. I want you to come up and try it with me.' This was only a partial lie. I never had pot myself, I bummed it off my friends. Virginia, however, had acquired her own stash.

'Why?'

'Just because.' He did not respond.

'Because!' I reiterated. I couldn't think of a reason, real or made up. 'I bet Mother will let you use her car, if you tell her you want to look at the college and visit me.'

We both knew that to be true.

'I'll think about it.'

'Well, think about it quickly. The offer is only good for this weekend.' I couldn't bear the thought of Chevy pretending he was going to come but never making it up here.

'Why's that?' With each question, I could sense his rising interest.

'I can't hold onto the pot any longer. I've got real pressure on me.'

'What day?'

'What's that?'

'What day do you want me to come up?'

This response I took to be a very good sign. I had to move fast. 'Any time Friday is fine. You can stay until Sunday. It'll be great.'

'Yeah,' he paused. 'Right.'

Our negotiation had been easier than expected. I'd thought it might take several phone calls – and the intervention of Father, and there would be a scene. But the fact was that Chevy was leaving the house, taking a trip, coming to see me. I felt a happy sense of accomplishment.

My emerging interest in Modern art had continued. A quotation from Eva Hesse accompanies one of her works in the art history textbook: 'Don't ask what it means or what it refers to. Don't ask what the work is. Rather what the work does.' This could have summed up Mother. It was impossible to figure out what she was or should be. The only part of her that was knowable was what she did. And that was evident when I saw Chevy steering her boxy green Volvo into the parking lot near my dormitory. So thrilled to see Chevy, I did not notice until the car pulled into a parking space that he had a passenger, a passenger with large-framed dark glasses, a passenger who seemed content to stay in the car until discovered. My mother sat there clutching a shoe box. Chevy got out of the car and stretched. His hair was long, scraggly, and oily, but his jeans and T-shirt had been so neatly pressed that the rumpled wrinkles from driving showed up all the more clearly. Mother loved to iron clothes, especially mine or Chevy's.

'Hey,' I called out. I knew better than to try to hug Chevy, although I realized at that moment there was no one else on earth that I could ever love as much as I loved him. And I admired his dedication to being so despondent.

He looked at me, glanced around the parking lot, then peered inside the car. He shrugged his shoulders.

'She was just sitting there when I got up this morning.'
'In the car?'
'Yep. With that shoebox on her lap.'
'Is it alive?' I asked.

'What? Is what alive?'

'Whatever's in the box. Is it alive?'

'Um, well, I don't really know, but could be, I guess. We just listened to music on the way up here. Didn't talk much.'

This did not surprise me. Father was the only real talker in the family.

My plans for the weekend were quickly disintegrating. The idea of smoking pot with Chevy, of going to see a French film with him and James and Virginia – all would have to be revisited in light of Mother's unexpected intrusion.

I made it over to the other side of the car and opened the passenger door. Mother slipped out of her seat and handed me the box. I accepted it gingerly, the image of Cleo the kitten rising between us.

'From your father,' she said. 'He brought this over last night.'

The box was heavy. On the top was written in thick block letters: 'For Cissy and Chevy.' I quickly lifted the lid – full of brownies, Father's specialty.

'He wanted you to enjoy them with your friends,' Mother explained.

I reached in to touch the brownies; they were warm, as if they had just been baked. I licked the tips of my fingers. The rich, familiar taste of chocolate reminded me of childhood moments with Father baking as he sang old-fashioned songs like 'Will the Circle be Unbroken' at the top of his voice.

'Do you want one?'

She hesitated. Eating Father's food was giving in to him, letting him remain a lingering participant in her regular life.

Chevy came around the car. 'Brownies,' I whispered reverently.

'Brownies.' Chevy replied with relief. He immediately took a large square from the box, and I followed suit. There was no way our mother could resist now. She extracted a small brownie from the side of the box. We stood in the parking lot bathed by the early autumn sun while taking shared pleasure in Father's rich chocolate brownies.

After she swallowed hers, Mother turned to Chevy.

'I'd like the keys.' Her tongue captured a wayward crumb resting on her bottom lip. She paused. 'Please.'

'Excuse me?' he reacted, patting the keys in his jeans pocket.

'Yes, I'm driving back this afternoon. Your father will pick you up on Sunday.'

Chevy groaned, 'Doesn't anyone around here trust me?'

Mother took the keys and got in the car on the driver's side. She rolled down the window. Her hand signalled us to come nearer. We walked over to her side of the car. 'It's not about trust, dear.' She took a deep breath. 'I need the car – to get home.'

'Laps,' I mouthed the word to Chevy. He rolled his eyes in silent agreement.

Mother fastened her seat belt, first appraising me and then him. 'George and Cecelia.' She paused for a moment. We stepped closer together, letting our elbows touch, bounce off one another, then reconnect.

'Take care of each other.' She glanced over our heads to the lowering sky then returned her gaze to us. 'Will you?' We both nodded obediently under the spell of her attention.

As she drove away, Chevy called out in his best Peter Pan impression, 'Second to the right and then straight on till morning.' With the certain sound of his voice, I suddenly believed that the weekend would have dimensions beyond what I'd been able to plan or imagine. James and Virginia would gorge on brownies with us after we got high. Then Chevy and I would stay up into the night talking in my room about lost kittens and marigolds, about swimming and brownies, about literature and life – about our mysterious past and undisclosed future.

Plan B+

They had moved out onto the new deck to get a picture of the whole group huddled around the keg as if it were a choice trophy. When the deck collapsed under the weight of fourteen adults with food and beverage, it seemed the keg might take off into the air like a missile or explode like a bomb. That's how Jill's sister Darcy described it afterwards. Jill had gone back into the house to look for the digital camera, which meant she didn't get caught in the crash. Darcy later said she couldn't remember hearing any screams even though two people, they soon learned, had died. All the rest were injured, some with concussions, fractures, and cracked vertebrae. Those words hadn't meant anything until Jill saw her husband's head in a bandage and his arms in matching casts in the hospital. When she kissed the patch of exposed white skin between his tightly closed eyes, she could tell Tom was awake from the nervous clicking sounds his throat made.

The doctor came in, wrote down notes on the pile of papers in his clipboard and pulled back the sheet at the end of the bed. Then, without a word, he took the tip of his pen and drew a line down the sole of the uncovered foot. Tom opened his eyes and wiggled his toes. The doctor chuckled. 'That's a good sign,' he explained to Jill. Her husband always hated having his feet tickled, but they smiled with relief as he waved his feet in the air. The doctor nodded and moved down the hall to the next patient.

That was the only smile Jill could remember for a long time. All her emotions had bled away, leaving a knot in her chest. The whole event should never have happened. She went over it every night before falling asleep, in her dreams, and when she woke up. They had not had a Plan B+ that day, which was what her father had insisted they always needed to have no matter what. He had been a fighter pilot, so whenever, even as young children, Jill and Darcy had an idea of something to get at the store or a party to attend, he asked for Plan B+. Any old back-up plan wouldn't do – it had to be a pretty good one in order to get their request approved. As the eldest, Jill felt the enduring tug of this responsibility.

But how could a person expect a brand-new deck to pull away from the house, collapse right from under them and kill a man who had survived bombing raids in Vietnam? Darcy reported she had seen their father fall backwards into the buckling lumber as she somehow managed to salvage her cell phone and dial 911. The keg landed right next to him, and a fountain of golden beer spurted into the sun-drenched atmosphere. They subsequently all smelled like they were drunk, which they had to explain away to the police. The party had just begun when their father broke his neck.

The children were in the front yard playing cops and robbers, so they didn't know until the ambulance pulled up that their parents, aunts, uncles, and grandparents were lying in the midst of rubble and shiny new nails. The incident hadn't made much noise. Only when the screaming emergency vehicles arrived did the kids figure out that something major had gone wrong. Jill, like her dad, was adept at managing situations, but she couldn't figure out what to do next. She just let the kids find out for themselves as adults were spirited away in orange vehicles with flashing sirens on top. The new neighbours, who'd been working in their yard, instinctively took in the children and let them watch cartoons.

Afterwards, when Jill learned that her father had died, she held her mother in her arms as if she were a sick child. 'It's going to be okay' she sought to offer comforting words – even though the loss was shattering to the whole family. She patted her mother's thin, rounded shoulders. Her mother's bones were so brittle that her doctor had prescribed extra calcium, but not one of them had been broken in the fall. She had slid right off the deck into the woods and lay there dazed in the hot sun on a bed of chicken wings and coleslaw until she was discovered by the paramedics. They took her to the hospital along with Darcy, who had fallen into soft flower beds. Neither one of them had been hurt beyond throbbing headaches and bruised muscles. Later they found out that their next-door neighbour had also died. He had three young children who had watched cartoons with the rest of the neighbourhood gang.

It all took place in a flash, and now it was a recurring bad dream. Beyond everything else that needed sorting out, the question plaguing Jill was what to do about her mother in the midst of this unspeakable state of affairs. She was scared to be by herself.

'I don't know what to do. I'll just be so lost in that house without your father,' she wept with her daughters at the hospital. 'I can't go back there. Not now.' Her faded blue eyes spilled out strings of tears.

'Well, I guess she could come to my place,' Darcy offered reluctantly to Jill later. She was referring to the one-bedroom apartment where she'd moved after she separated from her husband. She had left him and all of their belongings a week before the fateful crash. Even though Darcy had started new medication for her depression, it did not seem to be the right environment for their mother. When Jill conferred with Tom, he sighed, refusing to offer an opinion on the matter. He had enough to do to keep up with his own injuries. Jill longed to ask her father for his unfailingly sensible advice – but that was, of course, impossible. Anyway, she knew without asking what he would want her to do.

So that's how it turned out that Jill's mother came to live with her family in order to regain her strength. The boys had to move in together to create a private room for their grandmother. 'It will just be for a little while,' Jill had whispered to Derek and Drake. They didn't argue with her, but that night they drew a line down the middle of Drake's room with string.

None of the members of the household could bear looking out back where the new deck had drifted away from under them and descended into a scrambled pile of loose lumber. There was a gaping chasm that they couldn't seem to get fixed. Jill kept the heavy drapes pulled closed. She and Tom were suing the construction firm, but nothing was happening very quickly. Tom worked from home because his broken arms made it impossible for him to drive to his job as a management consultant; he was able to manoeuvre around the computer with his two little fingers and thumbs. The lawyer for their stricken neighbours had been in touch with an attorney, and Jill and Tom heard one Monday morning in August that they might also be sued.

Everything that had once seemed so special about their lives became a nightmare, all due to a single accident at a party. Tom and Jill went through the motions of taking care of their children and resumed some of the normal habits of life. Jill was glad each day to head to her job as a buyer at Macy's. She was in charge of purses, hats, and scarves. She liked accessories, letting others worry about the main items, the business suit, or evening gown. Her co-workers moved around her quietly in sympathy for her recent loss and current difficulties. She tried to carry on normal conversations about movies and Hollywood stars.

'Do you think Tom and Nicole might ever get back together?' she asked Nancy, who was in charge of cosmetics.

'Tom?' Nancy replied in a bewildered tone. Jill realized that Nancy thought she was referring to her own husband.

'Tom Cruise,' Jill quickly clarified things.

'Oh,' Nancy raised her eyebrows knowingly. 'They both moved on some time ago.' She stacked makeup boxes on the counter. 'But they sure did look good together.'

Nancy and Jill began their routine walk around the floor of the store before it opened. Jill pulled a hat off the display and placed it on Nancy's head.

'Pink's your colour. Why don't you ever wear it?' Nancy gazed at herself in a three-way mirror.

'I guess I always thought it was for little girls.' She adjusted the hat to the side. 'But I see what you mean.' She checked the price tag before putting it back on the shelf. She then fluffed her black hair as if she'd suddenly become prettier. That was Jill's effect on people – to give them a lift, to make them feel better about themselves. She looked at herself in the mirror next to Nancy and saw her own smaller, pale reflection with more freckles covering her nose than she had remembered.

This was about as personal as her interactions got at work. And when she arrived home, everyone was out of sorts. It seemed they waited each day for her to straighten things out. Tom wandered through the house like an exhausted zombie and spent most of his time entering data into his computer in the wood-panelled den. He only responded to direct questions. The boys argued constantly but couldn't abide being separated from one another. Her mother stayed up in her room until Jill came home from work, when she offered to help fix dinner.

'I bought you a scarf today, Mother. I thought it might look good with that turquoise outfit.' Jill was determined to make her mother feel better. She needed more colour in her life. Her preferred attire recently had been a droopy beige bathrobe.

'Teal,' her mother responded, sniffling over the chopped onions.

'What's that?'

'Teal, the pantsuit is teal.' Her mother sniffed again. 'You, of all people, should know that.'

'Well, teal then,' Jill responded patiently, not even bothering to defend herself. 'I still think it will blend.'

'I don't have any place to wear it.' Her mother scraped the onions into the electric frying pan.

'You could wear it to a bridge party.' Jill tried to be optimistic although her mother hadn't left the house since the funeral, a private family gathering, except to go to the physical therapist and get the newspaper. 'Or to church.'

'I'll give it some thought.' That was her only response. Jill turned up the heat on the frying pan until the onions spit oil into the air.

They continued to work on dinner together in silence. Her mother prepared a salad while Jill cooked the pasta and marinara sauce. She wasn't even hungry anymore. It hadn't occurred to anyone in the house to get dinner started before she got home from work. Not that Tom would've been much good at it in his current state. His primary contribution these days was to toast bagels in the mornings for breakfast. Jill would fix the boys bag lunches for day camp at the nearby lake and drop them off on her way to work. When it came time for them to get out of the car, they kissed her earnestly. She rubbed her wet cheek and watched them vanish into the woods. Those morning kisses were the best part of her day until she picked them up after work, and they ran to her breathlessly before their squabbles resumed in the backseat.

Setting the table for dinner, Jill realized that she didn't know what her mother did for meals when she wasn't there. The older woman stooped towards the kitchen counter as she sliced the tomatoes; she appeared to be curling into herself.

'Mother, have you taken your calcium today?' Jill desperately wanted her mother to get stronger.

'Of course, dear. I'm not totally helpless, you know.'

Jill turned on the overhead light. Otherwise, the kitchen was dark and dismal with the floor to ceiling drapes covering the sliding glass doors, which had to be kept locked so no one would inadvertently walk out there and fall into the cavity layered with exposed lumber. Jill would not let the children play near the shrouded doors. She had intended to redecorate with sheers after the deck was completed to bring more sunlight into the house.

Last April it had been Tom's idea to expand the deck so they could have relatives and friends over in the evenings and grill hamburgers. In May he enlisted his father-in-law and his brother-in-law, Darcy's soon-to-be ex-husband, to help design it. Later that month, they'd cleared the overgrown bushes out back. By June, Tom had researched various construction firms and selected the one with the most residential experience. They began work immediately and completed the job in good time. This was the first major addition to the house since Tom and Jill bought it five years ago when the boys were toddlers. Tom had gotten a bonus at work. They decided to handle most of the costs with cash up front so they wouldn't have to worry about bills when it was finished. That was the first of many missteps that plagued them.

Darcy came over to collect their mother to drive her to the doctor. Jill had Friday off this week, and she planned to spend it by herself. She'd already delivered the children to day camp, Tom had been picked up by a co-worker to go to a retreat, and Darcy had agreed to take their mother to lunch after the doctor. She was also accompanying her to the lawyer's office on the way back. There had been some kind of hitch with the will that Jill had not paid much attention to.

With the house finally empty, Jill looked around with profound disappointment. Newspapers were piled high in the hallway, and the degree of dust and clutter was worse than usual. Lately, it had proved to be a constant, futile battle to take care of their things. She started a load of white clothes. It did seem like her mother should at least manage the laundry while she stayed with them.

Jill went upstairs to brush her teeth and looked into the bedrooms along the way. The boys' room was a wreck. Toys and books and abandoned Legos were in a state of messy confusion. She couldn't even locate the magic string that separated their staked-out territories. She poked her head in her mother's room. There, in contrast, everything had found its place in the midst of Derek's Batman décor. His grandmother had created a little writing and reading area by the window and a tidy sleeping nook in the corner. It all looked very permanent, like she might be planning to stay for a while.

Jill had intended to go to the grocery store, but instead she stumbled across the hall into the master bedroom and lay down on her unmade bed and closed her eyes. This respite seemed like the first moment to herself since the deck crashing; she wanted to cry but was too tired. She desperately missed her father, whom she hadn't even let herself think about, and the order he had given to all of their lives. Her mother was depressed and adrift without him after forty years of marriage. If Jill could rewind what had happened, she'd do it all differently, but she wasn't sure what her Plan B+ should have been. She fell into an unhurried slumber that was full of dreaming sequences with brightly coloured fabrics on rows and rows of racks. Her own face was lost among them.

Jill woke up to the sound of voices downstairs. She felt guilty for having taken a long nap when there was so much to get done around the house, when everyone was relying on her to be organized and productive. She straightened up the bed and combed her hair and proceeded downstairs. She shook her head to clear it of leftover sleep. Darcy was sitting with their mother at the kitchen table in front of the closed drapes. They sipped from steaming mugs of coffee and talked in vexed tones. Her mother was wearing her pantsuit with the new scarf.

'I don't know what your father was thinking. He always took care of everything for me. I never had to worry about a thing.' She removed her glasses and rubbed her red eyes with the back of her hands. Jill sat down at the table with them; they hardly acknowledged her presence.

Darcy looked distracted as she played with the tangled fringe on the placemat. 'Well, you know Dad. He was always so careful. Surely, he must've had a pretty good plan or else he never would have done this.'

Jill stared at one then the other of them. She still felt groggy from her nap.

'What did your doctor say?' she questioned her mother, who propped her head up with both hands.

'He said I'd be good as new soon. But I don't know what he means by that. It's been a long time since I've been new.' She added in a weak, private voice, 'And I sure don't feel that way now.'

'In other words, he said you were doing fine.' Jill added as an afterthought, 'The scarf looks nice on you. You're right about the suit; it's not turquoise after all.'

'Oh. Thanks.' Her mother didn't seem at all pleased by the compliment or the doctor's report. She massaged her temples with her index fingers. Jill could see that the grey streaks in her hair were now turning powdery white.

Darcy then began to describe the course of their day.

'After the doctor's appointment we went to the Cheshire Cat Café.' Jill got up to pour herself some coffee and then rejoined them at the table.

'You know how I've always liked their pecan chicken salad,' her mother mused. 'We even saw some of the church folks there. They were very nice to me and quite solicitous. I promised I'd be coming back to church and Sunday school soon – if someone would be kind enough to drive me, that is. The food there was as good as ever.'

Jill was glad that something had pleased her mother but irritated about this new chauffeuring expectation, even as she acknowledged her mother needed more in her life than their jumbled dark house day in and day out. Whenever her father had been home between trips, he had driven her everyplace, even to the beauty parlour, although she had a nice new car of her own.

Her mother took several deep breaths and a sip of coffee before resuming her summary of the day. 'Then we went to see the lawyer, Carl Fisher. He's only a bit older than you, Jill. Before him, his father had been our attorney. Didn't Carl Jr date one of your friends?'

Jill shrugged her shoulders. In fact, her best friend Louise had been in love with Carl for years, but he'd never even noticed her, which Jill had not appreciated about him. Louise deserved better treatment. She and Tom used a different lawyer.

'What did Carl have to say?'

There was silence. Finally Darcy murmured, 'Well, it was somewhat confusing.'

'Yes?' Jill wasn't certain where this was going. She added sugar and cream to the coffee in her mug although she normally drank it black. She took a long sip of the coffee. It tasted sickly sweet, but she knew she needed the caffeine. She swallowed some more of it. The knot in her chest tightened.

'Um, yes, it seems that Dad left a portion of his estate to…to some other people.' Darcy was staring at her hands, now folded in her lap, as if she were ashamed of something she'd done.

'Some other people?' Jill sputtered coffee into the dim kitchen air.

'What kind of people?'

'Carl's been looking into that. And it seems like they are… um…Vietnamese people?' Darcy stated this like it was an unanswerable question. She kept her eyes lowered.

'Vietnamese people?' Jill repeated, shaking her head to indicate this would be impossible. Then she stopped herself. 'How many people are we talking about?'

'A woman and two children.' Darcy spoke quietly, still not looking at her sister, 'Yes, it seems he left the old farm property on the lake to them.' Jill added more cream and stirred her coffee vigorously into a whirlpool that spilled over the edge of the mug onto the table.

Their mother had said nothing during this exchange but grabbed a napkin and applied it to the creamy puddle of coffee on the oak table. Her hand was trembling. Darcy cleared her throat and elaborated, 'They are essentially homeless. According to Carl, Dad's been supporting them for years.'

'And how many years is that?' Jill inquired suspiciously, pushing the sticky coffee mug away from her. She'd had enough. She hated that Carl knew all of this about their lives before she did. It was humiliating. She felt robbed. The farmhouse was falling apart, the land had been neglected, and her father had complained about the taxes. But it had belonged to his parents. She and Darcy had often played in the as kids. In fact, it was across the lake from where Derek and Drake now went to day camp. Jill always assumed her father was saving it for his grandchildren, for her children.

'How many years?' she repeated the question, now nervously curious about this state of affairs.

'The woman since she was a young girl. Evidently, she's his child. And the children are her children. Carl has been in touch with them. Dad had been trying to get them to come to this country. The woman claims she suffers from discrimination since it's clear that they're partly white – with blue eyes and freckles.' Darcy added quietly as she covered her nose with both hands. 'Like ours. Carl had a picture of her. She's a few years younger than us.' Their mother had untied the scarf from around her shoulders and was mopping her face with it.

Jill bowed her head and closed her eyes as if she'd spontaneously decided to pray. She stayed very still until she heard a car pull up into the driveway. Through the front window she could see Tom getting out. With two arms in slings, he was struggling to maintain his balance. He nodded goodbye to the driver then stood in the driveway. His solitary figure looked stiff and remote, like that of a lost stranger. She had no idea what had been going on in his mind lately. Before the deck project had consumed them, they had often relaxed together on the old, small deck with wine in the twilight as they talked about their plans for the future and shared stories about their children. All of that seemed so long ago.

'Let me see if I've got this straight.' Jill spoke quietly and deliberately. She didn't acknowledge Tom as he came in the door. 'Dad had another family in Vietnam at the same time that he had us.' She laughed bitterly. 'A parallel family?'

Both Darcy and their mother nodded their heads in gloomy

unison. Tom had walked up behind her. Her thoughts were now gaining momentum, the caffeine pulsating through her body. Her mother had wadded the scarf into a small ball. She pulled it apart and twisted it around her hands.

'*That* was his Plan B+? Have another family just in case we didn't work out? I get it! A pre-emptive strike!' Jill choked on the next words, 'And did you happen to find out anything about this person's mother?'

Darcy sipped some more coffee and turned her gaze towards the covered sliding glass doors. 'Carl hasn't found much on her. He thinks she may have been a…a prostitute. Or at least that's what she turned to in order to support herself. Dad apparently didn't have much further contact with her after his assignment there. He tracked down the girl in an orphanage when she was about twelve years old.' Darcy relayed all of this in a flat, depressed voice with impersonal language that must have mimicked the words of Carl Jr.

At that, Jill got up and bumped directly into Tom. He groaned as he turned to protect his arms. She glared at him. 'How could you have done this to me?' She reached across the table to pull open the drapes. The late afternoon summer sun, a harsh, relentless spotlight, caught them in its fierce rays. They all peered outdoors, searching for the missing deck, but there was nothing beyond the brilliance of the sun. Tom blinked and squinted at Jill, watching her with astonishment as she stomped around the kitchen. Still at the table, Darcy straightened out the placemats, and her mother stared at her gnarled hands tied up in the scarf. Jill grabbed her keys from the hook by the door.

'I'm going to go pick up the boys. At least they are where they're supposed to be. Unlike everything else around here.'

She let the door slam behind her. Once she got in the car Jill knew that she had behaved in an irrational, inappropriate way. It was her mother who should be most upset by this news; she'd been agitated yet mostly silent, as if there was nothing left to say. No wonder she didn't want to be at her own house. There was no telling what other ghosts might be lurking around that their father had left behind.

Now all of a sudden, Jill had a throbbing headache. Along with everything else, she was beginning to feel responsible for this new person, the abandoned woman who was her half-sister with two children, cousins to her own children. She pictured them all coming to live at her house, crowded together like first-generation immigrant families. Darcy would probably decide to move in as well. And why not? With Jill there to do the laundry and cooking? The deck would never, ever get fixed. Their former lives had expired, along with her father and their future.

The whole crash with the inevitable medical bills and lawsuits had made Jill feel responsible for everything. Tom, on the other hand, ignored the complexities of life. He could barely manage to talk on the phone and didn't always return calls to the lawyers, doctors, and contractors. It must be nice to have your arms broken and your ribs so bruised that you couldn't do much of anything and everybody else has to take care of you. She was exhausted from sleeping with him because he couldn't turn over easily, and she had to help him out of bed to go to the bathroom and get dressed. Otherwise, they didn't touch very much. It was even painful for him to kiss her. She lay next to him at night on her stomach listening to the strangely reassuring sounds of her sons as they argued with one another in the room across the hallway.

Jill turned up the air conditioning full blast and steered the car quickly through their subdivision to the highway. Driving fast helped her collect her thoughts. Here, she had an idea, a new plan. An exchange program. She'd go to distant, now peaceful Vietnam all by herself, and the other family could come here. Someone else could sort out the rubble of their lives.

Jill got to the day camp parking lot earlier than usual. The boys and other campers were nowhere in sight. She parked the car near the familiar lake and walked down to sit on a bench and wait for them. Sweat trickled down her neck. The slant sun reflecting off the lake stung her eyes and transformed the water into slick shiny crystal, which beckoned to her. She hadn't gone swimming the whole summer long. Nothing had been much fun lately. She remembered when she'd been lifeguard there during the summers in college, and on breaks she'd take long leisurely swims. Those summers had been the best time of her life, her body tan and sleek, admired by all, especially Tom, then manager of the nearby club, who promised her a lovely, carefree future. Now she rested her perspiring arms on the ledge of her stomach, which had not ever gone flat again, not since Derek had been born.

Jill stood up, removed her sandals, tucked her keys in the sand under them, and waded into the water up to her knees. Cool ripples lapped against the edges of her khaki shorts. She wanted to sit down in the wet sand but instead inched further out. Some kids were on the floating dock at the edge of the enclosed swimming area. She knew she could make it out to them. It was okay to swim in her clothes. They'd even given her that kind of test at the last session for her lifeguarding certificate. She sank into the welcoming water and began what used to be called the Australian crawl. Air filled her pockets, and the slight wind helped her glide effortlessly along.

As she swam closer to the dock, she could see one head bobbing in the water and waving a hand excitedly. The children on the dock ran back and forth in a frenzy. At once she recognized all of the telltale signs and gathered her strength. Her lifesaving skills returned instinctively to her. With quick grace, she moved in the direction of the waving hand that disappeared then reappeared. As she got closer, she saw it was a young girl who sputtered in the water. Jill approached her from behind and expertly pulled her head into an armlock and then started to swim towards the shore. After a stroke or two Jill realized that she was losing strength as the girl fought against her with flailing arms. She decided instead that she should swim toward the nearby dock. She pulled the girl in that direction, her legs now worn out from the unaccustomed strain. The children on the dock were jumping up and down, creating haphazard waves in the lake. When she reached the dock, Jill pushed the young girl towards the ladder. They both hung on, gulping for air. Up above her she could see shadowy faces looming down towards her. One belonged to Drake.

'Mom! What are *you* doing here?' he exclaimed in a strange, tormented tone.

She caught her breath as she looked around her. There was the lifeguard stand nearby with a young man, bronzed and incredulous, perched on it. The children now sat quietly with their toes dangling in the water. The rescued girl, laughing hysterically and pointing at the others, had pulled herself up on the dock.

One of the older boys must have noticed Jill's consternation. 'We were playing sharks and minnows, Mrs Chisholm, and Cherie was the last one out there. None of us could catch her.' He paused. 'But you.' Even in the cool water, Jill grew hot with self-consciousness. When she frowned, he added in an encouraging voice, 'I guess that means you won. Would you like some help getting on the dock?'

The girl twirled around in sunbursts above her head. Jill did not dare get out of the water onto the dock in her wet clothes. It would only add to her embarrassment. She caught her breath and whispered to Drake, 'I'll be waiting for you in the car.'

Jill retreated toward the shore with a weary back stroke, her legs barely able to kick. She glared with envy at the innocent clouds that floated across the sky into the sinking sun. Her soaked clothes tugged her downward. As she neared land, she flipped over and executed a sleek surface dive into the murky, comforting lake water. She didn't want to resurface.

When her stomach scraped the sand, she pushed her heavy body out of the water, picked up her shoes, retrieved her keys, and shook off like a rain-drenched dog. With the sun falling into the lake behind her, she walked towards the car while squeezing water out of her shorts and T-shirt. From the trunk she extracted an old picnic blanket that she wrapped around her shoulders. She sat in the driver's seat and half listened to the dismal news on the radio. Her own family and friends had been featured on local stations earlier in the summer after the deck crash.

Jill leaned her head back and closed her eyes against the dazzling, chaotic afternoon. For the first time in her life, she understood how it was that she always ended up with all of these needy people around her. She felt compelled to save them – even when she couldn't, even if they didn't want to be saved. Hadn't that been what her father believed, that he needed to save all of Vietnam? When those efforts failed, he took another approach, his Plan B+. Just trying to get through it, to save himself, would have to suffice. Yet he had ended up with more on his hands than he'd anticipated. He couldn't hold on and he couldn't let go; he couldn't do much of anything until he died, leaving it to the rest of them to figure out a plan. There's just not a way, Jill recognized, to devise alternatives for all that could happen.

Jill checked her watch as she kept a lookout for the campers. She turned off the radio. Tomorrow was Saturday. She intended to go to work and let Tom, her mother, and Darcy decide what the next steps would be. All she needed to do for now was to take care of herself and her boys. With day camp over for the week, ragged clumps of children emerged from the dusk-covered woods. Derek and Drake dashed towards her, toting soiled towels and leafy art projects. Releasing the car door, she opened up her arms to them and enfolded their wiggling, wet bodies with her inside the blanket. The knot in her chest relaxed some at last. They snuggled together for a brief, merciful moment. She felt so grateful for her children. At this age they could still quickly forgive her, no matter what she'd done in life.

Quantum entanglement

Living in the library had its luxuries.

During the school year the library stayed open 24 hours. They had recently installed showers for staff who rode bikes to campus; lockers were available for free. Almost every day there were receptions or a luncheon following a speaker, so food was plentiful. With her backpack and jeans, Corey looked like just another graduate student. On the weekends, she scoured the refrigerator in the staff lounge for abandoned leftovers. As a sign of reciprocity, she also cleaned the refrigerator. She was used to that kind of work from various restaurant jobs. And change, if necessary, for vending machines, could be found near the belongings of undergraduates who carelessly tossed things aside as they went about their social lives and academic crises. In short, Corey had everything she needed, including a wealth of good reading material.

She'd been sleeping in a library carrel assigned to a faculty member who must've gone on sabbatical. The carrels had combination locks, and she had cracked the code. This professor kept a few personal items and books on postmodernism there. Corey had heard about such ideas when she was in college, before she dropped out to find her elusive passion. She'd also worked as part of a maintenance crew at a drug recovery centre for a time, seeing herself someday as a social worker who could truly help people.

After the start of the semester, when there had been no evidence of activity in or around this particular carrel, she set up the desk area as a counter for notebooks and the filing cabinet stocked with toiletries, a few dishes, a towel, and a shawl. She also stored books on a shelf – and she created a nest of sorts with her yoga mat on the floor where she could sleep, if not in the basement near the café where large lounge chairs pushed together formed a makeshift bed. Exhausted undergraduates pulled all-nighters nearby.

The living conditions of the library provided simple solutions. She'd even formed casual connections with some comp lit doctoral students who assumed she was writing an endless dissertation on Gabriel Garcia Marquez or Mario Vargas Llosa – names that sounded noteworthy in their foreignness. She spoke Spanish fluently, thanks to those childhood years in migrant camps where her parents worked alongside the orange pickers. Her mother and father had dropped out of college to seek another kind of learning experience. They lived, so they said, 'on the road,' a lifestyle that had given her a love of reading and appreciation for impermanence. Corey wondered what they were up to now.

As a child, Corey had also spent countless hours at the local public library, where her parents dropped her off for entire afternoons in the summer. Among her favourite books had been *From the Mixed-Up Files of Mrs. Basil E. Frankweiler*, the chronicle of Claudia, who, believing that she is misunderstood at home, convinces her younger brother to run away with her. Their destination: The Metropolitan Museum of Art. During their stay at the museum, they stumbled upon a secret involving a beautiful sculpted angel with curious markings on its base. With the help of Mrs Basil E. Frankweiler, the children learned that some secrets can be beautiful and even change you forever.

Corey had secrets too, not all of them beautiful, most rather tedious in their reminders of bad fortune. Her last lover, in fact a graduate student in women's studies at a college across town, had ended up going to jail for multiple shoplifting infractions

'I just needed a lift,' Zelda had explained helplessly. She'd begun to hoard stolen cosmetics.

'Get a life,' Corey muttered in order to keep from yelling.

Evicted by their landlord, Corey was once again left with no permanent place to call home, her possessions piled up on the curb. She took only what could fit into her backpack along with the yoga mat.

Corey didn't think anyone at this university library was on to her. They had their own preoccupations with complaints about the costs of books and journals skyrocketing and the computers constantly breaking down – not to mention the stories of men exposing themselves in the stacks. Even the custodians didn't pay much attention when they encountered her late at night. She'd learned at an early age not to do anything that directed unnecessary attention her way. If staff or students thought she was the least bit odd, such could be attributed to her newfound study of postmodern literary theory with all of its nonsensical *non sequiturs* about the ambiguity of the signifier. While stacking up the professor's books, she'd leafed through them a bit to get the basic philosophical particulars. Her interests were wide-ranging.

Lately Corey had become friendly with Nicholas, who worked behind the circulation desk. He kept logs on the database of what was checked in and checked out. Occasionally, she stopped by to ask about a book on Cervantes or Santayana. Nicholas seemed to be constantly behind, the books stacking up on the cart next to him.

'Need any help?' Corey inquired one day, late in the afternoon before the influx of students after classes and dinner.

He looked up at her blinking, as if awakened from deep sleep. She had seen him reading books during his break in the café downstairs – slim books that could have been poetry but seemed to include photographs, planets, and charts.

'What's that?'

'Just wondering if you're going to the poetry reading tonight.' She handed him a flyer that she'd found in the lobby.

'Nope,' he replied without elaboration. When she didn't move away, he added, 'I have errands to run.' Corey stepped back, reminded that Nicholas had a life outside the library.

The evening poetry reading featured a visiting writer who read poems about animals. One named 'Dog Dreaming' caught her attention when he spoke about it being 'so little that was tamed.' The very idea of these poems seemed simple to her at first. But the poet, an elderly gentleman, had vast blue eyes – and there were all sorts of distinguished looking professors along with a bevy of students who sat in rapt silence, nodding their heads and clapping at the end of the reading. Merwin, the poet's name, made her think of Merlin. She would look up more of his poetry in the stacks.

The food for the reception after readings was always good, and she helped herself to another plastic plateful of crackers, a variety of fancy cheeses, along with some grapes and strawberries. Her diet had become essentially vegetarian over the past three months. As she'd lost weight, her skin had become a bit sallow, the colour of slightly aged pages in a library book. Corey had read an article that someone had left up on the computer about the importance of vitamin D, provided by the sun. She was afraid to go outside since she didn't have a student or staff ID card to re-enter, and her visitor pass had expired. At least she'd stopped smoking as there was no easy escape from these confines.

Late that evening, she stopped by Nick's desk after the circulation department had closed down. No one was in the library but a few staff and the regular all-nighters. She sat down in the large black office chair, allowing it to envelop her, enjoying the idea of proximity to Nick's being. She had seen him go through the stack of books, checking their spines, leafing through the pages, and then sorting by call number on the cart. There was a full cart right next to her. She began the process that she'd observed him follow. If she could complete some of his work, it would lift a burden from him – one that must be overwhelming given his rounded shoulders and tired eyes. This cart contained science books with curious titles about cells, electrons, galaxies, and the uncertainty principle. When the security guard walked by, she turned to smile at him.

'Just trying to get through the backlog,' she stated with an efficient nod.

'I know what you mean,' he replied. 'It never stops.'

'You too?'

He nodded and shrugged his shoulders. Hers was a familiar presence in the library, one that everyone recognized even if they couldn't quite place her.

She felt too conspicuous to return to Nick's cubicle every night. Yet, over time, she developed a rhythm. He kept an old-fashioned spiral bound calendar on his desk. She flipped through it, noting at the end of each month a set of double-digit numbers. His actual entries were minimal: Tuesday mornings blocked off for 'staff mtg-' and occasional Wednesday afternoons for something labelled 'Misty appt.' Every two weeks there were dollar signs on Friday, presumably for payday. His only picture on the shelf next to his desk was that of a silver grey kitten in the arms of a child. She decided that the kitten, perhaps now grown into a cat named Misty, needed to go the vet every so often for a chronic condition. She liked Nick's attentiveness to small creatures.

Corey's regular visits to Nick's desk followed by occasional 'good mornings' became the standard pattern of her week. Her evenings were equally predictable. She'd learned the name of the security guard.

'Getting caught up?' Julius inquired as he walked by, never stopping to chat.

'Busier than ever!' she replied with gusto.

'I know what you mean,' he agreed. 'Don't work too hard.'

Corey found solace in organizing the books in order of call numbers. She also watered nearby plants that were withering. Performing these tasks for the library justified her existence, her dependence on this ecosystem for food and shelter. Besides, she figured she was getting a first-class education, from linguistics to physics to poetry, depending on the lecture topic for the day in the nearby meeting room.

When the Faculty Senate held its meetings, she'd taken to sitting on the periphery of the group. Everything from recycling to honorary degrees got discussed and debated.

'What area do you represent?' A bearded young man in jeans with a sports coat inquired.

'The libraries,' Corey responded without hesitation. She smiled. 'I feel like I live here.'

'Yeah, I know what you mean. Would you care for some more punch? Or wine?'

She grinned, unexpectedly. When he handed her a plastic cup full of a red liquid, she inquired. 'And you?'

'Social sciences,' he said cryptically.

She looked at him blankly.

'You know…like political science and sociology. Or in my case, anthropology,' he explained. 'Cultural,' he added as an afterthought.

'Of course.' She swallowed the rest of the liquid, glad it was wine, and nibbled at the cheese and crackers.

'How very interesting.' She turned back to the cheese table. She didn't want him studying her too carefully. She considered herself a person without a culture. After the Florida migrant camps, her parents had settled in the distant cold quiet of the Canadian woods. Corey felt close to them even though they were far away.

After gathering her backpack from the nearby chair, she remembered her plan to wash clothes that night in the large bathroom with the showers behind the staff room. The undergrads had not discovered it yet. She had learned that she could start the shower with all of her clothes on, use the soap to wash them down, then take them off layer by layer and hang them on the hooks nearby. She'd created a bathrobe out of a man's discarded flannel shirt (XL) and an old scarf. Usually her clothing was dry by morning.

Some classes were held at the library, and Corey had begun

to sit in on one that taught the basics of computer research. She could get into the Google website, where she established a password. The reference librarian who taught the course stood over her shoulder.

'Tell us about your research project,' she requested one day.

'Information technology in the twenty-first century.' The librarian didn't move. 'And how it intersects with postmodern Spanish poetry,' Corey added. The librarian nodded with approval. Corey had learned from the various lectures that everybody studied several topics at once. She'd started reading even more about postmodernism in the staff room during breaks. They usually had leftover treats there.

The entire spring semester moved forward with a rhythm that was satisfying. She wondered how her former partner, Zelda, was doing in jail. Their lives had parallels in terms of confinement. But shoplifting – and multiple infractions? Corey had learned from her parents how to scrounge without actually stealing.

From the carrel window, Corey could see intricate buds blossoming into dogwoods and flaming azaleas. She set aside the thought that at the end of the term the 24-hour schedule of the library would be reduced for summer hours. A new plan would arise in due time. Her presence was now taken for granted by everyone who assumed she was a student or staff member – or even a young, anxious faculty member. She was beginning to give some thought to planning her own library lecture on postmodernism although she was very busy with taking care of Nick's data entry that had accumulated and attending sufficient lectures and readings as she scavenged for food. She was even teaching herself PowerPoint. At many of the receptions, wine bottles were left behind for the caterers to pick up. She'd started collecting some of those, along with plastic bags full of cookies, crackers, and nuts. She stored the cheese in a tin container just above the air conditioning vents. The library was kept too cold for comfort.

Corey had been deliberately reading through the books on the shelves behind Nick's desk where the kitten, Misty, watched her beguilingly. Medical volumes on arthritis, diabetes, and leukaemia took up a bit of space. A few books must have been Nick's personal copies as no call numbers appeared on their spines. She scanned the book flaps; quantum physics caught her attention. One featured a scientist named Schrödinger – and something about his cat, supposedly both alive and dead. He also argued that tiny invisible electronic particles once linked continued to interact even when separated at great distances. They were entangled. She felt that way about Nick – that he was very present even when he was absent, especially when she sat in his chair.

Nick kept a to-do list in the stack of papers on his desk. During her regular visits, Corey glanced over the list, seeing if she could decipher it while attending to as many tasks on it as she could. Some items referenced meetings or messages that needed to be returned. But others involved skills and tools at her disposal. She figured out how he inspected the call numbers for the books then entered them into a database. His list included items like:

> *Arrange books by call number*
> *Prepare budget report*
> *Check on Misty*

She liked his handwriting. The letters leaned forward with long *l*s and large *g*s. Sometimes he doodled in the margins as if he were daydreaming, the squiggles shaped like atomic particles or constellations. Everything about his desk had a cosmic air, as if life's little problems were nothing in the larger scheme of things. Yet during the day, when Corey peeked at him across the circulation desk, he often had a worried look on his face. Perhaps there was simply too much to do in his galaxy; perhaps he needed more help.

With the semester moving into its final rush and the library abuzz with nervousness, she started making a point of visiting his desk every evening. Some of the comp lit grad students offered her a pizza one night as she walked by and tried to strike up a conversation with her. 'Here! Have some. Come join us.' She paused for a slice. A girl with a long dark ponytail asked about her classes.

'Gotta get back to work on my dissertation,' she demurred. Corey had heard this sentence so often that she pictured the graduate students forming some kind of old-fashioned assembly line, all of them required to amass intricate widgets.

These activities gave her life the kind of symmetry that other people, she figured, get out of jobs and church. She had work to do too. Arranging the books in the right order was simple. Accomplishing the other tasks took more careful consideration. At first, she was stymied, eventually realizing that Nick first entered the data on a form before the computer, and she could check the call numbers on the form. With practice, she was able to imitate his notes and handwriting to insert corrections or edits. The work was very relaxing in its repetitiveness. She didn't know why it seemed so stressful for him. She watered the plants on his colleague's desk taking care not to drown the African violet. She leafed through more of his books about quantum physics where particles behaved like waves.

Gradually, she got braver with little things she could do, such as sharpening his pencils. He kept yellow number two pencils in a cup on his desk. Once they got worn down, she stored them in her backpack and replaced them with new ones from the supply shelf in his area. She also cleaned out his coffee mug. She'd started reading a bit more about Schrödinger and his theories of remote systems. Einstein, she learned, scoffed at Schrödinger's quantum entanglement theories referring to them as 'spooky actions at a distance.' Yet Corey had faith in what Schrödinger was talking about. He'd won the Nobel Prize after all.

Sitting at Nick's desk, she began to feel a kind of easy intimacy with him and to imagine things they might do together – taking Misty the kitten outside to play, buying some pet toys, watching TV together. Theirs could be a full and happy life. Indeed, they could job share – giving them each resources and the added advantage of time, that special resource that everyone seemed to crave so much. Unlike others in the library, Corey had plenty of time on her hands. She tried to keep busy though, so as not to think about Zelda, still presumably in jail where she belonged, stealing jewellery and cosmetics that had piled up around them until Corey herself felt out of place even before she became actually displaced by the landlord.

She often returned to her carrel just before dawn, sleeping until nearly noon. The afternoon was when the library was at its most active with students, classes, meetings, and receptions. She especially liked the art exhibitions and sometimes helped to get those set up, just pitching in wherever she was needed. Corey was not afraid of any kind of work at all. Her parents had trained her well in this regard too; even in their remoteness, she abided by them. She had never before found a place that resembled the predictable yet busy patterns of the migrant camps until the library came along. As the semester drew to a close, however, things were starting to get frenetic. It was an especially lively place at night, hard to distinguish between undergraduates partying and studying, all of them attached to cell phones, laptops, and devices of every shape and size. She, who had none of those, felt like an alien from another planet invading their space.

In late April, Corey noticed the summer hours posted, indicating that budget cuts meant the library would close every night at 9pm and not open again until 9am. She also picked up on reports at the various meetings she attended that layoffs were imminent. She'd started keeping notes at the meetings, which gave her something official to do. When she heard that the circulation department was preparing to downsize, she left a folder with the notes on Nick's desk; it was information he needed to know. He rarely attended any of the meetings. In fact, she felt certain she knew more than he did about the inner workings of the library. He did not interact much with other staff. He left reliably every day at lunchtime, coming back an hour and fifteen minutes later. Once when he was gone and the rest of the staff busy with the circulation desk, she got up the nerve to check on his desk during the day. He'd circled the word Misty three times on a legal pad. The little electrons swirled all around it. Was the kitten ill? She pondered its worrisome condition.

Sometimes when carts were parked in the stacks, she also shelved books. During the staff workday, she volunteered to move all of the books from the fifth floor to prepare it for renovation. She was given a blue T-shirt. Afterwards, the barbeque dinner outside on the plaza made it worth her time and trouble. Security officers, including Julius, joined in; she felt safety in numbers. He grinned at her, 'Glad to see you're taking a break for once.' She laughed agreeably in return.

Nick had also been on the blue-shirt team, which won the competition for the number of books handled. She saw him on the edges of the crowd talking into his cell phone looking distracted. She decided to bring him a cup of iced tea. It was a hot day. The sudden brightness of the sun caused her eyes to sting.

'Finish the budget report?' she inquired as she handed him the tea.

He looked at her with some vague recollection. She held out her hand, 'Corey. Stacks.' She'd seen other people in the library introduce themselves that way.

'Oh. Yes. All completed. Now we just have to see what the furlough plan means for our division.'

'Well one extra day a week in the summer might be kind of nice.' Corey had no idea what that would mean for her – except that she'd see him less. Already the weekends dragged on and on with that overnight security guard watching her with more scepticism.

'Yeah, my ex-wife is now actually working overtime because of all the layoffs at her bank. No extra pay just extra work,' he added with irritation under his breath. She didn't know much about the outside world.

'Really?' Corey responded, wondering why that mattered much. She tried to shade her eyes from the glare of the sun.

Then he added, 'And the day care centre is cutting back its hours.'

'Hmm, I see.' She was trying to piece together the entangled puzzle of his life.

'How's your cat doing?'

'Excuse me?'

'I couldn't help noticing the picture of a kitten on your desk.'

He appeared to stop his introspection and examined Corey more carefully. 'The cat is dead.' He crushed the Styrofoam cup in his hand, tossed it into the nearby garbage container. 'Feline leukaemia,' he added as he walked away. 'Belonged to Misty, my little girl.' Corey blinked back tears from the piercing rays of the sun.

The following night in the cubicle behind the circulation desk, Nick stayed late. She could see him from the bank of computers where she was revising her postmodernism lecture, as if she were a TA called upon to handle the whole class at the next session before the end of the term.

Nick worked more rapidly than usual. The entire cart of books was easily managed. Since he was there by himself, when the cart was completed, he rolled it over to the intake area and returned with an empty cart. On that empty cart he loaded many personal items: his calendar, the picture of the cat, and his books on physics. Corey's chest ached. What was happening?

He piled more books on to another cart, volumes that had been accumulating in the corners of his cubicle, ones that Corey had not known how to handle as she went through his things. Leaving the library computer on, she quietly made her way over to his area. He did not look up.

Corey bent down to pick up a pile of books. She added it to the cart. He grimaced in recognition.

'Furloughs are one thing,' he stated flatly, 'Layoffs another matter altogether.'

She winced.

'Was it something you did – or didn't do?' she asked with a tremor in her voice, wishing she'd worked harder at night on his behalf.

'Nope. Just budget cuts. But you're probably safe. They always need students and shelvers. But for me, well… They gave me until Friday to get through the backlog. Then I'll be paid for a month.' He pushed hair out of his eyes, which she could see had become bloodshot.

'That's tough,' she empathized. 'Spooky.' She didn't want to think of them being too far apart.

'Not sure what that means for my future – or how I'll take care of Misty.'

She could sense his aloneness in the vast universe of complex processes.

'I'm sure you'll find something,' she tried to be reassuring. 'Such great experience.' He sighed with scepticism.

'Thanks,' he mumbled. This was the first courteous word she'd heard him utter. It gave her courage.

'Maybe you'd like to drop by my place when you finish up?' she suggested. They were both on their own. 'It's nearby.' As far as she could tell, they had nothing to lose – but maybe something to gain. She rested her elbows on the piles of books and further extended her invitation, 'For a little wine and cheese.'

'Whatever,' he replied with a shrug of his shoulders, regarding her with curiosity. Corey moved quickly, 'I'll just be a minute. Let me just save my lecture on the computer.' Maybe later he could even help her with it.

Earth Day

Earth Day was a bad day for the restaurant. Festival visitors wandered inside to use the restroom or to request water, but that was about it. A few customers bought the special oatmeal applesauce cookies, and one couple with a child ordered three grilled cheese sandwiches on whole wheat. Marlene wrapped the sandwiches in waxed paper. The father also bought lemonade plus a bag of the cookies, not chips, for the biggest sale of the afternoon. Just outside the restaurant door, farmers and vegetarian chefs had set up stands offering free samples of organic produce, artisan cheeses, and gourmet foods.

At the end of the afternoon, Marlene threw the leftover grease down the drain out back. The hamburger meat had to get tossed too; it was several days old. She wouldn't mind giving the raw meat to the dogs who played catch with their owners in the park, but that somehow seemed against the unspoken rules of Earth Day.

She'd already decided to lock up the restaurant before closing hours anyway. Paul, the weekend waiter, had left after the few lunch customers paid their bills. He mentioned he was going to meet friends in the park to play Frisbee. He was a good, if quiet, kid. Marlene gave him an extra ten bucks as there had been next to nothing in tips that day. Last week Paul had uncharacteristically announced that he was saving up to buy a guitar.

Marlene put on her grey sweater, which felt itchy and dull now that April had arrived. Outside, the spring air lifted her wispy pewter hair and blew it in her face; she needed a haircut. There was lively folk music in the park. Babies slept in fancy strollers, and toddlers scooted underfoot. Their parents looked like they belonged together, even if some of the couples were two women or two men holding hands.

Big posters of the Earth decorated the park, although gusts of wind blew them loose. A folk singer led the crowd in old-fashioned songs like 'Puff the Magic Dragon.' Marlene hummed along to the lyrics, '*Dragons live forever, but not so little boys...*' while searching for Paul in the park. She tried to keep an eye on him as his parents worked extra shifts at the hospital to make ends meet.

Marlene sat down at an empty park bench near a sombre family spread out on a bedspread, a faded patchwork quilt with holes in it. The two children of almost the same size sneezed and sniffled. Allergies were bad this time of year with pale dogwoods and purple azaleas in full bloom. The parents hunched separately on opposing corners of the quilt. All four members of the family had curly, uncombed blonde hair that framed melancholy faces. Marlene was seated close enough that her work shoes, comfortable black Reeboks, touched the edge of the blanket.

The youngest child, a girl, stared right into Marlene's face. She didn't bother to smile. Marlene remembered the bag of oatmeal applesauce cookies at the top of her purse that she was bringing home to her mother, an invalid. Each cookie was carefully wrapped in cellophane with a gold label to keep it fresh, the ingredients listed in small print.

'May I give her one?' Marlene asked the child's slender mother, who accepted a large, wrapped cookie and inspected it closely through the wrapper.

'They're fat free,' Marlene added. 'It's a special recipe. No milk or eggs. My mother, you see…she's on a limited diet.'

The woman shrugged her thin shoulders. Marlene shook the bag in front of the child, who sniffed at it. The other child watched with interest. He stood up on skinny legs and poked out his scrawny hand. Marlene extended her pudgy hand out, too.

'Glad to meet you,' she said formally. The boy pulled his hand back but took a step towards Marlene.

She didn't normally think of herself as someone attracted to children, especially those who came into the restaurant. They spilled drinks; one even vomited into his food last week. The parents whisked him away without stopping to clean up or to pay the bill. But the fatigue of this family in the midst of Earth Day festivities filled Marlene with a vague sense of recognition. Her own small family, really just her mother and herself, found celebrations to be exhausting affairs. People acted like Earth Day was a party for the world. Yet even she, a college dropout who didn't read much but the local paper and sometimes *Time* magazine when left on the counter by a regular customer – even she knew Earth Day was pointless. Global warming was spreading across the planet with a vengeance like those monstrous oil spills and harsh pollutants in the air.

'What's your name?' Marlene asked the boy. Now that the two children were standing in front of her, she could see that he was taller than the elfin girl.

'Edward,' he replied soberly, still staring at her.

'Eddie, would you like a cookie? They're homemade.'

'Edward,' the small girl corrected Marlene. She was dressed in a flowery cotton dress that made her look like a scruffy fairy. When she reached out her tiny hand, Marlene touched it with her own rough fingers, calloused from old burns.

'And you? What's your name?'

'Flossie.'

'Flossie,' Marlene repeated. The name reminded her of a childhood friend in a bygone era.

Marlene placed the paper bag near the girl's hand. She grabbed a cookie but handed it to her brother.

'And what about my Papa? Can he have one too?' The man was reclining on the blanket with his knees up, his eyes partially closed. His knuckles were bruised.

'If he wants.'

The little girl extracted two cookies from the bag. After unwrapping them, she knelt down beside her father. She stuck a morsel between his lips before placing one in her own mouth. The father never opened his eyes. The thin mother, closer to Marlene, stared off into the distance.

Edward leaned against the bench next to Marlene. He carefully opened the cookie wrapper.

'Do you live here?' he asked. He was fidgeting, moving from foot to foot.

'Not so far away,' she replied. 'But I have a restaurant close by.'

He glanced around, crumbs falling from his mouth as he whispered, 'Do you have a bathroom?'

Marlene surveyed the park. There were numerous port-a-potties scattered throughout with long lines in front of them. They all had 'Earth-Wise' written in bold green letters on the slanted tops decorated with drawings of the sun and trees.

'They stink,' he murmured, not looking at his mother. She was now sitting up very straight on the blanket, her posture like the girls who played violin at the free summer concerts in the park. There were no curves or bulges to her – in contrast to Marlene whose body spilled out in every awkward direction.

'Ask your mother if you can use mine at the restaurant,' she offered.

He chewed silently for a moment, still squirming. The little girl, Flossie, spread her small body across her father's chest. His hand, barely moving, patted her back in time to the guitar music.

'Please. I need…I need to go.' He turned his head impatiently towards his mother. 'She has a bathroom. Nearby.' Marlene thought Edward was too big a name for such a young child.

The mother stood up, unfolding her long, lean legs in black dancer's tights. Her arms stretched over her head toward the navy blue sky. She pulled a pink knitted shawl around her waist and nudged the boy with the sharp point of her hip.

Marlene, weaving her way in the direction of the restaurant, stepped around family groupings on blankets. Earth Day was starting to turn chilly. Babies wailed, screeching electronic sounds emerged from a jazz combo just tuning up, and pungent incense burned into the early evening air. Marlene felt an unexpected connection to all of these activities now with Edward and his mother following her. She was glad that she'd cleaned the restaurant earlier – although when she unlocked the door and opened it up, greasy smells released themselves into the open air. Marlene removed her frayed grey sweater. She realized with embarrassment that she carried these smells on her clothes, in her hair, and layered on her skin.

Edward darted around the tables as if following some inner navigation system, like those in fancy cars. At the door of the men's room, he hesitated, looking toward his mother. When she nodded, he shoved the door. The mother sat down at the counter, her head clasped in her hands.

'He's such a worry to me.' She rested her forehead on the shiny Formica surface.

Marlene turned toward her, surprised. 'He looks like such a lovely child,' she responded, offering a glass of water to the woman who seemed too weary for someone so young and pretty. She also tossed a package of saltine crackers in front of her.

'Looks deceive.' The mother opened up the package of crackers and ate them quickly. Marlene noticed that the woman's fingernails were long with chipped pink polish. Her fatigue was catching

'Would you like to have him?'

'Excuse me?' Marlene stepped back. The mother coughed into her hand and wiped her nose with a napkin.

Nothing was making sense to Marlene. Her thoughts rambled to her stepson who had left along with his father, her second husband. She hadn't seen or heard from them in years. They had moved out west; restaurant work could be hard on a family. The boy would now be about the age of Paul, the waiter.

'That was just a joke,' the mother replied without a smile. The little boy, Edward, emerged from the hallway, regarding his mother with suspicion.

'Where's mine?' he asked, staring at the crumpled cellophane on the table.

'You already had a cookie,' his mother retorted with irritation.

'Would you like some milk?' Marlene bent down close to his grimy face. 'Chocolate milk? And I have more cookies and crackers.'

He frowned at her with hungry green eyes. In the unforgiving fluorescent light, she could see that he was wan little fellow, veins running across his forehead. A sharp crease formed between his white eyebrows.

'I also have vanilla ice cream,' Marlene added.

'We're vegan,' the mother muttered.

Marlene stood very still and waited. She had a customer who said the same thing when offered cream for his coffee but sometimes took it anyway.

The boy looked at his mother. Her back was no longer straight as a board. She rubbed her cheek with the soiled napkin. Edward reached over to pat her wild hair.

'Two scoops,' he answered, holding up two fingers of his other hand. 'Peace,' he added with the hint of a smile. The mother sighed and shrugged her shoulders.

Marlene headed into the kitchen to collect the food. From the storage room, she retrieved paper napkins and silverware. She added cookies to a small plate. The oatmeal, milk, and ice cream would be good for Edward's bones. When she re-entered the dining area, he sat at a table all by himself with his own back straight, hands folded in front of him.

'She went outside to call Flossie and Papa,' Edward explained, glancing over his shoulder.

Marlene could see the woman talking on her cell phone on

the other side of the glass door. She wondered if Paul was still out there with his friends. The day had become too windy and full of shadows for Frisbee. He was at that age where life could easily pick him up and toss him around.

Marlene placed the plate with ice cream and cookies in front of the little boy and poured a glass of chocolate milk. She sat down next to him. His mother's fuzzy pink shawl was draped across the back of Edward's chair. Marlene stroked it, the softness reminding her of the newborn kitten she'd once adopted from a pet shelter. He'd disappeared a week or two later.

Now that the sun had started to set, the Earth Day families were departing, leaving piles of trash behind in the darkness. The small boy turned his head to check on his mother, who was just outside the door facing the other direction.

'She'll be back soon,' Marlene stated. 'Eddie.'

He drank the whole glass of milk in a series of noisy gulps so fast that Marlene was afraid he might choke. When she got up to put away his dishes, the mother was leaning against the front window under the awning. Her arm moved back and forth in a regular pattern. A small spark followed these motions. Marlene did not allow smoking anywhere near the restaurant; that's how she'd lost her first husband – to lung cancer. He was gone much too quickly. The second husband had disappeared quickly as well, along with her stepson, but for reasons she no longer remembered. Her spirit was drained from all these separations.

Marlene rinsed off the dishes and left them to soak in the sink. When she returned to the boy, his head drooped to the table. Removing the pink shawl from the back of the chair, Marlene draped it around his shoulders. As she did so, he lifted his arms to her. Eddie was much too big for Marlene to pick up. She knelt down, enveloping them both in the shawl and holding him close to her heart. When she heard the whine of the door opening behind her, Marlene tightened her arms around the boy – to protect him from the deepening shadows of Earth Day.

Spectacular lies

Each night before she went to sleep, she tasted the stars. Sometimes they were thin and sharp like a lifesaver that she'd been sucking on; other nights the lustrous insides were round and cold like a sweet drop of white chocolate. Blaise tried to swallow the smaller stars to feel them inside of her, but she could only taste the shape, size, colour, and texture as they shifted with the moon over the course of the month. She slept with her blinds open so that her tongue could touch the stars, tickling the roof of her mouth in just the way she imagined sparkling champagne might on New Year's Eve.

By day, Blaise avoided her mother, who spent her time answering newspaper ads. Not ads really – not like 'DWF seeks travel companion (M or F but not married),' which were the ones Jesse's mother examined each day. Jesse reported that her mother had made a New Year's resolution no longer to have drinks after work with married men; they were too tortured. This decision was disappointing to Jesse and Blaise, who liked to spy from the kitchen the strange males who kissed Jesse's mother in front of the fireplace. Jesse and Blaise invented families for the men. Most of them drove a Camry, which corresponded with a house in the suburbs, the way they figured it. Jesse's mother was now on the lookout for men who drove SUVs. They were more adventuresome types.

But those weren't the kind of ads that Blaise's mother answered. She read *The New York Times Book Review* where people working on biographies of poets, scientists, and explorers submitted queries. 'Anyone with personal anecdotes about Jacque Cousteau, please send them to me for a study I am doing of his life and work,' or, 'I am compiling a history of the suffragist movement, so would like access to any papers on this subject from the early twentieth century.' Blaise's mother arranged and re-arranged the clippings like a stack of cards in a never-ending game of solitaire. Then she taped them to the wall in the living room above her computer. There were no sofas or easy chairs in their apartment, just two matching workstations in the living room. Blaise longed for an ordinary household.

On the first Thursday of the New Year, when Blaise arrived home from school, the latest edition of the *NYTBR* had appeared. Her mother received the *Book Review* early, before Sunday, because she had a subscription just to it. She was not concerned with business or politics in the other sections. Blaise perused the new clipping: 'I want to write the story of Amelia Earhart's final flight. Anyone with any information about the preparations for the flight, please notify me. Thank you very much.'

The inquiries were always concise and polite. Blaise re-read this one. Her mother watched from the entryway, her amber eyes radiating energy, as if she had just accomplished a feat of enormous consequence. Each week she devised answers to the queries and sent them to the address indicated.

'Why do you suppose anyone would want to write more about Amelia Earhart? Aren't there enough books about her already?' Blaise scowled in disapproval.

'Because those things are important to do. Just like Sarah Bernhardt and Simone de Beauvoir – the story of all of their lives must be told, over and over again.' Her mother, who tended to be illogical and optimistic, smiled as she spoke. 'She was a great person.'

'Who?' Blaise had to constantly check on reality, as her mother tended to shift from one topic to the next without notice. Blaise felt pulled off balance.

'Why, Amelia, of course.' The eyelids closed tightly as if to conceal inner radiance, then opened wide again. 'That's who we're talking about, aren't we?'

Her mother added nervously, 'Did you mail the letters today?' Blaise disregarded the question in order to continue the quarrel.

'If she was so great, why couldn't you have named me after her.' This was a constant controversy between the two of them. Blaise kept a mental list of great people she should have been named after. Marie Curie, for example. To which her mother responded:

'Philosophy is more important than science. Besides, Pascal was both a scientist and a philosopher. A child prodigy, he was.'

'Or what about Louisa?'

'Pure sentimentality. Anyway, get satisfied with Blaise. It's unique.' She paused to ponder her daughter's leftover scowl. 'Surely you agree it's better than Ludwig or Wolfgang.' That was the way her mother liked to argue – from a position of absurdity. 'Don't you think?'

'Emily,' Blaise shot back emphatically. She struggled to get the last word in these discussions. 'Celeste,' she muttered inwardly the name she had secretly given herself.

'The heart has its reasons...' This familiar refrain steered her mother into the kitchen where she filled up the tea kettle with water.

Blaise grabbed her backpack and stomped towards her bedroom. She pounced on the bed and searched longingly out the window. The stuffed backpack spilled its contents of books and papers and rumpled, stamped, rectangular envelopes on the floor. It would be hours before the stars arrived. She envied Jesse, who claimed that her mother had chosen an outlaw's name for her. Because she'd been named for a philosopher, Blaise felt pressured to have serious, brilliant thoughts. She'd been told by the gifted and talented teacher that she that she had a high IQ, so there was no excuse not to reach her full potential. She ought to be able to come up with important ideas to contemplate. But all she could get her mind to focus on was the pair of boots on sale at the Rack Room for 25 per cent off. She had hoped against all hope that her father would buy them for her for Christmas, but she only got a card from him. Her mother received a monthly check, but Blaise was not allowed to touch it. She wanted to send an inquiry to the *Book Review*: 'For a memoir I am writing about my father, please tell him to send me a recent picture. I haven't seen him in a very long time.' Would her mother respond with a real picture or some made-up fantasy?

Blaise searched her room for any small token of her father, but his fleeting presence in her life was confirmed by only a few deteriorating photographs. In one, he held her newborn body against his wide chest. She tried to decipher his body language which might provide the key to a secret code. His tight, straight smile signalled unspoken worries while his grey eyes focused on a faraway object. She wanted to remember how massive his hands must have felt as they supported her malleable back and soft infant head. Blaise threw the photograph on the floor with the other papers. Everything was topsy-turvy. Only the stars kept her on track. She even studied them and the planets in school.

How could he have let her mother give her the name of Blaise anyway? What kind of insensitive beast was he – to name her after a man, a dead, ancient one at that? His other children from his first marriage had sensible, feminine names like Caroline and Anna. She didn't think Louisa would have been such a bad choice. It wasn't pure sentimentality – those four sisters plotting escapades. Their father was mostly gone also. Plus, people always spelled her name wrong – B-L-A-Z-E – like she might be a horse instead of a teenage girl.

Blaise sat up to peer in the mirror above her dresser across the room. She frowned at her reflection, knowing full well she'd never have a boyfriend. Her future prospects were dim, despite the IQ tests. Jesse was in with the group of slow learners, but her destiny unfurled before her like one of the dazzling scarves in her mother's closet. Who'd want to kiss a girl with a name like Blaise and big hips and no boobs? Her own mother was utterly useless in terms of planning a reasonable social life. With all of her clippings stuck to the living room wall, it was impossible to invite friends over. Jesse's apartment was more suitable for a happy and fulfilling life.

The ring of the telephone into their normally hushed apartment startled Blaise. She lifted the receiver just as her mother was responding in a distant but civil tone.

'Yes. How are you doing?'

'I'm calling about Friday night.' Jesse's mother spoke quickly, 'I have some plans.' The two mothers rarely talked to one another except to arrange sleepovers. 'Tomorrow, that is.' She paused. 'I see.' These words made Blaise flinch. Her mother never even tried to encourage people to express their thoughts. 'It's about the girls.' Jesse's mother paused to take a deep breath. 'Well, actually, just Jesse, I suppose.'

Usually the two girls spent Friday night at Jesse's place eating pizza and watching horror movies that terrified them.

'I was wondering if they, I mean if she, could stay with you this Friday.'

'That would be fine.'

'Oh.' Jesse's mother clearly expected people to be more talkative. 'Are you sure?'

'Yes, of course. We'll expect Jesse for dinner.'

Blaise hung up the phone despondently. She sat down, her bare feet pushing back the loose papers, photographs, and stamped envelopes under her bed with the others. She preferred to spend the whole weekend at Jesse's and to read *Cosmopolitan* beneath the covers about how to have a wild sex life. True, on those nights she missed the stars. Blocked by the window shade in Jesse's room, their secret stories were withheld from her. But there were other pleasures – like listening to the laughter and whispers in the living room. Blaise would close her eyes and imagine touching and tasting the stars as they cascaded through the dense atmosphere of her mind.

Rolling over onto her stomach, Blaise pushed her broad hip bones into the folds of the comforter. She unfastened her too-tight jeans as she yawned sadly into her pillow. When would her father rescue her from this dreary life? No wonder he'd left them. A house in the suburbs would be just fine for the two of them, Blaise and her father. Jesse could come to visit, and they'd take long walks in the neighbourhood, looking inside people's picture windows to examine how they conducted orderly suburban lives. Her mother wouldn't be bothered by her anymore. And Blaise wouldn't need to worry every day about mailing letters full of invented truths. She'd change her name and get the boots for her birthday, even though it would be summer by then.

After school that Friday before Jesse's mother came home, the two girls investigated her chest of drawers and tried on her lingerie over their jeans and T-shirts. All the while, Blaise knew that back in her own apartment, just one floor below, her mother was stationed in front of the computer, staring at those inquiries, and writing people she'd never meet about things she knew nothing about. On credit card applications, her mother listed her occupation as 'freelance writer.' But responding to random queries was the real way she occupied herself when she could be trying out new things in life, like finding a man.

First, however, Blaise knew she'd have to convince her to get a haircut. Her mother's style was very straight and severe around her tight, tired face. She used to be pretty but had given up trying anymore. Blaise believed her mother needed a new outfit, something that would make her feel young and alluring again – like the kind of thing they were trying on right then and there. She twirled a black lace camisole on her index finger. What if she stuffed it in her jeans pocket, later planting it in the dirty clothes basket for her mother to find the next time she did laundry? Just then the two girls heard Jesse's mother open the apartment door. They tossed the lingerie back into a drawer and ran pell-mell down the hallway towards Jesse's room, where they flung themselves on the bed in a tangle of giggles.

'Do you think this one is short enough?'

Jesse's mother stood up straight, letting her ample chest protrude against the tight knit top. A pile of discarded garments grew around her feet. This was going to be a real date with dinner and dancing, not just drinks at a bar with the girls staying at Blaise's apartment for the night, according to the terms negotiated by the two mothers. Jesse nodded, sucking on a strand of blonde curls while Blaise shook her head decisively no. She thought Jesse's mom should look as sexy as possible. According to *Cosmo*, men liked short dresses, especially if dancing was involved.

'How 'bout this one?' She selected a black filmy item from the pile. It had lavish lace on the top.

'That's a slip, honey bunch.' Mrs Jennings used lots of pet names. She had asked Blaise to call her Wanda since she technically wasn't a 'Mrs' anyway. Blaise did not like the name Wanda. It was too common for Jesse's spirited mother.

'Oh.' Blaise tried to recover. 'Well, it's pretty enough to be a dress. And nice and short.' Mrs Jennings watched her from behind the closet door where the full-length mirror was hung. 'Maybe you could just wear a blouse over it,' Blaise suggested softly, as if to herself.

Jesse laughed with a sneer as she spit out the wet curls. She knew Blaise had no experience in these things. Her mother turned to give her a stern look, then fixed her attention on Blaise, whose neck was starting to feel prickly hot with the three of them all crammed in the bedroom together.

'You know something. That's not such a bad idea.' Mrs Jennings eyed the black item under discussion.

'It would be really sexy,' reasoned Blaise. 'Like this one in Cosmo.' The picture showed a woman lounging on a sofa with just a slip and pantyhose. Her lips and legs were parted.

Mrs Jennings pulled her dress over her head and tossed it on the bed. She wore skimpy underwear that revealed parts of her body that Blaise did not recall ever seeing on her own mother. She sucked in her own protruding stomach. Mrs Jennings reached for the slip and stepped into it.

'Like this?'

She turned a full circle. Her hips were nice and slim. Blaise wanted to look just like her, the way Jesse was starting to shape up. The slip clung ever so slightly to the rounded parts of her.

'Yes, you look very, very sexy.' Blaise asserted. Jesse snickered again, but now Blaise knew that she'd found the right solution for Mrs Jennings. 'Just put on black hose, and you'll be perfect.'

Lately that was all Blaise could think about – how some people looked sexy and others didn't. She knew what category she and her mother fit into. They were condemned to a life of cotton underwear. Her father must have figured out their fate as well, which was why he had decided to escape. Maybe he would like Jesse's mother. The four of them could all live in the suburbs together.

'Then that's what I'll wear. You have great taste, sugar.' She walked over to Blaise and pulled back her stringy beige hair into a ponytail. 'And beguiling amber eyes, you know.' Blaise turned away embarrassed. Slippery perspiration beads squiggled down her forehead. She peered into the mirror across the room. Fatigued eyes were reflected back to her – just the way her mother's looked. She'd been trying to stay awake at night to observe the movement of the stars in order to plot their paths. She now imagined dancing elegantly with them against the black velvet sky trimmed with lace.

'So what are you two girls up to tonight?'

Blaise did not like it when her mother tried to manufacture conversations. It was awkward and embarrassing, plus there was the worrisome matter of the unmailed letters.

'We'll just watch TV in my bedroom,' she replied in a terse monotone.

Her mother did not approve of television, but she usually allowed Blaise to do what she wanted to do, especially when Jesse was over.

'How 'bout some dinner, Jesse?'

'No thank you, Mrs Terrell. My mother got us some roast beef sandwiches from Arby's. We already ate.'

Blaise's mother looked annoyed.

'They were five for $5.00. We had a coupon,' explained Jesse. She and her mother were always bargain hunting. Blaise knew this would not impress her own mother, who often served up fruit and cheese and apple juice to her guests, while she drank tea in carefully calculated sips.

Blaise worried that Jesse would no longer like her when they got older. Everything about her life seemed tarnished and lopsided while Jesse spun around her in bright circles. Still Jesse saved her a seat in the school cafeteria at lunchtime. Blaise tried hard to participate in the conversations with the other girls, which was why she stayed current on all the *Cosmopolitan* issues. It put her ahead of those who only read *Seventeen*.

'Hey, Jess. Let's go.' She needed to direct Jesse away from her mother so that she wouldn't see their life up close. 'It's time to watch *Seinfeld*.' The two girls abandoned Blaise's mother staring at the computer screen. She kept all of the lights on in the living room so that it was as bright as a spaceship. Blaise liked the way Mrs Jennings lit only a few mood lamps. By contrast, the two computers were brilliantly hygienic. No wonder she and her mother had grey complexions, washed out like the black-and-white photographs in old *Life* magazines.

Blaise purposefully kept her room messy as it was her impression from reading Ann Landers that teenagers were supposed to do that. Jesse reviewed the squalor with admiration. She vaulted on the double bed amid an assortment of battered stuffed animals, found the clicker, and turned on the TV. An overeager laugh track exploded in the empty space between them. Blaise kicked her entire backpack under the bed.

'Doesn't your mother ever do anything but sit in front of that computer?' Jesse mashed the mute button.

'Sure she does,' defended Blaise. 'It's just that…well, when we're around that's what she does…you see…so she won't be a bother to us.' She didn't like other people analysing her mother's habits. She needed to reassure Jesse that everything was perfectly normal in their home.

'Like what else?' persisted Jesse.

'Lots of things. All of the things that most people do. In

addition to being a writer, she's an artist, you know.' Blaise fervently hoped that identifying her mother as an artist would excuse her peculiar behaviour.

Jesse did not seem impressed with art. 'Doesn't she ever have sex?'

Blaise lay down and covered her face with a pillow. They often speculated on Jesse's mother's sex life, but they'd never discussed her own mother's private behaviour.

'Well, you know, not since my father.' Her muffled voice sounded distant, even to herself.

'He's been gone for years,' Jesse argued.

'Sometimes they meet to discuss me,' Blaise countered. She threw the pillow to the floor.

'And have sex?' Jesse was incredulous. 'Where do they meet?'

'Oh.' Blaise bit her lip hard. 'I…I never get to go. My mother doesn't want me to see him.' The metallic taste of blood coated her tongue.

'Maybe she just hates all men.'

'Yeah, right. Then why would she name me Blaise. Pascal was a man, you know.' She blotted her upper lip with the sheet; a tiny streak of blood emerged.

'Whatever.' Jesse turned up the volume. They obsessively watched *Seinfeld* reruns, memorizing the dialogue.

Blaise only half listened. She propped up her head on the pillow and gazed out the window. There were no stars out yet. Often they waited until late at night – as if to offer her dessert at the end of a dreary day.

'Put down the blinds, will you?' Jesse did not like blank windows. 'It's cold in here.'

Blaise sat up and tossed her a crocheted comforter. Her grandmother, her father's mother, had made it for her when she was a baby. But she was dead now.

'Use this.'

'It's itchy. Plus you know I don't like it when you leave the blinds open.' Jesse was starting to shake. She sucked noisily on the ends of her hair. Every now and then Blaise had an inkling that Jesse didn't know absolutely everything about life. 'People will watch us.'

'Don't be ridiculous. Anyway, I have to.'

'Why?' Jesse's voice had turned inward – like that of a tired toddler.

'It's just the rule in my room.'

Jesse shifted over on her side, away from Blaise and away from the window. The two girls were still fully dressed. They did not like to change their clothes in front of one another.

Now Blaise could see some stars. They were shy, and she had to wait patiently for them to appear one by one. She made up stories about them, about the one she called Celeste, creating secret tales of romance – about how they mated with one another and stayed together for life just like certain species of birds and apes. She'd been studying evolution in science, and she'd concluded that stars were more highly evolved than humans. In her mind, on this night, they accompanied Mrs Jennings while she danced in a sexy slip on her date.

The bed was starting to tremble. Jesse had been so quiet that Blaise assumed she was asleep. But now faint kitten sounds escaped from her. Blaise lay perfectly still. She didn't want to know what Jesse was thinking about. It felt scary to imagine Jesse or her mother ever being sad and lonely. They had everything – pretty clothes from discount warehouses, sexy bodies, admiring looks from men. They had each other while Blaise was all by herself, except for the stars. She would not let Jesse distract her from this time of evening intimacy with them.

Soon the trembling stopped, and Jesse breathed heavily through sniffles. It was safe to assume that she was asleep. When she was all alone, Blaise sang to the stars. She didn't know much rock music; besides it was too noisy. The stars wouldn't dance to it. She half-sang and half-hummed the love song from *The Music Man* video that she had watched over and over again: *'Goodnight my someone, goodnight my love. Sweet dreams, my someone, sweet dreams, my love.'* She envisioned her voice traveling to the stars and then bouncing back to earth into her father's house so that he could hear her clear silver voice.

Jesse moaned and stirred restlessly beside her.

'I have to pee.' She grabbed her bag of clothes as she proceeded out the bedroom door. Blaise knew Jesse would change in the bathroom. She turned off the TV so that the room would be nice and dark. She would go to sleep in her clothes. Sticking out her tongue, she tasted the sharp, bright sugar crystals on the points of the stars.

When Blaise woke up her room was dark and chilly. She reached across the bed to touch Jesse's warmth, but no curled body rested nearby, just the old comforter in an abandoned heap. Blaise sat up with alarm. What had happened to Jesse? Had she returned from the bathroom? The luminous numbers on her clock radio read 12:05am. She longed to drift back to the safety of sleep. The stars were still in the sky. But now her insides were all woozy, the way she imagined Mrs Jennings felt when she went dancing and had too much to drink. She glanced once more at the stars, grabbed the blanket, and managed to propel herself out of the bedroom.

From the hallway Blaise could see all the lights on in the living room. Her mother often stayed up the entire night. Usually there was just the clicking of the keyboard at a steady, hasty pace; tonight, voices dominated the normally quiet spaces. She peered into the kitchen. At the scratched oak table sat Jesse with her mother. They were drinking hot tea. The kettle rattled on the stove top. Blaise felt sick to her stomach. When she was not around, her mother was likely to say the most outrageous things. Blaise pulled the comforter around her shoulders.

'I don't know if I will get it though,' Jesse speculated in tearful tones. She gently tugged a slick dark blonde curl out of her mouth and inspected it. Blaise's mother nodded sympathetically. 'You have to pay extra just to try-out. Then there's the cheerleading uniforms. They don't ever put those on sale.' Her voice faltered as her hair collapsed around her distressed face.

'You'd be a splendid cheerleader.'

Blaise was shocked her mother even acknowledged the existence of cheerleading in the world. She listened with concern.

'Are you feeling better now?'

Jesse nodded demurely. She wore a faded flannel nightgown. Her socks had holes in the toes. She seemed to have shrunk in size since earlier in the day.

'Didn't your mother tell you about all of this?' The amber eyes blinked rapidly with worry.

'Not really, not much anyway. We just learned about it in health last year.' Jesse crossed her arms over her abdomen and moved her head in slow motion while she inspected each object in the kitchen as if it were a treasure. Blaise watched her take in everything. Stacks of books threatened to tumble over. Freshly stuffed, neatly addressed envelopes stacked on the counter awaited some otherworldly destination. Finally, Jesse's eyes registered the presence of Blaise in the hallway. Her mother shifted in the chair to look. They both then stared at their tea mugs, as if they had been caught in the middle of a midnight conspiracy.

'Hey,' Blaise uttered foolishly. The blanket slipped from her shoulders to the floor. Despite her wrinkled jeans and sweatshirt, she felt naked and cold all over.

'Want some hot tea?' her mother inquired. When Blaise had been small, she and her mother had tea parties at all times of the day and night. Lately she'd decided that she hated tea.

Blaise did not respond. Re-establishing the blanket over her shoulders, she took a seat at the table. Before her sat a large pale blue box. She shuddered. Sanitary napkins. Things like this were not supposed to happen out in the open. Last summer, she had stared out the window in stony silence when her mother tried to explain it all to her.

Her mother poured spicy, aromatic tea into a mug and handed it to Blaise. The steam hung in the air between them. She then silently excused herself from the table, headed towards the living room where her computer flickered. Exiting the kitchen, she paused to massage Blaise's shoulders and pat Jesse's head. A minute later, the customary clicking resumed. Blaise and Jesse drank their tea in silence.

The next morning at breakfast, the sanitary napkin box had disappeared. Jesse complained of cramps. Blaise did not respond. How was it possible that this beautiful girl could invade her home, have her period before Blaise had ever had one, get up and talk with her mother in the middle of the night, then complain of cramps the next morning? She ate her cereal and noted that the pile of letters now had stamps on them.

'I think I'm going to check on my mother to see if she's home.' Jesse's eyes were streaked with red lines.

'Better not go up there yet,' Blaise warned. Sometimes the date was still in the apartment. Mrs Jennings usually was tired and cross when she got up – and not particularly sexy. Jesse looked like she might cry.

'Let's look out the window. Maybe,' Blaise suggested hopefully, 'there's a car that we don't recognize.' They liked to be spies together. Jesse did not seem to mind unadorned windows during the daytime.

In the living room the lights were on, but the computer was off. Blaise's mother slept through the mornings.

The two girls rubbed their foreheads against the cold window. Wintry winds blew torn Styrofoam cups into the street. No new cars were parked there.

'You know, your mother is pretty nice.' Jesse rubbed her abdomen in gentle circles.

'Is that so?' Blaise replied noncommittally, hoping that a car, any style or model, would materialize to capture their joint attention.

'Yeah, we talked for a long time last night.'

'What did you talk about?' This conversation made Blaise nervous, but she couldn't help pursuing it.

'All of those clippings.'

Blaise swallowed hard. 'What about the clippings?' she whispered.

'I asked her why she did that. What she did with them.'

'Hmm. Really.' Blaise had never had the courage to ask her mother that question directly. She resented Jesse's open curiosity. 'What did she say?'

'At first she just said, "the heart has its reasons…"'

Blaise groaned. 'Ugh, those philosophers again!' Her own stomach was starting to tighten up in cramps. She tried to picture sexy Mrs Jennings in that silky black slip with a man's arms wrapped around her, his breath hot like smoke in her ear.

Jesse maintained her focus. 'But then she said something about, well something about she was doing it for you.' She paused as if trying to capture a thought that had escaped. 'So that you could learn about their spectacular lives.'

'For *me*?' Blaise was shocked. She never thought of her mother as doing anything for her. 'Don't believe it. It's only for herself, not for anyone else.'

'Well, that's what she told me, and I *do* believe her. We looked at the ones about Amelia Earhart and Emily Dickinson and Juliette Gordon Low. She said that they were all elec–electric. Or something like that – one of those vocabulary words.'

'Eccentric.'

'Yep, that's it.'

'Well, so what?'

'"That's what girls have to be," she said. "Ec–eccentric."'

'She oughta know.' Blaise remained unimpressed. But the image of her mother talking about cheerleading and telling Jesse stories over tea made her feel forsaken. Besides, Jesse had not been told the whole truth – about how her mother answered these requests for information with made-up stories. How could you ever explain anything like that? It was spectacular *lies* not lives. Blaise's sore lip throbbed with the thought of that kind of nearby eccentricity. She bumped her head hard against the windowsill in order to feel the painfulness of reality. Jesse was watching her.

It was time to change the subject. 'Anyway, maybe we should check on your mother.' The street below was coming alive, and the rest of the world was moving beyond them. 'I don't see any SUVs.'

Jesse did not respond. She fingered a new, dry curl, clenching it between her large front teeth with enormous concentration. Their faces had created a steamy smudge on the windowpane.

'I bet my dad has a SUV by now.' Blaise spoke with superior confidence, as if he might rescue her at any moment from the edge of the cold abyss.

Jesse released the curl as she emitted a high, disturbed laugh. 'Why don't you just give up on him? He's never coming back to you.'

Blaise would not let Jesse, whose own father was in prison for forgery, upset her today. No wonder she had given up; he was a convict. But Blaise's father was a lawyer who prosecuted criminals. The two had absolutely nothing in common. Blaise pressed her shoulder against the window, blocking Jesse's view.

'It's like this,' she explained deliberately, the way her math teacher taught fractions. She'd thought this issue through many times but had never told anyone but the stars. 'If he doesn't return, then I've lost nothing by believing he would. If he does come back, then I'll feel happy – you know, satisfied – that he and I, well, that I never let him go.'

Jesse collected all of her curls into one enormous blonde bouquet and wrapped them around her pale pink hand. She stretched her neck to look past Blaise toward the empty street below. Their shoulders touched, pulled apart, hesitated, and then touched again. Their merged shadow, cast on the living room wall, hovered protectively behind them.

'Well, let's go upstairs. We need to make sure my mother's okay,' Jesse suggested in a new quiet voice.

Blaise nodded in acquiescence. 'I wonder if the outfit worked.' She felt responsible for how well things had gone the night before.

As the two girls left the living room, Blaise switched off the lights. The smell of sweet spiced tea lingered in the air. She reached into the kitchen to collect the letters and stashed them in her back pocket. Maybe she'd mail them this time after all – so that her mother could keep on believing whatever it was she needed to believe. Like the planets, Blaise had her own trajectory to follow. She grabbed her jacket from the hall rack, turning to survey the familiar surroundings. The blank computer screen emitted deep, empty knowledge into the living room. When she returned everything would be turned back on again, predictable and bright just like the stars she loved. All day long, she hoarded their penetrating light inside of her until at night, once again, they appeared in the lavish sky to dance across silky black infinity.

The family plan

I had liked it better when Olivia added up the round figures in her head, her mechanical pencil tucked in her hand, her hair slipping silently from behind her left ear, which curled inward upon itself. Lately she had taken to entering code in a complicated calculator, one with graphing capabilities, and fabricating spreadsheets to be printed out by churning machines. She mechanized the balance of payments in my life while I sat and watched, longing all the while to trace with my little finger the ridges of that delicate ear.

I considered late spring, this budding season, to be our anniversary. It's when Olivia and I first met just over a year ago, right after 15 April, the time of year I'd previously assumed all people in her profession went on vacation – just as psychiatrists take the month of August off. George, my long-time tax accountant, told me to look her up: *Olivia I. Jenkins, CPA, Certified Financial Planner*, her business card read. Worn out shoeboxes, loaded down with more debits than credits, troubled George. My wife Jan was expecting us to go on summer excursions, yet we hadn't even paid off our Christmas bills. Jan said she worked all year round; she needed some time to stop thinking so hard. It sounded sensible to me, but George rubbed his face as if he had a migraine when he added up my tax bill. I hadn't paid our estimated taxes over the course of the year as he'd instructed me to do, so I had to come up with it all at once, plus a penalty. I wanted an extension from the IRS.

'Get some help,' he stated abruptly. 'Now.' His wiry hair jumped out in all directions. The year before he had been less agitated.

'Can't you help me?' I pleaded. It would be hard going through all of this with someone else. George had been my accountant for nearly ten years. I'd seen his hair turn from glossy black to distressed grey.

'You need more help than I can give you,' he replied in an unnecessarily gruff tone. I was reminded of my brother who had gone to the family doctor for an annual check-up, with a mild case of indigestion; he had then been referred to an oncologist. I rubbed my abdomen and clenched my jaw in order to resist his dire diagnosis of my condition. George's ink-stained fingers shielded his eyes from my appeal. He told me what to do next.

I wrote out the check for the tax bill, which I did by charging it against my home equity line of credit, which brought me to the max, right along with my American Express bill. The interest fees were high, but at least I was generating frequent flyer miles so that Jan could make our vacation plans. She had the idea of the Pacific Northwest firmly implanted in her imagination.

Eventually I took out Olivia I. Jenkins's smooth, glossy card that I'd kept tucked in my wallet next to the worn credit cards. The words, now smudged, presented a wondrous juxtaposition of the exotic with the routine. What did the 'I' stand for? Isabella, perchance? With every purchase I had rubbed her name tenderly with my thumb. I conjured up someone serious and young. Women of my generation, those like my wife, did not go into financial planning as a profession. Journalism possibly, maybe medicine and architecture for adventurous spirits – but financial planning was too tiny a sphere for women who wanted to break into the world of work. Take Jan for example. She was a photographer. She liked large vistas. She gazed out our kitchen window and deciphered the eccentric habits of squirrels and birds. She yearned to travel to distant lands with expansive skies. Big places made me feel small, imprisoned in myself, claustrophobic.

'We need to diversify your investment portfolio.' Olivia was always professional in our meetings, her office cool and orderly. I found her composure reassuring. I had stopped on my way over and picked up two lattes and zucchini bran muffins.

'Wouldn't you like something to eat or drink?' I gestured to the modest spread before us. Olivia didn't look up from her calculator. Instead, she drank bottled water in unobtrusive swallows. I felt reproached by her silence, wounded by her drinking habits.

'Okay. What do you recommend?' I gulped the hot coffee recklessly.

'Well, we want to go with a high performing mutual fund with plenty of growth opportunities.' Her dense unplucked eyebrows gave authority to her green eyes.

'Yes, obviously.' It was always best to agree with her. She handed me a stack of brochures, which I studied with exaggerated interest.

'Now, let me see your checking account. Have you been paying off your bills as we agreed?' She tapped her pencil against the calculator.

I appreciated the impatient way Olivia talked to me. She reminded me of my third-grade teacher, Mrs Pruitt, who always had a special place in her heart for me, even when I neglected my homework for TV and science fiction. I had to believe that Olivia could be forgiving as well.

'Umm, I skipped this month because of the high insurance premiums.'

'You need to get a smaller, less expensive car. Those payments and the insurance on the SUV are killing you. The gas too.'

I had figured it out. For as long as I stayed in financial trouble, I could spend time with Olivia. We met monthly for at least an hour. Sometimes longer. In between our meetings I came up with reasons to contact her. Just last week I had left her a voicemail that inquired, 'Do you think I should be worried about the Federal Reserve and interest rates?'

She usually did not return my calls unless there was some specific urgency. She knew we'd be meeting soon. This morning when I arrived, she responded immediately, so as to demonstrate how important she considered my questions.

'Alan Greenspan and I will worry about the Federal Reserve. You worry about sticking to your household budget.' She continued without even the briefest pause, as if she'd rehearsed her lines. 'Wouldn't your wife like to join us at some point?'

My stomach growled. I sank further down into the chair across the desk from Olivia, reaching for one of the muffins dominating the space between us.

'We recommend a family financial planning session,' she emphasized.

'She's very busy right now. You know graduations and weddings and all that sort of thing. It's good that she has this work on Saturdays, don't you think? So that we can pay off some of these bills.' I wanted to persuade Olivia that we were all trying to achieve the same goal. Her eyes refused to meet mine. Globs of moist muffin crumbled into my lap.

'Well, we could get together one evening during the week, if you'd like. I do that sometimes.' She scrutinized the straight columns and rows with renewed attention, as if contemplating a crossword puzzle in the Sunday paper. 'It works best for both the husband and wife to be here at the same time. There are decisions that might be important to her.'

'She has photo shoots at nights sometimes too. Our communication is excellent.' I swished the coffee around in its cup. 'Don't worry about that.'

We'd had this conversation before. She undoubtedly felt some special obligation to provide information to Jan. Women tended to watch out for one another that way.

Olivia clicked some more lead into her mechanical pencil, then returned to checking her numbers while I consumed the second muffin. This methodical realm of calculations was where she seemed most contented. Her gold and black earrings peeked out from her wavy brown hair. It was the same colour as mine. She wore no makeup and no other jewellery. No wedding ring. I was having a hard time extracting information from her, except that she had attended business school at the University of Tennessee. Her diploma was on the wall. She graduated from college *summa cum laude* in 1988, ten years after me.

Olivia concentrated on my ledgers. She stuck a diminutive tongue in between her teeth, orderly teeth that looked like they belonged at a beauty pageant. She must've worn braces as a child. No one could have been born with such perfect teeth. It was apparent that her mother and father had taken good care of her. They were future-oriented too. Her fingernails were carefully trimmed so as not to interfere with the keys on the keyboard or calculator. I suspected she could play passionate concertos on the piano with the same focused energy. She turned away from me as she faced the computer. Her hair, short and curly in the front, now made my heart quiver as the waves cascaded down her back, concealing her neck. The sleek strands rolled under in a very natural and satisfactory manner. Jan's blonde hair was short and straight. It worked better for photography that way.

Olivia sighed. She seemed disturbed that we had been planning my life together for thirteen months now, and I still had an outstanding balance on my credit cards. She took it personally. She had been especially stern after Christmas when she made me go through each of the statements with her. I had begun putting charges on the bill that I thought might catch her attention – over $100 at Victoria's Secret and nearly $500 at the jewellery store on the town square. I wanted to display my romantic disposition. Jan had been more pleased with her gifts this year than ever before in the fifteen years we'd been married. She was the envy of other women in our subdivision. One day after school last week I had stopped to buy her scarves and stationery as well. I often browsed through the shops and galleries on the town square near our house. Olivia seemed to me to be the kind of woman who wrote deep and revealing letters. She would understand the necessity of those expenses. Her hair would look lovely tied up in a colourful scarf, her curls hoping to escape the precise bun, the tender part of her neck revealed.

Some beeps on the computer forced her to slow down. She sat back in the chair and spoke sadly.

'Yes, it's just as I expected.' It seemed that all her pushing and probing had uncovered a dark spot, a malignancy. She turned to face me with grave green eyes.

'Even if we liquidated all of your assets, which of course we would not do, you'd still be carrying some debt. It's a good thing you have a sound retirement plan.'

I wiped away muffin bits from my mouth and returned her troubled gaze with an optimistic smile. There were some small but significant advantages to working for the public school system, beyond getting the summers off.

'I'm printing out a list of things for you to do. We talked about updating your will last year. Please take care of that soon. You also need to stick to your budget. And,' she added with emphasis, 'you mentioned last month that you might teach summer school.'

'Well, you see, Jan wants to take a vacation. Out west. She has some cousins with a cabin, so we can stay there for free. Plus, we have all those frequent flyer miles. It's a bargain.' I nodded my head vigorously. 'Hmmm.' Olivia sounded unconvinced, even distracted. Maybe she was thinking the same thing I was thinking. We wouldn't see each other next month.

I wanted to reassure her. 'I will bring my laptop, so we can communicate by email.' She frowned under her bangs. 'I mean, if you need me to make any financial decisions, that is.'

'Gary, I don't know what to tell you. You've got to get focused on your finances. Take these materials with you when you go away and see if you can get a handle on your spending habits. Will you do that?'

This question made me feel so much better. She was worried about me. I wondered if she ever thought about me at night.

Here was the other good thing about consulting her this past year: I had joined the health club, as she could easily see from the monthly charges. I was in the best physical condition I had been in since graduate school, so my sex drive was in overdrive. Jan and I now had more sex than the average American couple, according to the latest polls in *The New York Times*. We were on par with the French, way ahead of the Japanese. Sometimes I caught Jan whispering on the phone to her best friend Lauren. They told each other everything. Lauren had to be impressed.

'Okay. That's what I'll do. I'll study all of these materials. When I get back at the end of the summer, you'll see some big changes in me.'

It had occurred to me that Olivia's interest in my financial condition might eventually diminish. She'd probably continue to see me monthly as scheduled, but over time – if I didn't show some evidence of reform – she would lose heart. I didn't want to think about that possibility.

'How about you? Any big plans for the summer?' I asked as I stood up and brushed the crumbs from my lap, trying to give the impression that I felt ready to leave.

'Oh, a little bit of this and that. Nothing major, you know.'

'Well, it's not a good idea to work all the time.' I picked up the empty latte cups. I had been forced to drink both of them and finish off the massive muffins. My stomach was bloated now and a little disorganized. My hands were starting to shake. The caffeine electrified my system. 'I'm a big believer in taking time away from it all.'

'Yes, I can see that about you.' Her implicit criticism made me want to kiss her right then and there. I needed to glide my rough, eager tongue over those white, polished teeth. Her quick tongue would touch mine with bewildered curiosity. It was thoughtful of her to form these opinions about me, as if my choices made a difference to her. I vowed to myself to do better, to win her approval, to seek her confidence.

On her invoice this month, I noticed that Olivia listed both her home and business phone numbers. She had changed her letterhead, a cryptic signal to me. She also indicated her email address and reference to a financial planning website. I assumed she lived near her small office in the strip mall; her house could not be too far from mine. The professional suite was nestled in between an upscale dry cleaner and a family hair salon. I was surprised that she didn't worry about the mixture of chemical fumes being dumped into the air that they all shared. Sometimes on my way home from work I stopped at the grocery store in between her office and my house. Sooner or later we should run into one another. It was our destiny.

Mostly on those occasions I hung out in the fresh fruit and vegetable bins, near the cantaloupes and mixed field greens. If Olivia only drank bottled water, she was no doubt careful about what she ate as well. No red meat for her. Jan was always pleased to see that I had done the grocery shopping but puzzled by some of my selections. At home, I took to cooking our meals – making pasta with eggplant and squash instead of sausage or ground beef. I served it up with red wine. Even during the week sometimes Jan and I drank an entire bottle of wine. This made us feel closer to one another and happier about life – until it was time to get up the next morning and I had to stuff unexamined AP English compositions into my briefcase.

I jealously noted Jan's quick commute to her darkroom in the basement. Most days she did not even bother to change out of her nightgown until lunchtime.

I had created careful rules about how much I could think about Olivia and what lengths I might go to in order to find out more information about her. I would do nothing intentional or overt. That was the most important rule. But I could set up circumstances in which we might run into one another.

When I left her office that day, someone seated in the small reception area glanced up from the thick novel she'd been reading. I could sense inquisitive eyes following my forward progression and noting the empty latte cups. The furtive glance belonged to a compact woman dressed in workout clothes. She and Olivia did not speak, but I could tell that they knew each other well by the discreet look that passed between them, one of those looks that women give each other. It's nothing a man can ever describe, but you know when it happens and you know it's about you. I felt pleased to be noticed in that way. Outside in the nearly empty parking lot waited a shiny black Jeep Cherokee with two imposing bikes on the top. There was no one in the car.

Driving home I contemplated our relationship. Olivia is the kind of woman who wants to have children. I can tell that about her, that she is already planning their educational trust fund. She has reviewed financial aid policies at colleges so she will know exactly how best to make this investment, even before the baby is conceived. She is not the sort of person to stop at selecting the finest preschool. She wants the whole future figured out.

I had thought Jan would want children when we first got married because most of her photographs were of round infant heads. She collected them and created a photographic collage that won an award in an art magazine. The heads varied so much in shape and size that they reminded me of a little boy's eclectic collection of balls from various sports teams. The pictures implied a nursery full of children and their toys, which would be no problem because Jan ran her business out of the house. Childcare costs would be minimal with plenty of quality time, especially because my summers were free and clear. But come to find out, Jan thought having children would limit her artistic expression. She would have to consider them as individuals rather than subjects for her work. Plus, according to her, I had plenty of bonding opportunities in my high school classes. Kids that age required my full attention. There was no need for us to supply our special combination of genes to the soupy mixture of the Earth's population.

Driving cautiously down the tree-lined street guarded by sidewalks in our neighbourhood, I pictured Olivia and me out walking our babies. She would eventually be grateful that I had found myself in financial trouble. It had brought us together. I thought we might have twins. They ran in my family. I liked those large two-seater strollers, the ones that runners used. I had inspected them at Walmart just last week. I was tempted to buy one, to charge it and to put it in the trunk of my car. Then when Olivia reviewed my credit card statement, she would see it listed.

'Are you and your wife expecting a child?' She would query in an offhand manner. It would be an appropriate question for her to ask because of the impact on my finances.

'Nope,' I would respond without explanation.

She would go back to studying the statement, her thick eyebrows twitching. 'Don't you think $349 is a lot of money for a gift for someone?'

'Yep,' I would agree. 'But it depends on who it's for.'

Then I would tell her that I had gotten a bargain on it and thought it best to buy it now – before prices went up. It was very sturdy. It would last a long time. It was an excellent investment.

I adored the way she'd appraised me then as if I had increased in value, her straight teeth shining. It would not come as a surprise when I stood up, pulled her by the hand and led her outside to my car and opened the trunk. We would gaze together at the majestic carton, our swelling hearts already infatuated with its contents. She might even ask me to unpack it right then and there in the parking lot. We would never need to spell out our feelings for one another. I would go home with her that day, to her tidy craftsman cottage that she was refurbishing. We would bring the stroller inside, she would guide me to her kitchen where we'd drink green tea and let me kiss her on the soft part of her neck, under the loose curls of her hair. We'd push the empty stroller into the bedroom. Our fate would be sealed. She would unveil the financial plan that she had created for the two of us and for the children we intended to have together. We would buy a luxury minivan, one with built-in double car seats. I loved this life as much as I'd ever loved anything.

Jan was on the telephone when I got home. She talked on the phone all of the time – to Lauren, to customers, to her sister.

She paid a lot of attention to her sister's children and took their pictures for free. They were displayed in plastic frames throughout our house as if they owned the empty space.

Jan gestured me towards her as I walked through the kitchen. I kissed her chin, then grabbed the newspaper and a beer as I pulled away and headed back out through the kitchen door. I preferred to be outdoors, sipping an ice-cold beer while sitting on a lawn chair in the driveway. The next-door neighbour's basset hound slouched over and drooled cheerfully on my leg then wandered off. Something needed to be done about the condition of our front yard. The grass had given up growing altogether.

Out of the corner of my eye I could see Jan coming out of the house, the phone still clasped against her ear, her short gold hair sticking out around it.

'I understand the weather in Seattle can be changeable in the summer.' She was talking to the travel agent, the one her sister had referred to us. A pause stretched over the phone lines before she continued, 'I wonder where we should rent a car.'

The voice on the other end crackled through the air. Great plans were underway. I drank my beer and watched the Farley children. They were creating a fort out of a deserted refrigerator box by covering it with spare branches and crooked twigs. Bessie the basset hound investigated the grounds around them with her lustrous nose. She sniffed all the corners, selected a site, and then squatted in the dead grass to pee. The children bumped into her and scooted through the moist soil in their bare feet. Smooth, wet toes glistened in the yellow twilight.

'Don't you think so, Gary?'

'What's that?' I replied, louder than I'd intended. The children all spun around to gape at me. I shifted in the chair towards Jan. I felt guilty, as if I'd been caught spying. The youngest girl, Kimmie, smiled warily at me.

'Don't you think we should fly into Seattle then rent a car and drive the rest of the way? The scenery will be beautiful.' Bored by us, the children returned to their construction project.

I shrugged my shoulders. Jan moved away from me and continued the conversation as she walked up the driveway. I heard her tell the agent goodbye. She punched in more numbers, listened for a moment, then put the phone on top of my car.

'Jan, I've been thinking…' She twirled back around, observed the children for a moment, as if posing them for a picture, then returned to my side. She grabbed the beer and took a gulp. She was always doing that, drinking my beer as if it were hers.

'Yes?' She returned the suddenly lukewarm bottle. Her hands, lost without phone, camera, or beer, flapped around her like worried wings. They made my insides feel loose.

'Maybe. Yes. Maybe you could just go on this trip alone. I should probably teach summer school after all. You know, to pay off some of our bills.' I kept my eyes focused on the activities of the industrious children next door who had forgotten all about me.

'Gary, you hate teaching.' Jan fingered the fiery opal pendant I had given her on her last birthday. 'All year long you can hardly wait until summertime to get away from it. In the summer the kids are worse than during the school year. They don't want to be there any more than you do.'

'Yeah, but the classes are smaller. I really do like teaching,' I countered. 'It would only be one or two classes.' A little boy in drenched jeans sat on the decorated box, which buckled under him. I leaned forward. I wanted to fix it for him, for all of them.

'Well, I don't like this idea.' The injured points of her voice pierced my eardrum. 'I thought we'd do something special together.' Her fingers, now straightening the drooping corners of my collar, rested for a moment on my shoulder.

'It would just be for a little while.' I patted the back of her hand as she withdrew it. 'You know, it might be good for you to have the time to yourself. Nourish the creative juices in solitude.' The other children piled on top of the small boy, and the fort broke apart into haphazard heaps.

Jan frowned with deep suspicion. She tugged on the gold chain of her necklace as if it were choking her. Her neck was turning heated red.

'We could use the money, you know,' I added.

Bessie was licking the faces of the spilled children while they giggled. I was not even certain I could still sign up to teach summer school. But all of the sudden I knew I wanted to do it very much. The students needed me. I was also thinking about getting a bike. On those long summer evenings, with Jan away, it would be the perfect time to get back into biking. I noticed my neighbour's old three-speed that leaned up against the garage door. It had a child seat on the back. That made biking seem less lonely, not such a solitary endeavour.

Jan released the necklace, stepped backwards, and reached for the phone on top of the car. She punched in some numbers. I could tell from the familiar melody that she was calling Lauren.

I whistled the stirring love songs of *West Side Story* as I drove home from school on the following Monday. The students were mounting a production for the spring musical, and I was the dramaturg, the literary advisor. The day had gone well for me. I'd added my name to the waiting list of those interested in teaching American Lit in the summer to rising high school sophomores. It was my best course. We covered everything from Longfellow to Morrison. Sophomores were not as cynical as juniors or seniors, those who thought they had found the answer to all of life's problems. Together, in the steamy days ahead, we would read Herman Melville and Emily Dickinson and Sylvia Plath. I would even sneak in poets from earlier eras and distant continents. We would memorize the verses together, the old-fashioned way. I would dazzle them with lines from Yeats. New insights about life would be revealed to us all this summer.

Pulling into the driveway I noticed two of the Farley children playing outside with the remnants of the box. They had torn it apart and were sliding down the hillside, as if on sleds on tough and dingy snow. Their T-shirts were covered with pine needles and bits of dead green leaves. When they reached the bottom of the incline, Bessie, having waited for them, chewed on their ears. I got out of the car and set my briefcase down on the cement. The bicycle stayed propped against the wall, just inside the garage. One of the oldest boys noticed me walking toward them.

'Hey Mr Flintstone,' he taunted me good-naturedly. Even Bessie looked amused at the play on my name. I resisted calling back, 'Flynt – it's Flynt.' The truth did not matter to him.

'How'ya doing, Joey?' I stood in front of him.

'Wanna take a ride?' He lifted up his cardboard panel and flapped it over his head.

'On the bike?' I stepped towards the garage.

'Naw, Mr Flintstone, on *this*.' He held out the torn cardboard scrap to me. 'It's a magic sled.'

'Oh, nope, no magic rides today, not on that thing anyway.' He looked disappointed in me. Peering into the garage, I felt obliged to cheer him up. 'But I might be interested in that bike there. Would you like to go for a ride on the back of it with me?'

He regarded me with amazement. 'I can't fit into that old thing anymore. It's for Kimmy. That's her seat now.'

Kimmy, in bib overalls, appeared on cue next to Joey, her cardboard panel pressed against her belly. 'She loves to go for rides.' The plump child smiled sweetly. Blonde curls fought with each other in the breeze.

'Well, maybe I'll do that sometime.'

Kimmy automatically released the ragged brown board. 'Now.' She took one step in my direction. 'I wanna go now.' She stuck her tight, determined fist in my loose grasp and pulled me closer and closer to the bike, until I could touch the rusted handlebars.

The old bicycle was a woman's model. I remembered that I had seen their mother riding it, with Kimmy on the back, and Joey at her side pedalling his own miniature two-wheeler. I picked up Kimmy, whose solid body carried pungent reminders of Bessie. She threw her arm naturally around my shoulder. Then she squeezed my neck roughly.

'Now,' she commanded again. I dropped her into the child seat. It fit her perfectly. No wonder she liked it so well. Kimmy was used to having her wishes granted. It might be all right for us to take a quick spin around the block, just to quell her little girl desires.

Joey supervised our departure. He grasped Kimmy's arm while I mounted the bike. Joey and Bessie ran along with us until the breeze swept them aside. Kimmy's sturdy frame helped to keep the bike balanced. I glanced back to check on her. Pale ringlets danced in the late sun. She closed her eyes and whispered complicated nonsense. I realized that I had left my car door wide open. White papers and crumpled receipts fluttered around the exposed interior of the vehicle.

Riding the bike felt like poetry to me. Not the way my students repeated the lines at the front of the classroom with uninflected voices, but the sweeping, distinctive words of Yeats and Byron and Browning, the rhymes and rhythms that revealed their special yearnings.

Never give all of the heart, for love

I recited into the wind, loud enough for Kimmy to hear:

Will hardly seem worth thinking of
To passionate women if it seem
Certain, and they never dream

I caught my breath and then continued the reveries of Yeats:

That it fades out from kiss to kiss.

I pedalled as fast as I could. My legs were in excellent shape from the Stairmaster at the health centre, but my stomach muscles strained from the added weight behind me. I struggled with the hills. Kimmy's index fingers curled snugly in my belt loops; her confident presence gave me the courage to go forward. The late spring wind filled my lungs as more words tumbled out of me.

*For everything that's lovely is
But a brief, dreamy, kind delight.*

Like riding a bike with a contented child on the back, that kind delight. It was tempting to ignore the stop signs at the corners nearby, but I glided to a swift halt. A Volkswagen Beetle, the ancient model, revved its rattled engine behind us. I pulled over to the side of the road. I didn't want Kimmy to be scared.

'Go faster,' she insisted as I turned to check on her. Her eyes blinked to filter out the late afternoon light. Her stocky legs pushed the air in time with me.

'Your mother will miss you,' I argued. 'We should turn back.'

'She's in the bathtub.' It sounded like she said. I realized with immediate dread that neither one of us wore helmets, but I started our forward motion again.

I rounded the corner at the end of the next block, using appropriate hand signals, and spun past the section occupied by newly constructed cluster homes. The small yards were landscaped with hot red azaleas and sun-bleached dogwoods. I had not come this way in a while.

As I turned the next corner, a familiar looking black Jeep pulled past me and curved immediately into a driveway and came to a stop. I followed it without a thought. Little Kimmy's fist sunk into the small of my back, pushing me along as the bike bumped over the cement ridge. My insides jostled about, I coasted to a halt alongside the warm Jeep just as the engine shut down and the driver's door opened. I recognized the limber ankles in black athletic sandals, the toenails painted a delicate pink shade, the colour of cotton candy. For a brief moment our heads were so close I could have kissed Olivia I. Jenkins right on the lips that closed tightly over her bright teeth. Olivia snapped her face away from mine. My mouth was parched from the words and wind, and I feared my breath was bitter.

'This is Kimmy,' I offered proudly, as if she had asked for introductions. Perspiration droplets spilled from my forehead on to my hands, now cramped from clenching the sloped handlebars. 'Kimmy, this is my…' I struggled to find the right words.

Olivia did not say anything. Another person who looked vaguely familiar emerged from the Jeep on the far side and came around the vehicle. I smiled at her. She stood possessively next to Olivia. I caught my breath, feeling forsaken.

'Go fast again,' Kimmy cried out, her eyes starting to turn from blue marble to metallic grey.

'We're out for a bike ride.' I explained. My heart beat ardently from the recent exertion.

Olivia's arm moved in our direction as she released the car door; she then reached over to grab the hand of her companion. Dangling silver earrings carved the air between us like lightening during a fierce storm. The two women seemed disturbed about something.

'It's just Kimmy.' Neither one spoke to me. 'She's…she's a neighbour's child.' I struggled to reassure them.

In a single motion, they turned towards the car. Olivia stretched into the backseat to grab groceries. They held the bags between them and me, but a loaf of bread toppled over the edge into the nearby bushes. They left it there. I reached out my hand, longing to caress the ends of Olivia's hair, the waves now brushing against her backbone, as she twisted away from us. She wore a tank top that revealed athletic shoulders, bronzed and capable, and the inkling of a resplendent sports bra.

I thought about the way their brick bungalow must look inside, furnished with antique oak tables, decorated with needlepoint pillows, scented with spring potpourri. These two beautiful women with no children walked towards their home. I wanted to be there with them, creating neat columns of figures that all added up properly and making sensible grocery lists. I dismounted the bike, wedged it between the bushes and the Jeep, and found the kickstand. I released the handlebars in order to rescue the abandoned bread.

'Be right back, Kimmy.' She nodded. The bike leaned lopsidedly towards the driveway. 'Don't move.'

When I arrived at the front door, Olivia and her companion had already vanished. The deadbolt clicked twice with insolent precision. Dejected, I sat down on the stone steps and beheld Kimmy scrutinizing me from the tilted bike.

'More,' she demanded, pounding her fist into the seat. The bike trembled under her weight.

I struggled to remember the final lines of the poem.

O never give the heart outright.

I wanted Kimmy to understand the tragic realities of love that Yeats depicted so completely. She would need these lessons later in life. She would be better prepared than the students I taught every day.

He that made this knows all the cost,
For he gave all his heart and lost.

Kimmie stared hungrily at the loaf of bread in my hands. It was the honey-coloured whole-wheat variety. I opened the plastic wrapping and squished several pliant slices in my right hand, my grasp sinking into the fresh, fragrant softness. I tossed the pieces into the air, then tried to catch them with my mouth. My teeth clutched one small bundle of flying bread, and I shook my head like Bessie with a new rawhide bone.

Kimmy laughed with serious pleasure at my accomplishments. 'More,' she cried out. 'I want more. Go fast.' The bike was starting to merge with the bushes. Small sharp leaves stabbed her flushed cheeks.

I jumped up to share the bread with her. Kimmy squealed as she reached for it, as if all her wishes had now been granted. I steadied the bike while she tore apart several slices. We relished pieces of it, chewing sloppily, stuffing mushy bits into one another's mouths. Savoury bakery smells clung to the sweat on our fingertips.

Our appetites appeased, I extracted the bike from the bushes and set it straight. I guided us down the driveway while Kimmy hugged the pilfered loaf against her little girl chest. As I leapt aboard, we bounced, swerving into the street. I pedalled as hard as I could. In the dim distance I was able to make out the silhouettes of Joey and Bessie, posted like shivering sentries at the next corner. A furious, elongated shadow swept over them. My legs slowed, but the momentum of the wheels drove the bike forward. Behind me, my determined companion scattered scraps of bread into the nightfall as we rode home together in solemn surrender to all that awaited us.

Free radicals

Her feet have grown too big for her sandals, but Pal is still small enough to lie down across the back seat. She searches for the ends of the lap seatbelt of the VW bus to clasp around her middle. The straps are loose, allowing her to tuck in her rag doll Laura Ingalls. Pal picks at the foam in the torn seat, forming little balls which she stuffs into the pocket of her shorts.

Solace rides up front with her mother because he gets carsick in the back. He has a map spread across his lap although he does not know how to read yet. He crumples the corners into his tight fists. Short, bug-bitten legs stick straight out in front of him. He wears her old pink tennis shoes. Every now and then, Pal's mother glances into the back of the van to check on her. Her mother's long blonde hair is pulled back into a tight ponytail and tugs her face into a frown. In the rear-view mirror, her mother's eyes have the same mad look that her father had when the van pulled away from the cabin, the look her parents give her when she won't let Sol play tea party with her and Laura Ingalls. But she's been nice to him today, so nobody in the family should be upset. Pal grabs a fistful of dry, yellowed foam and tears it apart, tossing crushed bits out the window.

She likes the backseat anyway. She can keep watch over her mother and Solace and also look out the side and back windows. Her mother and brother's heads still as carved Indian statues are fixed on the twisting shady road ahead. Eli, their musty old black lab, sleeps in a heap in the middle seat.

When they left the commune, her mother started up the van with a roar, making it go so fast on the gravel road that rocks spit out from the tires. They did not pack suitcases – just cardboard boxes with jumbled-up clothes. That must mean they'll be coming back soon. Last time, they were only gone a week before Papa collected them, and they returned to the old family ways in the cabin. But now she can see the photograph albums in a wooden crate next to Eli with pictures spilling out from when she was a baby. Hugging Laura Ingalls, she gets on her knees and turns to the back window; her father is nowhere in sight.

When they pulled away, Pal had thrown him a kiss. He rubbed his cheek as if he'd been stung. She put her arm out the side window and held up her fingers in a 'V,' her special sign. Her real name is Peace and Love, but Solace couldn't say that when he was a baby, so they call her Pal. Papa did not reply with a peace sign. Maybe he couldn't see her face through the grime on the window. He stooped to pick up a handful of rocks. She ducked down in her seat to shield Laura Ingalls, still peeking over the top. He threw the rocks into the woods. She lay down and closed her eyes until the van got to the smooth highway.

Thinking about Papa all alone, Pal swallows a cry, which gives her the hiccups. She likes the stories he tells about brave robbers who steal from the rich and give to the poor. His voice is soft but big. When he talks, everyone in the commune listens; she climbs into his lap to feel his deep chest vibrate. His breath smells sweet like dandelion tea, his long hair like incense. Inside the van, a hot summer wind whips through the window tangling her yellow hair with the yarn hair of Laura Ingalls. She hiccups into Laura's back so that no one will hear her. They might think she is crying. She keeps watch out the back window until they pull up to Aunt Mary's house. Pal does not want to get out of the van, but the hiccups have made her stomach hurt, and she has to pee. She grabs Laura Ingalls by the arm and steps carefully over the crate, letting smelly old Eli sleep in the van. She also leaves behind her sandals that are too tight. The paved driveway burns the bottom of her feet. She starts to run.

Her mother and Solace head towards the house. She doesn't like her aunt's central air-conditioned and heated home with more bedrooms than people living there. Already, she misses the cabin in the woods where on cold nights the four of them sleep in one bed under quilts with Eli on top and Laura Ingalls tucked safely underneath. Nothing could be better than that. When she hears her mother's voice calling her, she runs faster, towards her father in the woods, until she wets her pants and falls down with Laura Ingalls on sharp blades of grass. Foam rubber balls fall all around her like dirty, leftover snow.

Now, at a stoplight in California while re-examining the directions, Annie takes off her shoes to wiggle her toes, swollen from the long airplane ride. She checks her makeup in the rear-view mirror of the rental car. Her eyes are crisscrossed with pink spider veins. Horns honk behind her. Flustered, her shoes still off, she pushes the accelerator too hard and moves forward with an unsteady lurch.

She eventually finds the subdivision her father had noted in his email after inviting her to California: 'Pal, with your beauty and brains and my connections, you'll go far.' He is the only one who still uses her childhood nickname. When she started public school, having left the commune behind, she decided to turn the 'and' in Peace and Love into 'Annie.'

Now, her father is offering to help her find a summer internship in Los Angeles. She drives slowly through the neighbourhood streets, all named for flowers and trees. The houses, pushed into a hillside, are large with shiny windows that look down on her. Annie inches forward, checking out the numbers on mailboxes until she comes to the right address on Bougainvillea Drive. Pulling into a circular driveway, she is confronted by an ivory stucco house with many sharp angles and a red tile roof. Carefully pruned crimson and orange shrubbery surround it.

Getting out of the car, she smells an unfamiliar sweetness in the air. Annie pushes her swollen feet into her new shoes and walks unsteadily towards the front door. When she rings the doorbell, there is the erratic yapping of a small dog. She breathes deeply and checks her watch, which her father had sent for her graduation from high school four years ago. He was not able to come to the ceremony because his new wife was expecting to deliver twins that spring.

The flower-drenched air in California makes her throat hurt and her eyes itchy. She steps away from the house. Just then a Ford Explorer pulls into the driveway, its horn honking. She smoothes her hair and swallows hard. All she can see is her own distorted reflection in the tinted windows – until the car door opens and her father, even taller than she remembers, emerges. He yanks off his sunglasses and walks toward her. Without a word, he pulls her to him. Her forehead presses naturally against his chest; when he gives her a bear hug her shoulders shake.

'What is it Pal?' he asks in a low vibrating voice.

Sobs emerge from her. She feels small again, her body taken over by an abrupt tornado. He pats her back, and Annie wants to fall asleep in his arms. Eventually, she manages to take in a deep breath to calm down, surprised that he smells like french fries instead of incense.

Behind them there is a rapid knocking noise. Her father releases her.

'I've got to unbuckle those rascals.' He opens the door to the backseat and sticks his head in. Soon two identical, dark-haired children pop out. The little girls, on either side of her father, gaze at Annie suspiciously. They hug Happy Meals. She dries her eyes with the back of her hand, feeling childish for crying in front of them.

'I just picked them up from preschool.' Her father nods benevolently, 'Ashley and Ansley, tell your big sister hello.'

They look in her direction, matching sets of grey eyes squinting against the brilliance of the late afternoon sun. The girls do not say a word.

'Hello.' Annie pipes up in the old habit of wanting to please her father. 'My name is Annie.' The girls look at one another with blank faces, shrug their shoulders, and turn away to run up the front lawn to the house. Annie and her father watch the synchronized bounce of their ponytails. He smiles with expansive pride that makes Annie feel lonely. She twists the watch around on her arm. A rash has emerged under the band, and she scratches the red bumps until they hurt.

'Hey, now, Pal.' He hugs her again, then pushes her away.

'Let me take a look at you. Aren't you something?' His eyes start at her feet, working their way up to her face. 'All grown up and glamorous.' He blinks. 'You look just like your…well, you look like a million dollars.' A blush creeps up her face. He rests his hand on her forehead as if checking for a fever, his touch surprisingly soft. Annie shivers when he removes his hand.

'Okay, now, Rachel won't get home from work until late this evening. She has a major court date next week.' Annie nods in response, rubbing her forehead where his hand had been. Her father's wife, who she has never met, is a famous entertainment lawyer. They got together when he moved to California from North Carolina.

'Let's check on those girls. They're full of mischief.' His voice picks up speed, 'I've called a babysitter so you and I can have dinner together later. Just the two of us – you know, catch up like old times.'

Annie sneezes, her eyes watering. The house looks very big.

'Dad,' she sniffles. 'I'm not feeling too great. Maybe I should stay in a hotel. I don't want to impose on you and your family. Or get your children sick.'

He appraises her, squinting in just the way the twin girls had. He whistles as he exhales.

'Don't be silly, Pal. You'll be fine as soon as you get some food and rest. You're part of the family.' Annie suddenly remembers that she did not call her Mother and Sol back in North Carolina when she landed at the airport. 'We've made plans for you,' he adds. His silver hair, still thick and curly but trimmed short, glistens in the sun, and his cloudy eyes penetrate her. She remembers how at Oasis, the commune, he was in charge of everything.

'Yes, I know. But...'

'Come on, come on,' he speaks hurriedly, 'Let's go inside.' Annie nods in half-hearted agreement, trying to ignore the growing soreness of her throat. Her father hooks his arm in hers. Walking past the fragrant orange bushes, she feels pale and poor in this lavish world.

The house is cold from an overactive air-conditioner and noisy from television commercials blaring in the background. In a spacious room with skylights, the girls lie shoulder-to-shoulder in front of a big-screen TV, a plump dog now quietly content at their feet. Her father leads her into the kitchen, which looks out on a diamond-shaped pool. He opens the refrigerator.

'How 'bout some juice, girls, to go with your snacks?' He calls out loudly. Within seconds, the twins arrive at the counter. Annie perches between them on a stool and slips off her shoes to stretch her puffy toes. The girls giggle as they dig into cardboard boxes, pulling out nuggets, fries, and plastic toys that look like miniature binoculars. Their father opens a packet of animal crackers and pours them some cranapple juice. The little girls abandon their nuggets and grab handfuls of the crackers, which they stuff in their mouths. Her father passes out napkins and swipes some of the nuggets. Annie wonders when he stopped being a vegetarian. Dressed in khaki shorts and a pink polo shirt, he looks like an attractive stranger, someone with only a faint resemblance to a family member.

'Here, Pal' Annie feels a sharp elbow in her ribs. 'You take some animals too.' Annie selects a giraffe and nibbles on its edges. She can't tell the two girls apart. Chattering about their day at school, they look at her with amused sideways glances.

Annie breaks off the neck of the giraffe and sucks it into a mushy glob. Smothering a yawn, she checks her watch then the kitchen clock. Only 5:30pm local time, it's much later for her.

Annie takes several long drinks of cranapple juice to soothe her throat, but it leaves behind a tingly sensation. The girls open the plastic wrap of their pink binoculars and peer at her through them. She wipes her lips with the napkin and smiles, first at one then the other, as if her picture were being taken.

'Say cheese!' the child on her right urges. The other one pushes her head under Annie's arm, looking up at her. The picture-taker makes a clicking sound with her tongue and drops the binoculars on the floor beneath them. She strokes Annie's golden hair with tiny fingertips as if she were a prized cat. Annie senses her father watching the three of them. She tries to hug the girls, but they topple off the stools, falling in a heap at her swollen feet.

'Ashley and Ansley, for goodness' sake,' her father scolds the children. 'Get up. Don't you want to show Pal where she is staying?'

'Yes, Papa,' one voice proclaims in a half-mocking tone.

The two children hop up and simultaneously pull on her arms. She resists at first then gives in. The girls' mouths, rimmed cranberry red, turn upward into exaggerated clown grins.

'Pal, you get to stay in the turquoise room,' the one on the right explains as she yanks Annie's arm.

'Turquoise?' She resists the urge to correct her name.

'Yes, everything in it is turquoise. Our mother picked out the colour,' the other one explains. The sameness of these two girls makes her dizzy, as if she were seeing double. '*Our* room,' they brag together, 'is purple. We picked it out ourselves.' Annie wants to join them in there. She envisions the three of them sleeping peacefully under matching purple comforters all in a row. But her blonde hair and translucent skin would be out of place between these tanned, dark-haired girls.

'Give me your keys, dear, and I'll get your things out of the trunk.' Her father stands in their path. The girls drop her arms but lean possessively against her. Annie automatically reaches into her purse. When she hands him her keys, she remembers what it feels like to have someone else in charge of her life.

Annie wakes up in the middle of the night with a headache. She had too much to drink at dinner. The beachside restaurant where her father took her was noisy, too noisy for much conversation. Bronzed, elegant people stopped by their table to greet her father, who explained to her that he was producing a documentary, the third in his series about life in the '60s.

'Cheers,' he toasted her, 'I'm so glad you've come to visit me and my family.' Annie forced a tired smile in return, wanting to feel a part of his world. 'You'll love it out here – the land of beautiful possibility.' She drank all of her champagne in a single, fizzy gulp to numb her sore throat.

A man from across the restaurant made his way over. Her father seemed eager to talk with him.

'Simon, this is my daughter. She's here for her spring break. Next year, she'll be going to graduate school – in communications,' he added, looking at her in the way he had the twins earlier. She blushed as the man studied her. Uncomfortable under his gaze, she reached across the table for her father's champagne glass.

'Glad to meet you,' he said at what seemed to be a distance. The glare of the setting sun made all of the faces in the room blurry, almost shapeless.

The man turned towards her father. 'Ted, I think I've got someone to back this project. I just need to get you to the studio to do the convincing.'

They continued to discuss documentaries as if she were not there. Annie drank the remaining champagne, staring at the flickering candle. After his family had left the commune, her father sold their land and moved west, where he transformed himself into a California writer and film producer. She had only seen him on occasional business trips he made back east; with each stopover he looked more and more like a movie star. She'd always wanted to visit him, but now it seemed that everything on the West Coast was overly bright – especially compared to North Carolina where large trees offered shelter from the sun. She gazed at the California beach glistening in twilight. Even the ocean was on the wrong side of her.

Annie gets out from under the hot turquoise covers to go to the bathroom. She searches for Tylenol in the medicine cabinet and takes three with a handful of water. Looking in the mirror, she sees her mother's worried eyes reflected back. 'What's between you and him is between you and him,' she had said when Annie first told her about the planned trip to California. Later, as Annie left in a taxi for the airport, her mother had called out, 'Take care of yourself, dear,' as if she considered her former husband a menace to society.

Annie's watch on the bathroom counter says midnight, but she knows it must be close to morning. Her stomach is unsettled and her throat thick. She leaves the darkened turquoise room to go to the kitchen for something to drink. The round black and white dog is curled up in a basket, his head cocked and alert. Annie is grateful that he does not bark as she doesn't want to wake up the household, especially Rachel whom she still hasn't met. On the wall are pictures of her father with the children and their mother at the beach; Annie's eyes sting as she examines their togetherness. She thinks of her own mother and brother back in North Carolina in an apartment too small for the three of them. Annie needs to save up money for her own place when she goes to graduate school. She seeks her own escape into the world.

She looks out at the pool as she drinks ice water. In the pre-dawn darkness, she is reminded of the sinkhole near Oasis where her family used to go swimming without bathing suits. Annie unlocks the French doors leading to the pool and sits down on the chaise lounge. A light breeze crawls up her nightgown, and she pulls her feet under it just as she had when a little girl cuddling in her father's chair with Laura Ingalls, now stored in a box under her bed back home.

Several rooms surround the pool, their drapes pulled open. Annie strains to look inside what she takes to be the purple bedroom, but it is too dim to see much. She gets up and goes to another set of French doors. She leans her forehead against the cool, clean glass. When she was little, she would crawl in bed with her parents and Sol, who was still breastfeeding. Annie would sleep in her father's arms so he would not feel left out. The arguments, spoken and unspoken, between her parents seemed to disappear when they were all in that warm bed together. Annie checks the handle on the French door. It opens more quickly than expected, and she nearly falls inside. With the hint of morning light, she sees that the room is spacious with a large, high bed on one side and two easy chairs on the other. She tiptoes over and sits down in one of the chairs that swivels.

This must be the gold room because everything shimmers in the early sun. Bodies breathe blissfully on the other side of the room. The duvet is so thick that she can't make out the forms or heads sunk into pillows. Feeling very tired and cold from the air conditioning, she creeps over to the bed. Three faces emerge from the covers – two little tan ones and her father's, which now looks pale and lined with worry. She slowly sits on the end of the bed. There is no movement in response. Lying back, she pulls up the edge of the comforter for warmth, inhaling then exhaling in time to the nearby breathing.

Annie awakens to the sound of giggles. A cold nose invades her ear, and small black eyes stare into hers. She sits up quickly. The little girls lean against a carved oak headboard and tickle each other. The dog settles into a big pillow next to her. She props herself up with her elbow, almost falling backward off the edge of the bed.

'Where's Papa?' she asks in a hoarse voice. The twins look towards the open bedroom door. Annie smells food cooking. As if reading her mind, one of them says, 'Pancakes and bacon. That's the Saturday morning special.' Despite her unsettled stomach, Annie feels hunger growing in her. She didn't eat anything on the airplane or much at dinner last night; she just kept drinking champagne. She scratches her wrist, remembering her watch is in the bathroom. The digital clock on the bedside table reads 10:10am She has completely lost track of time and can't figure out if it's day or night in North Carolina. She closes her eyes, wanting to return to the forgetfulness of sleep, but the cold black nose scrunches into her ear again, as if telling her a wet secret.

One of the girls places a yellow-haired rag doll into Annie's arms. 'We named her Pal. After you.' Tears rise in her eyes, grateful for their acknowledgement of her presence. She hugs the doll against her chest.

'Let's go get breakfast,' the slightly taller twin says. Following them, Annie drifts sleepily into the kitchen, still holding the doll. The dog tags along. Her father glances up from an electric skillet.

'Morning, there, my girls.' His voice is energetic, but he looks tired to Annie. He has set three places at the kitchen counter, and they climb on the stools, the binoculars from the day before under hers. He tosses a piece of bacon into the dog's mouth. 'There you go, Dylan, some for everyone.' Annie does not remember the father from her childhood being so indulgent. Back then, he had conducted himself like a ferociously moral Russian philosopher, careful in all of his habits.

'Dad, I mean Papa, when did you stop worrying about free radicals?' Annie asks in a louder voice than she'd intended. He looks into the frying pan,

'Well, let's just put it this way, Pal, when I freed myself from being a radical.' Then he expertly flips pancakes on to the platter. She has never seen her father cook before – or thought of him as seeking freedom.

The girls reach eagerly for pancakes, and Annie joins them. Everything is delicious – banana and nut tastes saturated with sweet maple syrup. To her surprise, Annie finds herself enjoying the salty, almost burned taste of the bacon. She does not allow herself to think of what her mother would say.

The chattering girls seem to accept her morning presence, but something is out of focus. Placing the doll on the counter, she reaches under her stool for the binoculars. Her feet have resumed their normal size.

'Where's Rachel?' she asks. The girls stop talking to look at their father and then at the telephone hanging on the wall. It's a natural enough question: Where would their mother be on a Saturday morning?

'Oh sometimes, when she works late, she sleeps at the law office on a couch. She knew she had to get up early today for an office retreat, so she left a message for us.' When her father smiles, his grey eyes turn dark in a look that Annie recognizes from the past. The house feels suddenly cold to her; she is still dressed in a nightgown. The little girls have left their sticky plates behind and taken the doll into the family room where they turn on the television.

Her father sits across from her. He rubs his forehead. 'I guess everyone tells you that you look like your mother?' Annie nods in agreement.

'But she's changed, too,' Annie muses. 'She got a promotion at Sears. She sells appliances now. Her hair is short and pewter grey. Sol looks just like you,' she adds, feeling the old envy of her brother.

'Well, you know, she was about your age when we first met. We fell in love so quickly that she moved to the commune with me, even though her parents forbade it. Then, before long, you came along.' Annie listens hard for the details. Last summer, she started piecing together the puzzle of her parents' life when looking through the old photo albums. From the dates on the back of photographs, she began to realize that her parents did not get married until after she was born. The picture of the two of them in their hippie wedding clothes looking down at their infant daughter was her favourite – her mother's golden hair covered with a crown of roses, her father beaming confidently at the child sleeping in his arms. She stays quiet, hoping to hear more stories of peace and love instead of bitterness.

'Listen, Pal,' he speaks in an intimate voice that makes her feel special. 'I was thinking about this summer and I was hoping, yes, wondering if you wanted to come out here and watch the girls for me, for us.' He takes a drink of orange juice. 'I'm doing this documentary. And Rachel works all kinds of ridiculous hours. Already, the girls are quite taken with you.'

Annie pays careful attention to what he is saying. Champagne headache, sleepiness, and the leftover sweetness of pancakes cloud her thoughts. What about the internships he'd mentioned in the email? She pushes aside the remaining crumbs of bacon on her plate. 'Excuse me?' she asks, taking a sip of orange juice, which makes her throat burn.

'We'd pay you, of course, so that you could save money for graduate school. It would be better than an internship in some dull office.' His arms sweep out expansively as if embracing her with the house and pool. 'Maybe you could even go to grad school out here. And live with us.'

Annie feels hot now. The tone in his voice and the practiced words remind her of the speeches he used to give at the commune. Her head and throat start to throb. She checks her wrist again for her watch but sees only the red bumps. Her father leans towards her on the kitchen counter, closely watching her face for an answer. She shakes her head in order to clear it. Eager to please him as in the past, she nods it up and down while lifting her hair to let the air conditioning cool her neck down. Then she hesitates, in wait. She knows his tactics; she also knows where it will lead her.

'You know we'd have a great time together,' he coaxes. Resisting his gaze, Annie peers through the wide end of the binoculars. In the distance are Ansley and Ashley, a lovely tangled heap stationed with Pal-doll in front of the large-screen television. She longs to be near them, to stay close to her father, to fill the neglected space in all of their lives. If only the binoculars could also allow her to see Sol and her mother in faraway North Carolina – and beyond them, into an uncharted future.

'Dad,' Annie starts, not certain what she wants to say until she says it. 'I can…' He smiles approvingly, and she speaks quickly, 'I can come for visits, but I can't stay all summer and take care of the girls or live with you.' The clarity and directness of these words surprise her. She feels her headache diminishing as her mother's tense eyes relax inside of her. Annie pictures how hard her mother had to concentrate when she sped off from the commune. 'I have other plans,' she adds. Her father turns away from her. He sprays hot water into the sink to rinse the breakfast dishes.

Light-headed with resolve, Annie leaves the kitchen for the turquoise room where she puts on her watch, still on North Carolina time. She brushes her hair, pulling it back into a ponytail. From the doorway, she observes her father sitting at the kitchen counter; holding the dog in his arms, he stares at the blue swimming pool. His shoulders, she can now see, are bent, diminishing, like those of an aging, dispossessed man. She resists the automatic desire to go to him, and she instead finds her way into the family room.

Annie holds up her fingers in a tentative 'V,' and the twins eagerly return matching peace signs as they make room for her in their midst. The three of them lie together on the floor watching Saturday morning cartoons eating Sugar Pops from the box, a treat never permitted when she was a child their age, back in the woods in North Carolina.

Suchness

Tatum jotted down her thoughts on a notepad, just like the one her mother used to have on hand for shopping lists. She also kept a daily journal in her composition book because she knew the truth: all feeling is really a memory. If you write down the feelings, the memories turn out to be true.

When the school security guard came to her room asking for details and a description of the strange man reported on campus, Tatum pulled out her notes and read aloud: *Tall and smart-looking. Shoulders rounded. His jacket, a windbreaker, dark green. In the library, at the computer near me, then in the coffee shop in town reading* The New York Times. *He looks alone, maybe even lonesome.*

'I've also seen him outside the dorm window,' Tatum informed the security guard. 'He looked right at me. After I closed the blinds, I peeked once more in between the slats, and he stood there as if searching for something he'd lost.' Tatum and the security guard both turned toward the still-darkened window.

'There have been other times,' Tatum added.

The security guard, who shifted her gaze back to Tatum, wore large glasses that made her eyes big and blurry. She wasn't very old; it didn't seem quite right to Tatum to call her Officer Reynolds, which was on the silver badge on her chest. Her first name was Cathy, but that doesn't seem right either.

'You've seen him other times recently on campus?' Officer Cathy probed.

'Oh yes,' Tatum replied. She was named after Tatum O'Neal, the child star who her mother liked to watch over and over again in a movie about a young girl and adventures with her father. 'I see the man often when I'm alone. He's always by himself too.'

'Has he said anything to you, gotten in your path, or tried to touch you in any way?'

'Oh no. He just follows me around and stares.'

Officer Cathy stared at her too, through those thick glasses. She was short, shorter than Tatum. Her shoulders were broad like a boy's, and her shoes were black and heavy. Tatum wondered if she had to run fast sometimes and if she knew how to use a gun, even though she didn't wear one. Tatum liked having her nearby.

'I may follow you around a bit on campus also, so don't be alarmed,' Officer Cathy informed her. 'That's just SOP.' When Tatum blinked blankly in response, Officer Cathy explained on her way out the door, 'You know, "standard operating procedure."'

Tatum lay back on her bed, satisfied. She didn't write in the same journal for this part. She pulled another one out from underneath the special satin pillow her mother had made for her.

What does it feel like to have the Secret Service around you all of the time, like presidents, their wives, and their children? SOP.

Officer Cathy asked me more questions. I think he has green eyes or maybe blue, not brown. But no glasses, except for reading. He usually has a spiral notebook and the newspaper all folded up.

Going to class now felt more interesting to Tatum. She thought she might see the man because she had written and talked about him, or she might run into Officer Cathy on her rounds. With the early, powdery pollen of springtime floating in the air, she felt lighter somehow. The pudgy weight she wanted to lose to make her mother happy didn't hold her back so much. Tatum felt less shy too. Back at home, she'd worn black jeans with dark tops and had frowned at anyone who came her way. Now it was easier to smile – because she knew someone was watching her.

On her daily walks, Tatum wore the long, colorful striped scarf that belonged to her roommate. Jen, who was studying Eastern religions, had renounced materialism; she'd tossed the scarf in a pile of woolens after the last snowstorm. Tatum kept it wrapped around her neck. She liked recycled things. Her favorite store in town was the All Souls Thrift Shop. Expensive clothes that the other girls discarded cost just a few dollars there. She didn't care if her classmates recognized their designer clothing on her. It meant they had a bond. In the evenings, for dinner, she wore some of her mother's cast-off blouses, shiny ones bought for parties before she got too sick to go out anymore.

On Tuesday Officer Cathy left a message that she had additional questions for Tatum. They met in her dorm room again. Tatum showed her what she had written in her journal, the main one. There was just one entry from the weekend.

Yesterday he sat on the bench by the pond. I think he knows my schedule, even weekends. His pants are khaki, and they look like someone ironed them. But his shoes are brown and scruffy.

Then on Monday, she had written:

He was not on the bench today, but I think I saw him in the hallway of the Hayes Bldg. He looks tired to me, as if he couldn't sleep.

'You saw him inside Hayes?' Officer Cathy probed.

'That's where my history course is,' Tatum explained, 'I was working on my class project. Mine is on the British Museum and whether or not the collectors stole ancient artifacts from Greece and Italy.' Tatum knew they did; it was not just a feeling; it was a fact.

'How close were you to him?' Officer Cathy asked in a tense voice.

Tatum's parents would not be pleased to learn that a tall man in a green jacket was following her around campus. They were counting on her staying safe while her mother had chemotherapy treatments. She was losing her hair, even her eyebrows.

'We brushed by each other in the corridor,' Tatum replied. Officer Cathy made a note on her small, spiral pad in a red pen. Just talking about him gave Tatum stomach flutters.

After curfew, she told Jen about the man. Jen sat on the floor in a lotus position, wearing only bikini underwear and a tank top. Tatum lounged on the bed, her entire body covered by a long T-shirt, one that had been discarded by her father. Jen listened so quietly that Tatum thought she might have fallen asleep while meditating.

The next day a notice in Jen's cursive handwriting appeared on the hall bulletin board: 'Watch out for stalkers! Report anything suspicious to school security.' She decorated it with a border of peace symbols. Tatum liked the way it looked. When Sara from the school newspaper called her up and asked for a description, Tatum held her cell phone against her ear and closed her eyes. She lay back on the bed.

'Yes, he's about forty, I'd say. Not nearly as old as my father,' she guessed. 'His hair hangs down in his eyes like somebody even younger though. Somebody who doesn't think to comb it every day.'

Sara assured Tatum that she would not identify her source in the story, but news travels fast in a small place. On Wednesday, when the paper came out, several people asked Tatum to sit with them at lunch. She hoped that Officer Cathy would notice all of her new friends. Tatum planned to bring her a cappuccino from the coffee shop in town, the one where the man watched her from behind his newspaper.

That afternoon Tatum worked on the British Museum project in the library. From the school computer, she downloaded images, cutting and pasting them with superglue on a poster board. The pictures were of ancient artifacts taken from the Mediterranean. *The British Museum is a thief,* she wrote in the heading. In smaller print, she added: *The English exploited other people in distant countries, even after they had given up colonization, stealing their history from them and claiming it as their own. Famous museums in America also knowingly took donations from rich people who bought stolen goods from Greece or Italy. They knew what they were doing. They couldn't help themselves. They let the facts of the situation get all tangled up with their desires.*

Tatum wanted to tell the tall man about these illicit acts. Maybe he was someone who used to teach here or the husband of one of her teachers who wasn't even aware that he came on campus, because he was supposed to be working at the Corner

Bookstore or in City Hall defending criminals. That was it. He defended criminals, and he needed to conduct research in the library on campus in order to understand the criminal mind.

Jen had started talking to Tatum about all kinds of things. That night she described her paper topic for the Eastern religions course.

'Suchness,' she stated matter-of-factly. 'It's Buddhist.' When Tatum took off her glasses, Jen looked small.

'Suchness,' Jen repeated from her distant bed. 'It means something like being present.'

'Whatness?' Tatum asked. She'd been reading *Portrait of an Artist as a Young Man* for literature, and they'd been learning about James Joyce and his kind of crazy epiphanies.

'No, it's *suchness*. Which is what *you* need,' Jen stated in a superior voice. 'We all do,' she added.

She read from the textbook: 'For Buddhists, truth and acceptance are the pillars of faith. *Suchness* is a term used to describe life as it is, the truth as it is. A flower is a flower. Without the knowledge of suchness, we find ourselves trying to make life into something that it is not through false desires and illusions.'

Jen stared into space, looking thoroughly pleased with this idea. She took a bite out of a peach her mother had sent in a basket from South Carolina with matzos. Being the Southern Jewish girl on campus who studied Buddhism gave her an air of importance.

'This peach is a peach – nothing more, nothing less,' Jen added solemnly.

'Suchness,' Tatum repeated. It sounded like a kiss. The word made her think about the tall man.

She wrote in her journal, while Jen took her shower.

Today he sat on the bench by the lake. I frowned at him rather than smiling. He moved slightly closer, then watched me when I got up and walked away.

For her very private satin pillow journal, she added, *I could tell he wanted to follow me. I want him to know about suchness, about the feeling of being inside a kiss, of expecting to be kissed.*

Tatum stopped by the security office the next day after classes. She'd hoped that Officer Cathy would ask her more questions and read from the composition journal that Tatum carried with her. But she needed to make late-afternoon rounds on campus.

'Would you like to come with me?' Tatum nodded agreeably. 'Let me know if you see anyone who looks like the man who is following you,' Officer Cathy instructed. 'You can signal to me by tugging on my sleeve. No need to say anything.'

There were not many men on campus, just the headmaster who always walked in a big hurry, along with some teachers and maintenance workers. No green windbreakers. They checked doors and looked behind buildings. Tatum liked being seen with Officer Cathy. She thought she'd like to have a job that required wearing a uniform. But not a nurse. Tatum did not like the sight of blood or even being around sick people. That was why she had been sent to the boarding school in the first place. When her mother got sick and had chemo last year, her father said it was time for Tatum to go to prep school, where she wouldn't have to worry about taking care of sick people.

She and Officer Cathy circled around the pond. They picked up trash along the way. Everyone in the school was supposed to do that. 'We're all responsible for where we live.' That's what the headmaster said at convocation every term. Peppermint candy cellophane, paper cups, and also a small, green, rectangular wrapper were in her path near the bench where she liked to sit. Tatum knew about the green wrapper from health class. The teacher had passed out condoms last semester and told the girls to open them up and to put the smooth latex on their thumbs, making them look like sad puppets with no ears or eyes or hair. She threw away the other trash but kept the condom wrapper in her jeans pocket. Touching it made her feel grown-up, more knowledgeable about the secrets of life.

Officer Cathy didn't ask many questions along the way. They walked briskly, checking the locks on the doors in the main buildings. It was after five o'clock, and the administrative offices were closed. Together they secured the back and side doors to the residence halls. Students were supposed to use the main entrances after 5pm. When they got to Buckley, Tatum's dorm, the basement door was propped open with a brick.

'This is not a good idea,' Officer Cathy pointed out, as if accustomed to giving lectures on safety. 'Anyone could get in here. Anyone at all.'

Tatum nodded in agreement. She took the brick from the security guard, placing it behind some bushes. 'Nobody will be able to find it there.'

'I'm going off duty for today. Stop by to see me tomorrow – or call me on your cell phone if you see him again, if he bothers you.' Officer Cathy's large, blurry eyes fixed on Tatum's for a solid moment before she turned away. Tatum wished she would hug her. Officer Cathy's arms and chest were strong, not fragile and tight like her mother's had become.

After Officer Cathy disappeared down the sidewalk, Tatum went to the front entrance of the dorm and headed down to the basement side door. She retrieved the brick and propped open the door once more. 'Life is transient,' Jen had told her. 'There is no such thing as security.'

Tatum changed into a clean silk blouse, another hand-me-down. On the way to dinner, she checked her mailbox. Nothing there, not even a postcard from her mother who sent one almost every day, collected from faraway lands where she'd traveled with her father before he retired from the newspaper – places like Hong Kong, Croatia, India, and Big Sur. Her mother stored the postcards in a small, wooden box along with her formal stationery. She wrote little wobbly messages, sometimes quotations, all across the postcard with no room left for the address. Then, she placed them in an envelope and mailed them to Tatum. Sometimes she sent several postcards in a single mailing with sequential, numbered messages, like those Tatum had received yesterday: '(1) There is a new robin making a nest in the bushes. I hope that she will lay her tiny blue eggs there. (2) And the skinny, hungry babies will be here when you come home. XOXOX your Mother.' The postcards depicted different views of the glimmering Taj Mahal, which the caption said had been built for love.

Tatum stuck the postcards to her wall with superglue that would get her written up once the residence counselors realized what she had done. But she didn't care. And Jen didn't seem to mind either. Sometimes she posted them with the writing side exposed, where there were quotations written in her mother's hand from *Alice in Wonderland* or *Little Women*. She had wanted a new picture of her mother, even if she didn't have hair anymore.

But her father would not send her one, not even by email. At spring break her mother had worn a lovely Asian scarf around her head, maybe from Hong Kong, with interwoven Oriental colors. When Tatum returned to campus, she'd begun wearing Jen's striped scarf; soon afterward the man started following her.

'Do you want to sit with us?' These were the pretty girls who liked to have hush-hush parties with beer in the study room of the dorm. Jen was always with them, and she scooted over to make another place. Tatum sat down next to her, and Jen adjusted the scarf around Tatum's neck.

'Like that.' She loosened the ends. 'So it doesn't look like it's strangling you to death. Now you can breathe.' Tatum felt Jen watching her closely as she took a deep breath.

'Have you seen him again?' one of the pretty girls asked her. Tatum thought she might like to get some new glasses like Officer Cathy's so that she'd look extra smart and they'd ask her opinion on all kinds of things. She could explain everything she knew – about how feelings can become whatever memory you need them to be.

Tatum shook her head. She was not supposed to talk about him with the other girls. Officer Cathy said she would do the talking as part of her investigation. Rumors on campus can rage out of control.

'My sister once had some people follow her at the mall. They stole her purse. She never got it back again,' one of the girls at the end of the table volunteered.

'We thought my younger brother got kidnapped once when we couldn't find him,' another girl stated. 'But he'd fallen asleep in the car.' She paused to chew on a cherry tomato. 'Good thing the windows were open, or he might have suffocated.'

'Did you know that they might let that guy John Hinckley out of jail?' Jen volunteered. 'Or I guess he's in a loony bin. He's the one who tried to kill Ronald Reagan. He's crazy.' Reagan had been president before Tatum was born, before they all were born. Everyone, even Jen with her suchness, wanted to tell a scary story.

'I found something down by the pond, near the bench.' Tatum pulled the condom wrapper out of her pocket and tossed it on the table next to the butter. All of the girls gazed at it as if it were a sacred relic.

'You touched it?' Jen whispered incredulously.

'It's just the wrapper.' Tatum replied. The dark-green rectangle was ripped carefully along the top. One of the girls pushed at it with her fork. Someone snickered. 'Maybe that should go in the school paper too. Under lost and found. You'll be famous, Tatum, one way or another. Just you wait and see.'

Tatum picked up the wrapper back up and stuffed it in her pocket. She tugged on the scarf as she stood up. 'I need to get to the library to finish my history project.' She didn't want to be the last one left at the table. Some of the other girls grabbed their backpacks. Tatum walked out first. She liked being at the front rather than the back of the group. She fingered the torn wrapper in her pocket.

On her way to the library, Tatum called her mother on the cell phone. Usually, she got up out of bed for dinner. They ate late at home. Her father answered.

'She's still sleeping,' he stated quietly. Tatum would not ask how she was doing. Her father sighed on the other end of the phone as if he too had just gotten up from a long nap. 'I'll tell her you called.'

'Dad.' She paused. Her father was older than her mother by a lot, maybe twenty years. He was the one who was supposed to die first. 'Yes, Tate?'

'There's a man following me on campus.'

'Are you sure?' he asked. 'Again?' he added.

'They wrote about it for the school newspaper. The security guard, Officer Cathy, she's on the lookout for him.' Her father was silent for a minute. 'SOP,' Tatum added.

'Well, Tatum, it sounds like you're doing the right thing. Notifying the authorities.' He paused to swallow. 'I'll call the headmaster in the morning.'

His voice sounded crackly, like that of an old man. Last time they were together, she'd noticed he was not as tall as he used to be. His gray hair had grown wiry and wild, not cut short when he traveled for the newspaper. As the foreign correspondent, he had seen the world, both its good and bad parts. Newspapers were his source of reality. What got printed there was what had actually happened.

'Dad?' She wanted to tell him something else, something that would make a memory for her mother too. But he'd already hung up. She wanted him to tell her mother about the colorful striped scarf she wore around her neck. Tatum wanted her mother to know that she was letting her hair grow extra long. And that she washed it every other day. She wanted her mother to know about the history project and that she was taking walks with Office Cathy. And she wanted her mother to know about suchness, about everything that was happening, even as her own world was slowing down.

Instead of going to the library, Tatum headed back to her room. She removed her bed comforter, satin pillow, and secret notebook and headed out. Down in the basement, the door was no longer propped open. Tatum recovered the brick from behind the bush and placed it in the doorway again. She walked to the pond, to the bench near where she had found the condom wrapper. Lying down, she tucked the comforter all around her. The sky was dusky, nearly dark, with the wind making tiny, turbulent waves on the lake. The air smelled fresh, like the first hope of springtime.

Officer Cathy, Jen, her father, the headmaster, the pretty girls, or anybody else who bothered to look would find her on the bench. And Tatum would tell them about the man – about how he had been there too, his arms holding her tight, his legs tangled up with hers, his face close, breathing hot breaths on her chest. When morning came, she'd write down the memory, that feeling of suchness, all deep and hard inside of her.

Summer solstice

That summer before the millennium, Meg used to go to the ballpark late in the afternoon while the sun still hung in the sky like a bruised lemon. She could taste its tart pulp in the humid air and smell its sour rind on the bodies of little boys who spun around her in stained white pants. It was hard for her to pick out her own son, his blonde curls flattened by a cap, so she was grateful when she could make out his name on the back of his spinach-coloured shirt. 'Jean-Luc,' it called out distinctively, mixed in with all those other Jasons and Joels and Jeffreys and Jonathans. When his friends' parents met her, they enunciated loudly and slowly, 'We are so glad to know you finally.' Their eyes signalled disappointment when she responded simply, 'Hello, nice to meet you' in a crisp NPR announcer voice. They had no doubt expected a provocative French accent.

Her daughter Francine and her husband Frank normally escorted Jean-Luc and his tribe of teammates to the park and then sat and talked with the other parents and noisy siblings in the stands. They all moved with calm assurance, like regulars at the local bar. When Meg arrived later, after work, Frank helped her remove the lawn chair from the car and placed it close to the fence a few feet from the stands. She settled into the scratchy plastic webbing with a novel in her lap. If she forgot the book, she felt disoriented. She panicked just like Jean-Luc used to when he couldn't find his stuffed dolphin at night. She didn't know what to do with her hands. They floated around her body, weightless.

'Mom, can I get a hot dog?' Francine whined almost immediately behind her.

'What does your father say?' She let him call the shots at the ballpark. He knew the rules of the game.

Francine proceeded to beg and beguile her father until he dug into his deep pocket and retrieved wrinkled bills and some change along with a few broken toothpicks.

'Get me a green – no, purple – Slurpee,' Jean-Luc commanded as Francine headed to the snack bar. He then tore into the dugout where the boys and the coaches bartered bats and balls and headgear as if they were negotiating transactions at the stock exchange. It was serious business.

'Mom, why don't you come sit with us?' She could hear Francine's voice hover over the crowd, its propellers sharp and shiny. She turned toward the top of the stands to see her youngest child's lips smeared with red and yellow, painted that way by the deteriorating hot dog. She just smiled in return and began the next chapter of *Anna Karenina*. She was making her way through the bookshelf on Tolstoy. She admired his convictions, his righteous clarity. When the serious grey-haired man behind her knocked the lawn chair as he jumped up and cheered, she remembered to survey the events of the field. She could see Jean-Luc scowling at her from first base. 'Pay attention, Mom, for once,' his fierce eyes screamed.

She placed the book under the chair with her purse and sat on her hands. The conversations behind her wandered randomly through aisles of the supermarket, hallways of the school, culs-de-sac of the neighbourhood. Various remedies for head lice were under discussion.

'I heard if you use that stuff too much it can cause brain damage,' one of the mothers reported.

'Well, if they can't go to school because they're infested, they're not going to learn much anyway,' a woman with a pointed chin and denim vest responded dryly.

Although she had seen both of them many times here before and they often smiled pleasantly at her, she didn't know their names. One of them offered to spray the batting helmets with disinfectant. So that became a topic of debate. She couldn't decide how she felt about it, but she had complete confidence in the other moms to figure out the right decision to make. They seemed to know what they were doing.

With the sun still burning, Meg was having a hard time connecting to this world that her husband and children so easily inhabited. If she ventured forth, she felt like she was on stage with the spotlights aimed at her. Every nuance of movement and tone observed, critiqued. She stumbled over her lines. A novel and her daydreams were more fitting occupations. In this setting, she felt cast in the wrong scene or act or even play. Somehow, she had missed the class in school that told you how to name your children, what colour nail polish to wear, and when to use bleach on the laundry. Where all of the other girls had learned these things was a mystery to her. They could even talk with one another freely at the ballpark about how sore their nipples were from breastfeeding or how long it had taken to conceive the last child. She was astonished by the ease with which they revealed their private moments and how steadfastly they organized their lives. Hers always seemed on the verge of spinning out of control. It was best to watch and wait – to see what the others did first.

On this longest day of the year, she didn't want to let it all slip by. It was the start of a new season. As the sun turned faint and lost its place of prominence, as the world cooled down around her, Meg found herself yearning to snuggle up next to Francine. To settle between her and Frank, their knees all touching. Just before the ballpark lights blinked on, when the evening breeze tasted like café au lait, she turned to them and felt Frank's eyes searching for hers.

Finally, as the sun sank behind the horizon, they both shed their sunglasses. She wanted to hear him describe once more how wise Jean-Luc had been to throw the ball to the catcher. 'He knew he could make the out,' Frank would state matter-of-factly. At that moment, she enjoyed the pride that mothers of astronauts must have. Your boy can do something that you never knew existed. It was a startling realization that these children occupied a different cosmos. That they had grown too large for your planet. That they somehow knew precisely, without even stopping to think, where to throw the ball, what its arc and trajectory would be, how gravity would grab it and place it in the mitt of a catcher, right where it belonged.

So sometimes, just as night began to fall around her shoulders, she would rise and make her way past the cushions and Cokes and jackets on the stands. As the planets stopped rotating and the sun stood still, Meg would squeeze in between Frank and his friend, Joel's father. She bravely asked the woman in front of her where the team pictures were to be taken and inquired conscientiously when it would be their turn for snacks. In the twilight, she could see her book and purse in a lump underneath the chair, glowing moon rocks far away at the end of a telescope. And from behind she would feel Francine rub her neck, her hands all sticky and warm, her breath a lemon drop in her mother's ear. When Jean-Luc crookedly grinned at her with approval from the field, she wondered with parental concern if it was time to think about braces for him. In the momentary quiet of the evening, Meg asked Frank's opinion, loudly enough so that everyone else could hear. He did not respond but circled her wrist tenderly with his thick fingers. She breathed deeply and struggled inside to find a smile for him. Just this once, she knew that she had gotten it right.

Acknowledgements

The magic of any family is its improvisational nature. The luckiest people on Earth are those who also enjoy enduring love and adventure. I count myself among such fortunate beings—further supported by an extended family of fine friends and fellow writers, too many to name. I wish to express deep gratitude to all.

I also wish to acknowledge the many places that have sustained my writing life, especially Emory University and The Hambidge Center for Creative Arts and Sciences.